NAN BRITTON:

The Most Hated Woman in America

By

E.S. Laurence

Cover image by: Austin Studios, 99D
Book design by: SWATT Books Ltd

Printed in the United States
First Printing, 2023

ISBN: 979-8-9892010-0-6 (Paperback)
ISBN: 979-8-9892010-1-3 (eBook)

ES Laurence Publishing
San Francisco, CA

eslaurence23@gmail.com

Dedication

In a nod of respect, I offer the following dedication, a slightly re-worded version of the one she included in her book *The President's Daughter*:

> *This book is dedicated with understanding and love to the many women whose struggles are usually not known to the world...*

PART I

The Aftermath

Introduction
1932: Getting America Back on Track

Much was wrong with America. Much was wrong with the Western world. Still shaken by the unspeakable horrors of The Great War, the first modern war, the Western psyche was now deeply traumatized by the Great Depression. With no end in sight, the nearly three years of abject national poverty had exacted a terrible toll on almost everyone. Too poor to buy food, men foraged for dandelions and tumbleweeds to feed their families. Women turned feed sacks into dresses and old tires into sandals. And schoolchildren played a game called Eviction. The land was void of trust, pride, and hope - as a widespread malaise took firm root in the souls of men.

One man, Warren G. Harding, the now-dead former President, was blamed for much of the country's woes. The country's deteriorating spirit mirrored the former President's precipitous posthumous reputational decline.

Harding, the first president elected after women got the vote, was a beloved statesman at the time of his unexpected death in 1923. Less than a decade later, revelations about his rampant womanizing, his cabinet's rife corruption, his incompetence, and his idiotic policies, recast the Harding Presidency as an unadulterated disaster.

In the public's mind, Harding was the chief architect of the current economic calamity. Harding was to blame for their now pitiful and dreadful existence. The ire he aroused was intense and never-ending, as the suffering populace was constantly reminded of his failings.

Newspaper articles were awash with reports of his Administration's massive thefts from the public trough, crimes so serious that they resulted in the imprisonment and suicides of many who had previously held prestigious posts in the White House. Harding's direct involvement in these scandals was unclear. But these were men he appointed, and at a minimum, his incompetence and laziness allowed this widespread larceny. Economists also pointed to Harding's economic policies of American isolationism and tariffs as chief contributing causes for the current depression.

In death he had become a pariah, so much so that public officials went to great lengths to avoid attending the consecration of his tomb in Marion, Ohio.

His name was, in fact, more in the public consciousness in death than it had been in life. In addition to the above scandals, two sensational books about him were selling well. The first was written by a woman, 30 years his junior, who alleged, in titillating detail, that she had had an illicit affair with Harding. The second was written, behind bars, by a scam artist and former White House employee. It claimed the President did not die naturally as officially reported. Rather it posited that his wife, upset with his excessive philandering, killed him.

Harding, though, still had at least one friend: Arkansas Congressman John Tillman. Tillman was determined to "set the record straight," restore dignity to the dead President and place the true blame for the country's problems where it belonged. He would lead the charge to get America back on track. He would, however, first visit a Senate Hearing investigating his old friend's Administration. A hearing certain to make his blood boil.

Chapter 1

Truth and Reconciliation

It is March 21, 1932. Congressman Tillman sits in the gallery of the Senate chambers waiting for the Brookhart-Wheeler Committee hearing to begin. The hearing's stated purpose is to investigate the numerous malfeasances of the Harding administration.

Tillman will have none of it. In his mind, there was no malfeasance. The Harding administration did nothing wrong. The hearing is a ruse and just a political hack job by loathsome heathens (i.e., Democrats). The malicious Democrats are simply trying to boost their standing and future prospects by unfairly denigrating the former President and his party.

Tillman conveniently ignores the numerous, prominent, and now well-documented, scandals of the Harding administration. And there are plenty of them - the Tea Pot Dome Scandal, thefts from the Veterans Bureau, widespread graft surrounding the Administration of Prohibition laws, etc. - all perpetuated by the Harding administration under the direction of his Attorney General Harvey Daugherty, the leader of an unscrupulous group within the White House commonly referred to as "The Ohio Gang".

Congressman Tillman, who is with his junior aid, is not the only one with a keen interest in this hearing. A chief object of Tillman and America's scorn, Nan Britton, sits on the other side of the gallery. Virtually overnight, Miss Britton went from a complete unknown to the most infamous person in the country. Her sudden notoriety occurred when news leaked of the book she had written. A book where she outlined what she claimed was her love affair with President Harding. A love affair that she asserted resulted in her giving birth to his child.

Everyone knows her story; few believe it. And since the publication of her book, *The President's Daughter*, Miss Britton has been labeled a sex-craved whore, pornographer, extortionist, addict, liar, and worse. She has, in short, become the most hated woman in America.

It has now been years since the publication of her book back in 1927 and her infamy has somewhat faded. Certainly, the passage of time has helped, but she has also been reasonably effective in laying low and staying out of the public eye. Nonetheless, extreme elements of a still angry population sometimes seek her out and harass her. Occasionally, and typically around election time, the most virulent send her death threats.

Deciding to break from her seclusion, on this day in March 1932 she returned to Washington D.C. She is with her sister, Liz Willits, in the gallery for the Senate hearing investigating the alleged corruption of Harding's Administration. Today, the dastardly Harvey Daugherty is to testify. She abhors Daugherty, probably more than she does Tillman.

Daugherty is a lowlife lying scoundrel, a slick confidence man who took unfair advantage of the man she loved. He double-crossed the President and lined his pockets with money earmarked for worthwhile public projects. Tillman, on the other hand, is a blowhard simpleton. He is a miserable, misguided human being, for sure. But he wasn't a double-crosser. Tillman didn't steal. And his message, as misguided as it is, is always clear.

Miss Britton is certain Daugherty was the kingpin for all the corruption in the Harding administration. She blames him not just for the President's woes but strongly suspects he also stole the money the President had left her. In her mind, Daugherty is the cause of Harding's downfall and her own.

However, she is shocked when she sees Daugherty enter the chamber. He is slumped over, his complexion blotchy and his hair thin. He looks weak and is disheveled, nothing like the confident conman she remembers. She surprises herself. She hates the man but seeing him in this state, for some reason, conjures up in her glimmers of sympathy.

Senator Brookhart pounds his gavel to begin the meeting. He administers the oath and then speaks to the witness.

Brookhart: Mr. Daugherty, our committee is here to investigate your alleged failures as Attorney General. These include your purported failure to prosecute multiple crimes and the alleged misconduct committed by you in your role as a senior member of the Harding administration. Do you understand the seriousness of what we are investigating?

Daugherty: I am well aware of your investigation. I take it very seriously and look forward to correcting the false allegations leveled against me.

Brookhardt: Very well. Please proceed with your opening statement, and remember you are under oath.

Daugherty: Thank you, Mr. Chairman. I appreciate the opportunity to talk about the Harding presidency and set the record straight. We had many accomplishments, often overlooked.

As you know, our Administration took over after the Great War ended, and the country was in a state of economic malaise. We immediately instituted policies and procedures to help the country get back on its feet. Among other things, we passed a new tax law, limited immigration, imposed tariffs, instituted the budget system, built highways, and created policies for new technologies like automobiles and radio. And our efforts were very successful. By the end of the Harding administration, which, of course, ended with the unexpected death of the President, unemployment was at an all-time low - just some 2%, and the economy was improving measurably. I am proud to have been part of that and believe the good people and policies we brought to the White House helped turn this country around. Now I am happy to take the Senators' questions.

Brookhart: Let me go off script a bit and start with some questions directed at your opening statement.

Daugherty: OK.

Brookhart: You mentioned people. Mr. Coolidge and Mr. Hoover, both of whom went on to become President, were key members of the Harding administration, were they not?

Daugherty: Of course. Mr. Coolidge was Vice President, and Mr. Hoover was Secretary of Commerce during our Administration.

Brookhart: And aren't our current policies, still under Republican leadership, essentially the same today as during your time?

Daugherty: They've been tweaked, but that is a fair statement.

Brookhart: Weren't these policies you initiated in 1921 designed to have a long-term effect?

Daugherty: That was the intent, yes.

Brookhart: Indeed, they were. I want to quote the preamble to the budget submitted under the Harding administration. "The positive fiscal impacts of this budget should endure and have lasting effects well into the next decade." Well, we're well into the next decade the preamble spoke of at the time. Do you know what the current unemployment rate is?

Daugherty: I don't know the precise number, Sir.

Brookhart: Unemployment is 20%. If you weren't aware, we are in the midst of a great depression, the worst our nation has ever suffered. So, your policies, now fully realized a decade after adoption, have created one fine mess.

The Chairman reaches for some reports.

Brookhart: A group of independent economists, no less than ten that I have found, believe that your policies, particularly your tax, and tariffs, contributed mightily to our current condition. All agree that these policies, if not the chief cause of the depression, certainly accelerated it and made it worse.

Daugherty: The economy is a complex animal, Sir. Many factors influence unemployment; most are well beyond the government's control. And I believe unemployment would be even worse now, maybe twice as bad, if not for our policies.

Brookhart: Very convenient belief, Mr. Daugherty. Are you an economist, and do you have any substantiation for it?

Daugherty: Not an economist, no. And substantiation? Well, kind of, it's based on my background of working for decades in the government. I sort of have a gut feel for these things. So, my statement is based on my vast experiences of being on the world stage.

Brookhart again lifts the reports he previously referenced.

Brookhart: Two economists rarely agree on anything, and here we have ten agreeing. Do you want me to believe your gut and not these renowned economists?

Daugherty: They're entitled to their opinion, but I believe otherwise.

Brookhart: I am sure you do. Maybe you believe in the tooth fairy too. I will reserve the balance of my time to later address your record on prosecution. For now, though, I turn this over to Senator Wheeler, who has specific questions about the misconduct you directed while Attorney General.

Mr. Wheeler leans forward and begins.

Wheeler: I'd like to ask about some people you worked with in the White House. Specifically, Albert Fall, Charles Forbes, Jess Smith and Charles Cramer. Are you familiar with these gentlemen, and did they work for you?

Daugherty: Yes. I know them, and they did work with me.

Wheeler: None of them could testify today. Do you know why?

Daugherty: None of them are available, Sir.

Wheeler: Correct. Both Mr. Fall and Mr. Forbes are in jail. Both were convicted of embezzling from the federal government while working in the White House. Mr. Fall for taking kickbacks on Government Oil Leases, and Mr. Forbes for misappropriating funds designated to build veteran hospitals. Isn't that correct?

Daugherty: I didn't closely follow their trials, Sir. I can't comment on the charges or the outcomes.

Wheeler: Mr. Fall is now the first cabinet member ever to serve a jail sentence. Isn't that true?

Daugherty: It might be. I don't know the history.

Wheeler: Do you know why Mr. Smith and Mr. Cramer are unavailable?

Daugherty: Neither is living, Sir.

Wheeler: Correct. Both committed suicide just as they were about to be investigated for fraud and larceny committed while working with you in the White House.

The senator reaches for his notes.

Wheeler: Smith allegedly sold confiscated liquor to gangsters, took bribes from bootleggers in exchange for pharmaceutical licenses to buy alcohol, and misused Government property for personal purposes. And Cramer was working with the now-convicted Mr. Forbes and was part of the theft from the V.A.

Daugherty: There were no trials, so none of those charges were ever proven, Sir. And I understand Mr.

Smith was not well at the time of his death. He may have wanted to avoid a prolonged and painful illness.

Wheeler: You seem to know a lot about Mr. Smith. Do you know where Mr. Smith killed himself?

Daugherty: In Washington, Sir. A hotel room.

Wheeler: Yes, it was in a hotel room that he shared with you, isn't that correct?

Daugherty is silent and angry.

Wheeler: I will take your silence as a yes.

Daugherty continues to fume but says nothing. Wheeler now holds up a document that he shows to Daugherty.

Wheeler: Mr. Daugherty, according to this contract, you were personally paid when you sold oil leases to the Japanese. Congress designated that the oil would go to the U.S. Navy and be used for our national defense. And contrary to this Congressional mandate, you sold it to the Japanese instead. You sold it to a foreign country, not the U.S. Navy, as required. Good lord, you didn't even sell it to a U.S. business. And you took a good portion of the proceeds. None of this was supposed to go to you. Can you explain any of this? Both the legality of you having sold it to the Japanese and why you personally took some of the proceeds?

Daugherty: It's been a while since I looked at that contract. I really can't comment right now.

Wheeler: Really? It's exhibit H of the evidence binder we gave your counsel two months ago. If you still need to read it, a copy of the binder is right next to you. Please turn to Exhibit H. Read it now. Take your time, Mr. Daugherty.

There is a long pause. Mr. Daugherty does not open the binder. Instead, he and his attorney have a whispered communication. Then Mr. Daugherty returns to the microphone.

Daugherty: On the advice of counsel, I will respectfully decline your request. My review would be meaningless as I would refuse to answer any questions related to that contract on the grounds that it might incriminate me.

Wheeler: Very well, let's finish up, Mr. Daugherty. Your relationship with Mr. Harding pre-dates his entry into politics. Is that correct?

Daugherty: We'd been friends a long time.

Wheeler: It has been reported that you once described Warren Harding as a sleeping turtle on a log that you pushed into the water. Is this statement accurate?

Daugherty: I'm aware of the reports, but I categorically deny ever saying such a thing. At least I don't recall saying such a thing, Sir.

Wheeler: So, which is it? Do you deny ever saying it? Or do you not recall, so maybe you did say it?

Daugherty: I'll stand by my original answer. Next question, please.

Aware that none of his questions will be answered, Wheeler decides to go for the jugular. In the form of repeated questions, he will list the litany of sordid payoffs Daugherty made on behalf of Harding.

Wheeler: Very well. Did you have dirt on Warren Harding? Were you his fixer? Were you paying off the women and whores he had affairs with? Keeping the affairs silent, paying for abortions? Did you pay off one of his lovers, Carrie Phillips, with a trip to Japan and a large sum of money? Were you basically serving as the President's pimp?

Daugherty is now furious and becoming unhinged. His legal counsel, aware of his stress, whispers in his ear. Daugherty nods, acknowledging the advice. Nan is also very upset once again hearing the rumors of Harding's infidelity. She still believes them false, that Harding was not a womanizer; she is about to blurt out something when her sister stops her.

In the gallery, Congressman Tillman, too, is becoming increasingly upset. He turns to his assistant and speaks to him in a loud whisper. "These guys are freshman senators. They're supposed to be seen, not heard." His aide responds dryly, "Apparently, they have other ideas." "Well, so do I," Tillman retorts. "This is the most despicable unethical political scam I've ever seen. They're destroying this guy's life. Someone needs to set the record straight." He gets up and storms out of the chambers just as Daugherty responds to the last question.

Daugherty: I refuse to answer the questions asked or any additional questions this committee may have on the grounds that they might incriminate me.

Chapter 2

Proud Horse's Ass

A few days later, Congressman Tillman is about to enter the House floor. His aide catches up with him. "Sir, may I have a moment please?" Tillman, though not happy with the interruption, says nothing. He does, however, accede to the aide's wishes and listens reluctantly. He knows this aide well and is quite certain he will offer advice he most likely will not take.

Having failed to convince his ill-tempered boss to abandon his plans to address the House, Tillman's aide is now desperately trying to persuade him to give a different speech than currently planned. He cautions him, "Sir, I would suggest something different, something less antagonistic."

As written, Tillman's speech is an angry rant that will do no good. On the contrary, it will rile many people, particularly women. His outrage will undoubtedly serve to defeat him in his re-election bid. Politically he has much to lose and nothing to gain. Though preferring no speech at all, the aide desperately offers a more benign substitute.

With some trepidation, the aide hands Tillman the alternative words he has drafted. "It's brief, and I think it gets to the point." Tillman reads the first paragraph.

"Mr. Speaker, I want to address the Senate's fact-finding committee charged with investigating the Harding Administration. I appreciate their work and diligence, but the hearing lacked the appropriate decorum typically seen in that fine institution. And we would all be better served with a calm, impartial look at all the facts. I am all for identifying and punishing bad players, but we must use a systematic and intellectual approach."

Tillman won't read anymore. He is incensed, "This is nonsense. It doesn't say anything." "Exactly," responds the aide. "There is nothing in it to upset anyone. You aren't going to accomplish anything anyhow. There is no need to piss off half the voting population and make a horse's ass out of yourself."

Tillman rips up the aide's speech and makes the baying sound of a horse as he enters the Chamber.

Chapter 3
Tillman's Rampage

Anger rules this day: a scorching hot spring day. John Tillman is about to address the half-filled Chamber of the United States House of Representatives.

The Speaker of the House is about to call on the Congressman, and Mr. Tillman is well prepared. He has sat alone in the bathroom stall for the last half hour, repeatedly reciting the speech he had memorized days before. He is confident and anxious, and now waits, pacing back and forth a short distance behind the podium.

He breathes deeply, looks up to the gallery, and snarls as he sees some of his many detractors. The gallery includes suffragettes and other critics, mostly women, who look down on Tillman with contempt. They rustle uncomfortably, knowing he is about to begin. They know him well. They know his tirades. He is an unapologetic and outspoken misogynist. They despise him.

Tillman steps forward as the Speaker pounds his gavel. "The House recognizes the distinguished Congressman from Arkansas. Mr. Tillman, the floor is yours. You have five minutes." Tillman stands straight and proud, lifts his chin arrogantly, and begins.

Thank you, Mr. Speaker. I wish to address this body regarding a depraved circus I witnessed the other day in the Senate. The event, falsely labeled an "Inquiry" by a few miscreant, inexperienced and misguided Senators, was baseless trickery. And they had the audacity to call their deceit an impartial investigation into the alleged malfeasance of the Warren G. Harding Administration. Poppycock, I say! Impartial investigation? My ass! It was a witch-hunt. And malfeasance? Complete and utter bullshit!

Excuse my language my friends. But I can assure you there was no impartial inquiry into anything that day, and why? Because Harding and the great men of his Administration did nothing wrong. They all served their country admirably and with distinction, which is what they are being punished for. No good deed goes unpunished, I guess.

The other day, I witnessed a pure and simple political hack job, the likes of which I've never seen before. The lying opposition, oh how disingenuous they are; they unconscionably and deviously framed my good friend, a great statesman – Warren G. Harding. An orchestrated setup – facts completely ignored. In their place, a diatribe and a fictitious plethora of unadulterated lies. Their most ignoble objective - destroy a good man now a decade deceased – blame a dead man for the world's problems when the real culprit was right before their eyes.

Tillman gestures menacingly toward the women in the gallery.

But I am here to save the day; and I am here not just to save the reputation of that great man. Oh, indeed, I am here to set the record straight about my good friend President Warren G. Harding, but more importantly, I am here to place the blame where it squarely belongs. You see, we must first diagnose the disease, and then we can cure it. And good friends, I have the diagnosis and the cure if the country is man enough to take the medicine.

Now, there's a lot of nastiness in the world today, a lot of finger-pointing, and right now, it is underhandedly directed at my friend, the late President Harding. Many falsely blame this great man for all the evils in the world today. Easy to blame a dead man, I guess. Well, I am here to defend that dead man. A distinguished man that I can demonstrate was innocent of all wrongdoing and who was a very good man. But more importantly: I know the real offender and the root cause of all our problems. I will tell you who they are, tell you the truth, perhaps the first to do so and reveal all. Let's go step by step.

Tillman pauses for dramatic effect.

Now we all know that hurricanes are, of course, given women's names. Why? Because they're irrational, unpredictable, angry outbursts of death and destruction. They wreak havoc on everything in their path. Well, that's what's happening in this country today.

Tillman boldly thrusts up a copy of a book titled, *The Strange Death of President Harding*.

> We learned a sad lesson from this book, one even I did not want to accept at first, but we must be honest with ourselves. And the horrible truth, as this book proves, is that Mrs. Harding, the First Lady, killed her husband, the President. She poisoned him.

May Dixon Thacker screams from the balcony. "That book's a lie. I know, I wrote it!" The Speaker hammers his gavel. Some security officers run to Miss Thacker, who is still yelling, "A lie, a damn lie!" She is now hysterical. "A lie, a damn lie," she continues. The Speaker strikes his gavel hard as he calls for quiet, "Order in the house!" Thacker screams as security approaches, "I re-worked the incoherent lunacy of a serial liar into intelligible prose. All still a lie, but I made it a best seller."

Security guards now have Thacker in their grasp. She struggles ferociously and screams while being dragged from the Chamber. "It's a pack of lies from a criminal. I hope he dies, and soon." She battles mightily, twisting to and fro, and briefly breaks away from the security guards. She runs to the railing and shouts to the Congressmen below, "And the bastard never paid me! Asshole! You're all assholes!" The security guards rush at her, grabbing her securely this time. They carry the still-screaming woman from the gallery. Her forced departure leaves the room strangely silent. Tillman pauses for a second, shakes his head, and gestures to where Thacker has just been escorted out.

Now you see why hurricanes are given women's names. That, my friends, is precisely what I've come to talk to you about today.

Tillman now raises his hands.

Now, I won't dignify the pornography I am sure you are all aware of by bringing it into these hallowed halls. You all know of what I speak. The shameful deceit of a book a woman claims to have written, that, in explicit detail, falsely accused our President of despicable behavior – enjoying, outside his marriage, an intimacy with a girl which purportedly led to his fathering a child. Something we know he could not have done. It was a most outrageous falsehood, conveniently written after the President died. When he was not around to defend himself. The utter depravity of the accusations here cannot be overstated. Pornographic lie after pornographic lie about a dead man. Could there be a more vile girl in the world?

Tillman shakes his head in disbelief.

Just empty steamy blasphemous lies designed to titillate the masses. It sold well, though, and why? Because of all our current societal degradation, that's why. And what has led us to this widespread social immorality? Well, I will tell you. Women took us down this treacherous road. And it's our fault. We should never have granted them the freedom they didn't deserve and that they clearly can't handle.

Boos rain down from the women in the gallery. Tillman looks up in the direction of his detractors.

You're all lying tarts, depraved seekers of base pleasures. In any other time, you would have been tarred and feathered.

The suffragettes and others in the crowd hiss and boo loudly and ferociously for several minutes. They scream obscenities and blow raspberries at Tillman.

I think the ladies doth protest too much. But they help me make my point.

The Speaker pounds his gavel and screams for order in the Chamber. Tillman returns to his prepared remarks while the crowd murmurs disapproval from the gallery.

And there is yet another woman that is part of this sordid tale: a beautiful woman with a tiny waist and generous bosom. She knew how to use her endowments and seduced our President when he was at his most vulnerable. And she did so on behalf of a foreign power. Now men will be men, of course. We all know that, and so did she. And this clever German spy, an expert in the art of false love, attacked our great President and our great Country.

One suffragette screams out, "Bullshit, Tillman!" The Speaker pounds his gavel, "Two minutes left, Congressman." Tillman continues.

It's time we put a stop to all this. What do these three transgressions have in common? It's obvious. A woman was behind each of them. Committing treachery to a great man, a great legacy, and a great country.

The gallery erupts once more in condemnation. The Speaker again pounds his gavel, "One minute, Congressman." Tillman goes on.

What I am proposing today is what my friend Warren Harding so eloquently proposed years ago: A return to normalcy. The mistake we made that has taken us on this road to anarchy and will destroy our democracy was allowing women the right to vote. I propose a full repeal of the 19th Amendment, and we must do so before it is too late!

More boos come from the gallery. The Speaker interjects, "Congressman, your time is up." Gallery members chime in, "Sit down already." Undeterred, Tillman continues.

Let's take away the women's vote now and return to normalcy. Restore American Values Now - take women out of the ballot box and put them back in the kitchen where they belong.

The Speaker screams, "Time," as a group of suffragettes stands and chants in unison. "Women work, women vote, women work, women vote, women work, women vote."

PART II
The Beginning

Chapter 4

School's Out
1912: Marion, Ohio

The campus at Marion High School is empty, as the school year has finally ended. The elated students, intoxicated with youthful desires, merrily begin their long-anticipated summer vacation. No one is more looking forward to this break than sixteen-year-old Nan Britton. Nan has plans, big plans.

She now lies on the floor in her bedroom, cherishing the old Warren Harding campaign posters that cover her walls. Having lost his bid for Governor two years earlier, Mr. Harding is no longer in politics. Nan, though, cares nothing about his politics or career. She simply loves the man, a man she has not yet met. She loves him anyway. She always has and always will.

The Hardings are one of the most prominent and well-known families in Marion. Everyone is familiar with them, and Nan has known of the handsome Warren Harding her entire life. As luck would have it, and to Nan's delight, Warren Harding's sister, Daisy Harding, is her English teacher. She's worked hard in the class and is more than just the teacher's favorite. She and Daisy are becoming fast friends. Nan is giddy about her relationship with Daisy. It makes her feel close to the family and, therefore, close to the object of her secret infatuation, Warren Harding.

Nothing diminishes Nan's obsession with the former State Senator and former Lieutenant Governor. Nan's father, one of the few aware of this, is bewildered and exasperated by his daughter's excessive interest in a married man more than 30 years her senior. His efforts though to dampen her enthusiasm have backfired spectacularly. The more he disapproves, the more intense her feelings for the man easily old enough to be her father.

Now alone in her room, she professes love to the Harding images on the posters that adorn her walls. She looks at the clock. It reads 6:45pm. She gets up, looks in the mirror, and makes a promise to herself, "Tonight is the night. You're not going to chicken out. You will finally speak to him." She nods and touches the reflection of her hand in the mirror to seal the commitment.

A short time later, a precocious and determined Nan rides her bicycle past the Harding home. As expected, she sees Mr. and Mrs. Harding sitting on their porch. Warren Harding is reading a newspaper while his wife, Florence, knits. Nan rides by slowly and enthusiastically greets the couple, "Good evening." Mr. Harding looks pleasantly at the young girl and returns the salutation, "Well, good evening, young lady."

Nan then stops, smiles, and looks curiously at Mr. Harding. She looks at him with her head tilted, falsely acting as if she has only a vague recollection of speaking with someone she might somehow know. It is all a pretense, of course. She knows precisely who he is, but to create the illusion of serendipity, she pretends to be not quite sure about his identity. After a moment of silence, she breaks the ice with a query she well knows the answer to, "Excuse me, Sir. Are you Senator Harding?"

Harding laughs softly and graciously responds, "I'm not anymore. But I used to be a State Senator. I was Lieutenant Governor too but lost my bid for Governor. Now I am just an ordinary Joe." "Ordinary Warren, I think," says Nan, laughing. Warren joins her in her laughter. Florence though is stone silent.

Nan continues, "And not ordinary at all, in fact extraordinary. Wow, Senator Harding or Mr. Harding, I guess. It is a pleasure to meet you." Nan gets off her bike and approaches him and shakes his hand. "You were a great Senator. Our state is so much better now." Mr. Harding is flattered to have such a young and attractive female admirer. "Well, thank you very much. It's great to see our youth today paying attention to the workings of government."

Nan, delighted to have Harding's attention, continues, "And you know, Mr. Harding, if you should ever decide to run for office again, which I think would be a swell idea, and if women get to vote as they say might happen someday, well then I'd vote for you, and I'm sure a lot of other girls would too." Harding laughs heartily, "Well, thank you. I'll gladly accept your vote, but I wouldn't count on women ever getting the vote if I were you. Seems a little odd to me."

Nan, thrilled with the Harding interaction, blurts out, "I think you're the bees' knees, Mr. Harding. I've plastered loads of your photos on my bedroom wall." Harding is more than flattered. His thoughts are now prurient and predatory. He's an unapologetic seducer, a compulsive philanderer and is delighted by this attractive young woman's clear infatuation with him. He can't help but think lewd thoughts.

"Really?" responds Harding. Nan nods and continues, "Yes. You're such a spiffy wise head. I hope to go to secretarial school someday. Maybe if I graduate, I could work for you?" Harding eyes the young woman. He is intrigued by her youth and can't control his erotic thoughts. Looking at her husband making a fool of himself, her, and their marriage, Florence sits silently, fuming.

Harding smiles, "That would be nice." He pauses, then says, "Hey, I've got an idea. Why don't we add to your photo collection? Right now. The two of us together - we could take a photo." Nan is ecstatic, "Wow! That would be the cat's meow!" Harding then calls out to his wife, "Florence, get the Kodak while..." Harding pauses and looks lecherously at Nan. "I'm sorry. What is your name?"

Nan enthusiastically tells him, "Nan Britton." Harding stares at Nan as he repeats his request of Florence, "Yeah, Florence, go get the Kodak while Miss Britton and I get set up for our photo." Florence is noticeably annoyed. She takes a deep breath, glares at her husband but nonetheless goes inside to fetch the camera. As she steps inside, a highly irritated Florence speaks to herself, "You're a dick, Warren. You look even stupider than normal, and now you're making me look stupid too."

Oblivious to Florence's upset, Warren and Nan remain on the porch smiling at one another while exchanging suggestive glances. Nan runs her hand through her hair, flirtatiously fixing it, ostensibly for the photo but more to tease Harding. Harding, needing little encouragement, looks at her lustfully and smiles. He puts his arm around her, guides his hand around her waist, and then reaches down and grabs her butt. Nan coquettishly squeals, "Oooh, Mr. Harding!" and then giggles like the young girl she is. Harding, looking at Nan lecherously, laughs.

Florence returns. Though still seething, Florence steels herself as she looks at the flirtatious couple. Boiling with internal anger, she, with careful outward indifference, perfunctorily snaps a photo of the couple posing - Harding proudly smiling as a coy Nan leans into Warren, looking mischievously at the camera.

Chapter 5
Sleeping Turtle

A few days later, Harding has another meeting. This one is scheduled and in his office. It is with his attorney Harvey Daugherty and Daugherty's good friend and colleague, Jess Smith.

Daugherty and Smith are on their way to that meeting. Daugherty drives with a certain arrogance as he is quite proud of his newly acquired Stoddard Dayton Coupe.

Though a licensed attorney, Daugherty now just works as a political operative for the Republican Party. He is as underhanded as they come. He collects dirt on friends and foes alike, manipulates the system, lies, squeezes colleagues, and, when necessary, resorts to physical threats to get his way. He is, in short, an accomplished bully: feared and disliked in equal measure. He is highly effective.

Daugherty pulls up to the Marion Star building and parks on a side street near the office. From this vantage point, one can discreetly observe the people entering and exiting the building.

Daugherty remains seated in the vehicle. Jess Smith is about to open the passenger door to go to their appointment when Daugherty interrupts, "Wait a second. Not yet." Smith looks at Daugherty confused, "What are we waiting for? Harding knows we're coming, doesn't he?"

Daugherty laughs sinisterly. "Of course. But Florence has got to leave first." He looks at his pocket watch. "She'll be leaving in two minutes for lunch. At exactly 11:38 AM. Woman's a nut case, superstitious beyond belief. The clock, more specifically the minute hand, controls her. She leaves when the minute hand hits eight; it's her lucky number. And she's got to start her lunch, actually, everything, while the clock is on the upswing."

Smith is perplexed. "What the hell's the upswing?" Daugherty laughs and says sarcastically, "It's when the minute hand heads north toward the top of the clock, from half past to the top of the hour. That's when the mojo is good." Smith looks bewildered, "And when the big hand goes from the top of the hour to half past?" Daugherty says, "Catastrophe. Start anything on the downswing, and the evil spirits will get you." The two laugh at the absurdity of it all.

At exactly 11:38, they see Florence leave the building. Daugherty looks at Smith. "What did I tell you?" Smith nods. "Well, the good news is that we're starting our meeting with Harding on the upswing. I expect miracles." Smith laughs at his own joke. Daugherty pats Smith on the back and says laughingly, "You're now a Florenceology disciple."

Smith shakes his head as the two men exit the car and head to the building entrance. "Why's Harding even got her in the business?" Daugherty looks at him askance, "You kidding? She runs the place and turned it around.

And it was her daddy that bought it for him. If Harding were in charge, he'd run it into the ground. He couldn't find his way out of a paper bag. He's a loser. And losing her daddy's money would be bad, really bad."

The two men enter and approach Harding's secretary, Mrs. Gladstone. Though she knows and despises Harding's guests, she remains professional. "I'll tell Mr. Harding you're here." She knocks on Harding's office door and enters, letting him know his two visitors have arrived.

The always affable Harding immediately greets his guests. "Welcome, gentlemen, and please come in. So nice to see you two." Harding motions the men into his office. He follows and closes the door behind them. Harding sits behind his desk while Daugherty and Smith occupy the guest chairs.

Daugherty starts with small talk. "So, how's life in the private sector? Do you miss not being in public office?" Harding nods and says, "Not at all. Actually, I very much prefer the private life. It's going very well here, thank you. Losing the Governorship may have been the best thing ever to happen to me. Running this small-town newspaper: it's great. Meet lots of nice people. And I think I am respected around town by just about everyone, even Democrats. It's refreshing after all the rough and tumble backstabbing of politics."

Daugherty smiles, "That's so great to hear. I've always thought that there's a lot to be said for the simple life. The dull routine of being a common ordinary man has its hidden pleasures. You just got to look for them." Smith nods in agreement, "Boring is good." Harding, a good poker player, nods stoically in agreement. However, he is disturbed by these accurate yet derogatory depictions of his life.

The three men sit for a moment in silence. Daugherty then takes out an invoice. "Here's an invoice for my services. I know it seems high, but we had some major accomplishments, and the bill reflects our successes on your behalf."

He gestures to the invoice Harding is perusing, "You're a great client. I love helping you out. And, of course, I couldn't put it all in writing. A lot of our work is very discreet." He pauses, "Discretion; we specialize in that." He leans forward and speaks in a hushed tone, "We paid for a couple of abortions and bribed a dozen or so ladies." "Ladies?" Smith laughs and then winks at Harding and blurts out, "Prostitutes. One, rest her soul, committed suicide, a Jennifer Stanton, remember her?"

Harding shakes his head, "Name doesn't ring a bell." Daugherty shrugs, "We went looking for her, and her friends said you had told her you would divorce your wife and marry her. I can't imagine she believed that shit, but apparently she did. And she was so upset when you never called that she killed herself. Too bad, but it did save us some money. One less bitch to pay off." Smith laughs sinisterly.

This revelation is shocking to Harding. He grimaces and utters little moans in sympathy. "I didn't mean any harm to come to anyone." Daugherty waves him off. "Oh, it's not your fault. Not at all. You can't control a woman's emotions. No one can." Harding is briefly silent but realizes he can do nothing, so he changes the subject, "But why didn't you just mail the invoice like you usually do?"

"I got other news that I wanted to deliver personally. The Party wants me to spend my time exclusively on politics." Daugherty gestures around the office, "And now that you're in the private sector, I can't help you anymore.

Sorry, I'll try to find a replacement." Harding is unhappy and surprised, "But you're my attorney."

Daugherty shrugs and points to the invoice. "I wouldn't exactly call this legal work. I'm more like a pimp, don't you think?" Daugherty laughs at his self-deprecating joke. "Anyhow, are you banging the ladies like you used to when you were in politics?" Harding shrugs without answering. Daugherty knows that women have lost interest in him now that he is out of politics.

"Well, I guess you've lost me, and the ladies too." Daugherty chuckles. "But you got this nice little business here, and you can spend more time here and at home with Florence. A lot of together time with your wife." He pauses. "That's sweet." Daugherty is goading Harding. He knows Florence is a constant irritant and that Harding abhors every minute he's with her.

To rub it in, Daugherty turns to his colleague Smith and pats him on the leg. "Don't you think that's sweet, Jess? Spending more time with the wife." Smith smiles, "Wouldn't know. I'm divorced. I was happy to get rid of my ball and chain." Smith laughs, and Harding takes a deep breath.

Daugherty and Smith have achieved their goal. Though he needed little reminding, their comments have gotten under his skin. Harding detests Florence, and being constantly around her is annoying. And his insatiable carnal desires are not being met. He is craving the freedom and easy sexual perks he enjoyed in his political life.

Daugherty leans forward and speaks directly to Harding, "Look, Warren, all kidding aside, you can do better than this." He motions around the room and continues, "And the Party is looking for someone to run for U.S. Senator from Ohio. Think about it. You got public recognition. You're tall, look like somebody, and for some reason, people like you. You got the public fooled. You might win."

Daugherty pauses so Harding can let the thought sink in. "And if you win, you'd have more prestige than ever. Imagine being a U.S. Senator. And you'd get to spend a lot of time in D.C. Great place: lots of gorgeous women there that like to spend time with powerful men. And it's just far enough away from here to keep the wolves at bay." Daugherty looks at and gestures toward a photo of Florence. Smith howls like a wolf, and the three men laugh.

Daugherty puts up his hand to keep Harding from speaking. "Don't answer now. Just give it some thought and let me know. I know the Party bosses would love it if you said yes. You'd be helping out the Grand Old Party. And then we could become teammates again. I could work for you. I'd like that." The two men get up and shake Harding's hand and leave.

On the way back to the car, Smith asks Daugherty, "Why is this guy so important to the Party?" Daugherty shrugs. "The Party couldn't care less about him. We want him, though. He'd serve our interests well." Smith shakes his head, "But he's a happy small-town newspaper guy. He doesn't have the balls for big-time politics if you ask me. A wishy-washy henpecked zilch."

Daugherty laughs. "The zilch factor. That's why I like him. Florence pulls the strings at home and here in the business. We pull his political strings." Still uncertain, Smith shakes his head. "He's like watered-down tea. We need backbone, some gumption, someone that's 100-proof whiskey – not this guy." Daugherty pats Smith on the back. "Don't worry. He's a sleeping turtle on a log right now. I am here to push him off. Then he'll have to swim."

Chapter 6
Day Five

Nan looks at her calendar. On it she has memorialized June 12th, 1912, her first encounter with Mr. Harding, as "Day One", and numerically counted off each subsequent day. Today is day five. She has been ecstatic since that encounter. In her mind, she has relived every moment, every glance, and every spoken word. She has relived it hundreds of times. Each recollection brings a soft smile.

It was, continues, and will always be, a wonderful memory. Nan wants more than a memory, though. She wants happily ever after with the man she has longed for nearly all her life. She is well aware of the significant obstacles: the 30-year age difference, his wife, and the certain destruction to both his career and their social prominence should they become a couple. All that be damned, she and the man she loves deserve happiness. And she knows he will be happy with her and only her. It will take time, diligence, and determination—all traits Nan has in abundance.

Five days have passed. It is now time for the second encounter, and, besides, Nan desperately wants a copy of the photograph they took together. Nan embarks on her pursuit.

It's late morning, and she rushes off to the office of the Marion Star newspaper. She steals her way to the outside back wall of the office and stands on her tippy toes. Peering into the window of Warren Harding's office, she secretly watches as Harding, editor of the Marion Star, discusses tomorrow's edition with a reporter. Though unable to hear their conversation, Nan is certain that the eloquent Mr. Harding, a gentleman she is sure is of superior intellect, is offering brilliant and sound advice to his employee.

The reporter leaves, and Harding turns to grab his coat and hat. Just before Harding can glimpse her in the window, Nan ducks from view and hunkers down with her back to the wall. Unseen, she counts backward to herself, "Five, four, three, two, one."

At the count of one, she starts running to the building entrance. Her plan and timing work too well as she nearly collides with Harding as he leaves the building. Both Harding and Nan are in a bit of shock. "Oh, excuse me," Nan proclaims, smiling at the man she loves. Nan continues, "Oh, Mr. Harding, what a pleasure. Nice to see you again. Sorry about nearly running you over."

Harding laughs a bit. "I was startled, but I doubt a collision with a pretty little waif-like you would do me much harm." Harding immediately recognizes Nan, remembers her infatuation with him, and instantly thinks lustfully. He, nonetheless, wants to flirt, so he pretends to have only a vague recollection of her. He hopes that this ruse will add to his allure. "Have we met before?" Nan nods enthusiastically. After a short pause, he blurts out, "Oh, of course, it's you! What a wonderful coincidence."

"Well, kind of," responds Nan. "I came by to get a copy of the photo we took together last week." Harding continues to play it coy, feigning not to remember. He thinks for a minute and ponders the query. "Photo? I am sorry. I meet an awful lot of people and take a lot of photographs. Please remind me of your name and where we met?"

Then he immediately gestures to her not to answer. "No. Don't answer. Give me a moment; I think I might remember." He deliberately pauses, acts as if he is thinking hard, and eventually says, "Yes, on the porch the other evening, and don't tell me your name. Let me see if I can remember that too." Nan looks excited as Harding fakes, racking his brain for the memory.

He vividly recalls her name. "Why, you are Nan, is that right?" Nan enthusiastically responds that he is indeed correct. "Yes, and do you have a copy of that photo for me?" Harding willingly responds, "I will, of course. Come to my office next week. Ask my Secretary, Mrs. Gladstone, for a copy. And by the way, she's my campaign manager. I'm running for U.S. Senator."

Nan is delighted with all this good news. She will get a copy of the photo, and the fact that Harding is again entering the political arena is, for Nan, joyous. "Oh, that's swell, Mr. Harding! I hope my encouragement helped persuade you." "Well, let's hope I do better this time," he says, trying to temper Nan's excitement, "And good thing you ran into me today. We leave for Europe tomorrow with my best friend Jim Philips and his wife."

Nan is completely in awe. Mr. Harding is such a worldly man! Few travel abroad. It's for the wealthy, sophisticated, and educated. It is an enormous endeavor, and he said it in such a nonchalant manner. For a man of his stature, such an exotic trip must just be a common occurrence. To Nan, this is too much. She looks at Harding with great admiration proclaiming, "Europe! Wow! A foreign country!"

A week later, Nan, following his instructions to the tee, is in Harding's office to get the photo. As promised, Mrs. Gladstone, a somewhat maternal woman, hands Nan a copy of it. "He told me to be sure to give this to you when you came by and to thank you so much for encouraging him to again run for office." Nan smiles broadly, now believing she really did have something to do with his return to politics.

"Golly, he's such a great man. I can't imagine who wouldn't vote for him." Mrs. Gladstone looks over her glasses at the naïve Nan. "Well, my dear little girl, I can assure you, there are more than a few that won't be voting for him. It's going to be a very tough election." On the spot, Nan volunteers, "Gee, can I help? I mean, I'll work on his campaign for nothing. I admit I don't know a thing about politics, but I know a good man when I see one and would do anything to help him."

Mrs. Gladstone knows this is an awful idea. Nan will only get in the way and make things worse. However, she knows her boss well. Though typically compassionate, she knows Harding's dark side. He is a lecher with unbridled sexual cravings for very young women and girls. Mrs. Gladstone knows the quickest way to turn the normally charming Harding into an ugly barking and bullying ogre is to get between him and his erotic desires.

Mrs. Gladstone, therefore, carefully chooses her words in responding to Nan. "We're just getting started, but sure, you can help, but only if you have time. If you're studying, Mr. Harding would prefer you to focus on your schoolwork." "Oh, I'll make the time," Nan quickly replies.

"Well, as mentioned, we're just getting started, but I'm sure we can find something for you to do if you want to swing by for a couple of hours an afternoon a week." Nan nods enthusiastically, "I'll stop by on Fridays." "That is fine dear. There will probably be more to do when Mr. Harding returns from vacation. I'm sure he'll find creative uses for your talents." "Oh," replies Nan, "I'll do whatever he wants!"

Mrs. Gladstone looks up at Nan and removes her glasses. "I'm sure he'll be most appreciative." Nan smiles, then looks concerned. She is worried Harding's European excursion and long absence will adversely affect his run for the Senate. "Should he even have gone on this trip? Won't it hurt his chances?"

Mrs. Gladstone looks at Nan. "Well, it might, but didn't he tell you?" Nan is perplexed. "Tell me what?" "Oh," replies Mrs. Gladstone, "He's on a sympathy trip. His friends lost their son, just a toddler. He's helping them ease their pain." Nan sighs in admiration. "Putting friend-ship over career. He's such a caring man."

Chapter 7

The Refreshing Sea Air

A month later, the luxury liner carrying the two couples (the Hardings and Phillipses) is on its return trip from Europe. Warren Harding and Carrie Phillips are alone and below deck. They saunter to a storage room door, look furtively around, see no one, and quickly enter.

Once inside, they cannot control their unbridled passion for one another. Harding stares stupidly at Carrie's chest as she unbuttons her blouse. Carrie notices and slaps him hard. "Your adolescence is overwhelmingly annoying. If you weren't so attractive, I'd have nothing to do with you!" She looks hard at the now dumbfounded Harding. She waits a second and then slaps him again. She pauses and then kisses him passionately.

The two giggle softly. The exhilaration of their upcoming intimacy is heightened by the chance they could be discovered by the crew or even their respective spouses, who aren't far away.

And unbeknownst to them, they are indeed found out. Florence happens to be strolling down the hallway on her way to the upper deck. She passes the storage room and stops on hearing the easily recognizable sounds of sexual grunting and groaning. And with a high degree of certainty, she identifies the groans as belonging to her husband and her friend. She is furious but moves on and goes up on deck.

Oblivious to his wife's tryst below, James Phillips lays comfortably on a chaise lounge on the deck. Nearby is James' and Carrie's four-year-old daughter, Isabelle, who plays with a coloring book. Still silently angry, Florence takes a lounge chair next to James and smiles sympathetically at him. James turns to her, "The voyage is helping so much. My darling Carrie seems more like herself now." Florence takes a deep breath and responds sarcastically, "Well, the sea air can be so refreshing."

In the storage room below, the cheating couple chuckle with conspiratorial delight. Having completed their illicit activity, they are giddy with guilty pleasure. On deck, James is somber. He looks toward Florence and cries, "I wish I were doing as well as Carrie. I'm not sure I'll ever get over the loss of our son." Florence gently takes his hand in sympathy.

Below deck, Warren and Carrie smile slyly at one another as they silently finish dressing. Warren opens the storage room a tad, sees no one coming, and motions to Carrie that they need to exit quickly.

A few minutes later, the cavorting adulterers act nonchalantly and join their respective spouses on deck. Florence turns to Carrie and makes a cynical inquiry, "Where did you and my husband run off to? You're not trying to steal him from me, I hope. I can assure you, he's most definitely not worth stealing." Carrie laughs nervously, then responds, "I just had to show Warren the beautiful porcelain pieces I got in Dresden. He is such an admirer of the finer things in life." Florence turns to Warren, then making sure she is seen, looks at Carrie's oversized breasts. "Hadn't you seen those yet? They're marvelous, aren't they?" Harding smiles apprehensively. "Indeed, they're quite the sight."

Wishing to change the subject, Carrie takes her husband's hand and clears her throat to get everyone's attention. "Now that I have your attention," she declares, "Jim and I have a very big announcement. We're moving to Germany next year. Isabelle and I are anyhow, for the school year."

Harding is shocked. "Really?" "Yes, really," Carrie responds, "We want Isabelle properly educated. We want her to grow up hearing Bach and Beethoven and reading Goethe and Schiller. I just so love Germany. Such a delightfully refined and sophisticated culture, Isabelle must be given the best."

Her comment is met with surprised silence, so Carrie nods to her husband, imploring him to add something to the conversation. Jim stumbles, then says, "Well, I'll miss them, but we think it's for the best. And they'll be back for summers." Carrie nods approvingly as Jim smiles awkwardly.

A few days later, the ship approaches the dock. Waiting for them is an ecstatic Nan and a reluctant Mrs. Gladstone. They hold up a handmade banner that says VOTE HARDING FOR SENATOR. Florence is the first to notice the sign and is not pleased. She points to it as she disembarks and speaks to Warren, "Looks like you have a fan club." Harding is also embarrassed by the display and grimaces.

Harding tries his best to remain polite as he approaches Mrs. Gladstone. He gestures toward the sign, "Thank you,

Mrs. Gladstone, but maybe we're jumping the gun a little." Mrs. Gladstone is similarly uncomfortable and explains, "Oh, this was Nan's idea. I suggested this could wait, but I can't control her enthusiasm for you. She's your first and, I think, most ardent volunteer. I think you'll find her energy to your liking." Harding smiles and looks in Nan's direction. "Well, thank you, Nan. You'll be a great addition to the campaign. I can't wait to get to know you better."

Florence looks at her husband scornfully as he looks lecherously at and unabashedly flirts with the much younger Nan. Florence remembers well the photograph she took of them a few months back. She was displeased then and even more so now, knowing that Nan has wiggled her way into her husband's campaign and is seemingly stalking him.

The four travelers awkwardly head off to waiting cars as Nan and Mrs. Gladstone walk behind them with their banner. Unaware of the awkwardness, Nan enthusiastically shouts and waves as they drive off. She chants an impromptu campaign slogan: "Harding's our darling. Vote for our darling, Harding."

Chapter 8
Double the Pleasure

Mrs. Gladstone sighs silently but smiles at Nan as she enters Warren G. Harding's campaign office, a converted office in the Marion Star building. "You've become quite a fixture here lately. Our most active volunteer. Mr. Harding is certainly getting his money's worth with you." Nan giggles. "I am so happy to be part of so important a project. It makes me feel as if my life has meaning. A chance to help out such a great man. It's wonderful. I love it here."

"Isn't your schoolwork suffering, though?" Mrs. Gladstone asks, reminding her of her initial commitment: "I thought you could only spare one afternoon a week. You're here almost daily now." Nan reassures Mrs. Gladstone, "My schoolwork is going well. Well, maybe a little less well than before, but English is my only important class, and my teacher is Mr. Harding's sister, Daisy, so she understands." Mrs. Gladstone responds skeptically, "Does she? It's curious then that Daisy herself hasn't volunteered."

Nan looks away sheepishly. She has deliberately misled Mrs. Gladstone. And she is quite certain Mrs. Gladstone is aware of the deception. Nan and Daisy's friendship is quite strained right now. Daisy is now aware of Nan's obsession with her married brother and strongly disapproves. Daisy has repeatedly and pointedly told Nan to pursue other interests and enjoy the company of friends her own age. And she has firmly counseled Nan to, by all means, cease working for the Harding Senate campaign. Nan has ignored all this advice.

And Daisy knows her brother well. She accurately described him to Nan as "an old bugger; a lazy womanizing alcoholic and a nightmare for any respectable woman." She continued, "And he's too old and too married for you. Should anything happen between you two, it would ruin you both and the reputation of our families."

Nan is oblivious to his faults and the potential consequences of her actions. She pointedly explained to Daisy, "I'm an independent young woman living in modern times and free to choose my own path. Isn't that what you taught me in class?"

For Nan, her love for Warren trumps her friendship with Daisy. If one must be sacrificed, it is the latter. Accordingly, Nan now spends most afternoons in Warren's campaign office. She looks in Mrs. Gladstone's direction, puts her purse down, and begins stuffing envelopes. "I'll just pick up where I left off yesterday. Will we be seeing Ohio's next Senator today?"

Mrs. Gladstone is busy shuffling papers. She pretends not to hear the question, so she does not respond. And she has now been interrupted by another of Harding's assistants that just entered the room. The assistant whispers in Mrs. Gladstone's ear, "Mr. Harding would like to see Nan. Make up some reason for her to come to his office." They both look at the clock. It is 11:40 AM, and they look knowingly at each other. Florence, as always, left for lunch two minutes earlier, at exactly 11:38 AM.

Mrs. Gladstone breathes deeply, gathers some papers, and then says, "Oh, Nan, I have to run another errand. Would you be so kind as to drop these papers off on Mr. Harding's desk? He's expecting these and needs to look at them right away." The reason she gives is weak and implausible. Mrs. Gladstone could have easily handed off the documents on the way to the other errand she claimed she had. Nan is oblivious to this reality; she's just delighted by the assignment. "I'd be happy to." She immediately grabs the documents and heads to Harding's office.

His door is ajar, but she knocks softly and pokes her head inside. "Excuse me, Mr. Harding, but I have some documents for you, Sir." Harding looks up, though expected, he is very pleased by the visit. "By all means, do come in, Nan. A pleasure to see you, and thanks so much for all your hard work. With your help, we might pull this thing off." Harding gets up, closes the door, and motions Nan to sit in one of the guest chairs. He moves the adjacent guest chair close to Nan and sits beside her.

"Now, what is it you came to see me about?" Harding asks. "Oh. Mrs. Gladstone wanted me to give these papers to you. She said they were important, and you needed to see them immediately." She hands over the papers, making sure she touches his arm. He takes the documents and gently pats her hand, "Well, thank you." He begins reading the documents and, while doing so, spreads his legs so their thighs touch. Their physical contact though somewhat subtle, is not at all accidental. And it is sensual for both and mutually desired. Nan smiles at Harding as he reads the papers (or, more accurately, pretends to read them).

She then not-so-accidentally lightly brushes the top of her hand on his upper thigh. Harding is ecstatic at the gesture. Nan looks away briefly and then smiles shyly. She then looks down at his crotch and notices a bulge, the beginning of an erection. She's pleased with this reaction but feels it is time to leave. She stands, "I don't want to be taking too much of your time, so I best be getting back to work now." Harding nods, "Of course."

He calls out as she opens the door to leave, "You know, we should have a celebratory dinner. Just a small group of us, and I'd like you to be part of that gathering." "I'd love to, but don't we need to win first?" "Nonsense," responds Harding, "We'll do it now before the election. The worst that happens is that we have two such dinners. Another after we win!" Nan laughs, "Double the pleasure; that sounds great."

Chapter 9
A Very Small Gathering

Harding, Mrs. Gladstone and Nan approach the Maître d' at a swish, intimate restaurant. He greets them, "Good evening, Sir." Harding replies, "Yes, good evening. Our reservations are under the name of Harding." The Maître d' notes the reservation, grabs some menus, and motions the party to a secluded booth.

Nan turns to Harding, "Who else will be joining us tonight? Will Mrs. Harding be coming?" Harding replies, "Mrs. Harding has her bridge club tonight. I invited others too, but they were all previously engaged, and I didn't want to put off our celebration. After all, the key members are all here."

Nan sits next to Harding, and Mrs. Gladstone is a comfortable distance on the other side of Nan. Harding smiles as the waiter approaches the table. "Let's order drinks." "Oh, Mr. Harding. I am not of age." Harding waves for Nan to stop her protest. He winks at her, "I will take full responsibility for your actions." He turns to the waiter, "Yes, why don't we all start with a Hanky Panky. A glass for everyone, please." The waiter nods and agrees to comply, "Yes, of course, Sir. A glass for everyone." Nan smiles a bit deviously.

As the evening progresses, Nan and Harding become increasingly cozy and playfully affectionate. They giggle, touch, and smile at one another. Mrs. Gladstone, at the same time, is increasingly detached from their conversation. She is very much the third wheel tonight. Harding arm-twisted her into attending, a necessary part of Harding's plans. She is the unwanted and ineffective chaperone. She hates the role and is angry that she's part of Harding's antics. She rightly feels exploited, having been unfairly pressured to attend.

As the evening ends, they leave the restaurant. Harding waves for a taxi. "We'll drop you off, Mrs. Gladstone, and then head to our neck of the woods," Harding declares. "Thanks, but that's not necessary. You know I'm in the opposite direction, so I'll just get my own cab," proclaims Mrs. Gladstone, coldly. Harding smiles, "Very well," as he and Nan enter the car. He looks lecherously at Nan, then briefly turns toward Mrs. Gladstone. Delighted to be rid of this third wheel, he says hastily, "See you tomorrow in the office, Mrs. Gladstone." He then turns his passionate gaze toward Nan.

The car carrying Nan and Harding is a few blocks from her home. Harding calls out, "Driver, please pull over and stop. We'll get out here." Nan looks curiously at Harding, who replies, "Like to stretch my legs a bit and work off that large dinner." He pays the driver. They exit the vehicle and begin strolling toward the Britton family home. "Oh, it's gotten a bit chilly," Nan says, lying. "May I take your arm?" Harding gladly accepts the offer and smiles at Nan. "It's been a wonderful evening. Let's hope there are many more just like it." Nan smiles broadly at Harding's suggestion.

They are near the Britton home. Harding looks at Nan and takes her hands. "Thank you again, Nan. It's been a delight having you in the office." "Oh, the pleasure's mine, Mr. Harding," she replies. They are now almost at Nan's home. Harding looks around, "And Nan, I don't want to be too forward or in any way inappropriate, but would it be ok to give you a small peck on the cheek?" Nan looks demurely at Harding and hesitates. "Actually," she pauses, "I'd welcome more." He smiles and looks at her. He draws her toward him, and the two kiss passionately.

PART III

Mr. Harding Goes to Washington

Chapter 10
Ohio's Best Day Ever: November 4 1914

Nan is ecstatic as she adds to the Harding homage that adorns her bedroom. Today is the day after the election and Nan is delighted to affix to her wall the lead story from the Marion Daily Star. It reads:

> *Warren G. Harding - Now U.S. Senator-Elect*
>
> *Four years after his failed gubernatorial bid, Harding achieved an amazing political comeback with a Senatorial win. "I didn't give up on Ohioans, and they didn't give up on me."*

Nan looks proudly at the news article she has just posted. She gently kisses the photo of Harding in the article, "And I will never give up on you, Senator-elect Harding." She moves back a bit, still admiring the piece she has posted, and proclaims to her empty bedroom, that this day is "Ohio's best day ever." She smiles and continues, "And now it's time for our second celebratory dinner. Maybe this time, I could be dessert!"

Meanwhile, another Harding admirer, Mrs. Carrie Phillips, is checking into the Lofts Hotel in Columbus, Ohio. She wears a plain dress and a matching hat. Her shapeless boxy dress hides her ample bosom and hourglass figure. She wears her hat quite low, the brim just above her eyelids. The reception clerk is filling out the paperwork, "Just one night, Mrs. Phillips?" She nods, "Yes."

He hands her the key and points toward the elevators. "Take the elevator to the top floor and turn left when you get off. We had availability, so I put you in one of our deluxe rooms. It has a very nice view. I'm sure you'll find it to your liking."

Carrie smiles apologetically and pushes the key back. "Thank you so much, but I have a fear of heights. Is there, by chance, anything available on the first floor?" The clerk, a consummate professional, accommodates her request. "Certainly, Mrs. Phillips." He scratches the completed registration information and writes in the new room number. "Here's a key to room 103, a comfortable and quiet room." She graciously takes the key, "Sounds perfect, thank you."

She takes the elevator up one floor, puts her small suitcase on the hotel dresser, takes out a pen and writes '103' on page three of her newspaper, then leaves her room. She takes the inner stairway to the lobby and leaves the hotel with newspaper in hand. She strolls down the sidewalk and sits on a park bench. She looks around, gets up, and returns to the hotel, leaving the folded newspaper on the bench.

Harding, wearing a trench coat and hat, strolls by the bench a few minutes later. He picks up and opens the discarded newspaper. He sits down and spends some time reading a few articles. However, his interest is not in the newspaper's prose but in the room number Carrie Phillips has written on the top of page three as prearranged. He looks around and sees no one. He is pleased. He believes he's not been noticed. He smiles to himself, gets up and heads to the hotel.

Harding arrives at the hotel some twenty minutes after Carrie re-entered. He moves with alacrity through the lobby with his head low. He goes up the inner stairs and knocks on room 103. Carrie, now wearing a sexy bustier, opens the door and greets him in a cultured yet erotic tone, "What took you so long?" "Sorry, my dear, I wanted to ensure I wasn't seen." They embrace and kiss. He disengages and smiles at her, "Well, mission accomplished again." He laughs, takes off his hat, and with Carrie's' welcome help, they begin removing his clothes together.

A short time later, the deed now done, the lovers lie together comfortably in bed. "You know," Carrie says, "I want to congratulate you on your victory. But honestly, I was hoping you'd lose. I wanted Hogan." Harding is stunned, "You wanted me to lose? You wanted Hogan, a Roman Catholic? How could you?" Carrie looks at him matter-of-factly, "I would have preferred anyone to you. I'd have even taken a Jew."

Harding is bewildered. "You do the nasty with me but want a Jew to have official power?" Harding laughs, "Totally irrational. But you can't help it; you're a woman." He kisses her, "You, my dear, are exhibit one as to why women should not get the vote." Harding laughs, smiles at her, and then gives her another kiss. "I do love you, though."

She returns the smile and embraces him lovingly. "I wanted you to lose because it would have been easier." "Easier for what?" Harding asks. "For us to marry. We must divorce our spouses. Then we can marry and move together to Germany. It is a superior place." Harding shakes his head. "That's quite a plan. You aren't serious, are you?" She looks at him sternly.

"Sure, I am," she replies. "It's a bit more complicated now, but it's just one extra step. You'll have to resign as Senator. They'll appoint a new one, and there's a Republican governor, so our party will still hold the seat." Harding is stunned. "You are serious!" "Of course, I am. We were meant to be together. We both know it, and you'll find life in Germany far more civilized than here. Germans are a higher class. And they all look like us. At least the important and powerful ones. They're our kind of people."

Harding stumbles for a response. "Carrie, let me give this Senator thing a try, at least for a while. Then we'll see." Carrie shakes her head and smirks, "Now I remember why I wanted Hogan to win. He was right. You've got no balls."

Chapter 11
The Boys Pay a Visit

Loud and repeated knocking startles and wakes freshman Senator Harding, who has been sleeping soundly on the couch in his office. The Appropriations Bill he had started reading lies on his chest, open at page one. His intention to read the bill comfortably on the couch went awry. He dozed off halfway through the first page and fell fast asleep. Abruptly awakened and groggy, the Senator looks at the door, and the direction of the continued knocking. "Just a minute, I'll be right there."

Harding opens the door and greets two serious-looking gentlemen in suits, white shirts, and ties. "Yes, how may I help you, gentlemen?" The two men display their badges; both are Bureau of Investigation agents. "Sir, may we come in, please?" Now ill at ease and very much awake, Harding replies, "Of course." One of the men closes the door behind him as Harding ushers them in, motioning them to the seats in front of his desk as he goes to sit behind it.

"Sir, I am Jim Thornberry, and this is my partner, Steven Grantz. We have some questions for you if you don't mind?" A somewhat anxious Harding tries to make light of the situation. "Sure, I hope I haven't done anything wrong." He laughs nervously but abruptly stops when he notices the two men remain stoney-faced. Harding is now worried. Perhaps he is in trouble.

"Sir, do you by chance know a Mrs. Carrie Phillips?" Thornberry asks. Harding nods, "Yes, I do. She and her husband are old friends from Marion." Thornberry continues, "And have you seen her recently?"

Harding leans back and looks around, thinking, "You know, I get back to Ohio regularly. Meet with constituents, family, friends, businessmen, politicians, and lots of ordinary folks. I can't remember them all." Fearing the Senator is about to incriminate himself, Thornberry holds up his hand to stop Harding. He nods to his partner, signaling him to hand Harding some photos and a piece of paper.

"Sir, if you don't mind, let me help you to recollect. Mrs. Phillips is a very attractive woman. She looks like a Gibson girl to me. I think you'd remember her. And according to our records," he nods at the documents just handed to Harding, "Looks like you've met with her at least a few times recently; at the Loft Hotel in Columbus, a number of times at the Stambaugh Hotel in Youngstown, and other places too." He gestures toward the list now in Harding's hands. "I understand it's a pretty special place, the Stambaugh. Couldn't afford it myself, but I hear it's very romantic."

Harding blushes, as it's clear these men know of his affair with Carrie. He's upset by the violation of his privacy. Without thinking, he exclaims, somewhat indignantly, "Are you two following me?" "Oh no, Sir," replies

Thornberry, as he looks at Grantz, who confirms this information, shaking his head too, "Absolutely not, Sir."

Somewhat relieved, Harding leans back in his chair, but then sits up, realizing the truth: "You're following her, aren't you?" "Sir, we don't like to use the word 'follow'," Thornberry says. "That's right," says Grantz, "We just keep an eye on certain people. That's how we put it. We keep an eye on some people."

"I think you know that Mrs. Phillips spends a lot of time in Germany," Grantz volunteers. Harding nods. "I do know that. Actually, it was while on a trip there with us that she became infatuated with the country. We all went to Europe to try to console Jim Phillips and Carrie. They had lost their toddler son earlier that year."

"That's very kind of you, Sir," Grantz smirks. "Sounds like she's been very receptive to your condolences." Harding blushes, and Thornberry jumps in, "Sir, we don't care about your personal life. That's not our business." Harding nods appreciatively, suddenly relieved. "But what we do care about is national security, and we are concerned that Mrs. Phillips may be working with the German Government."

Harding is stunned. "I really don't think so." "Sir, as you know, Germany is embroiled against our allies in a great war in Europe. There is talk we may be entering the conflict, and we are concerned about information, confidential information, you might inadvertently tell her that she might pass on to our adversaries." Harding is genuinely flabbergasted. "I've never revealed Government secrets to her or to anyone." "That's good to hear, Sir," Grantz says skeptically.

Harding nods, pauses, and then asks, "You think she's a spy?" Thornberry shrugs, "It's possible. We really don't know, but just be careful, Sir. That's all we are saying." The men stand up to leave.

Harding walks them to the door, "Of course, I'll be careful." "Thank you, Sir. And here are our cards." Both Thornberry and Grantz hand Harding their business cards. "Give us a call if she does anything suspicious or asks inappropriate questions." Grantz adds with a smirk, "About government stuff, Sir." He laughs quietly. "We aren't interested in any personal favors she may want from you." Harding glares at Grantz and puts their cards in his pocket. "Rest assured, I'll call you if something comes up that you need to know." Thornberry, trying to be more diplomatic, says, "Thank you, Sir, and thank you for your service to our country."

PART IV
Love and Happiness

Chapter 12

The Second Celebration: July 30 1917

It is time for a real, albeit delayed, second celebration. And this one will be very special and more deserved. Harding was, of course, victorious and it is time for him to realize the spoils of victory. And this time, it will be a most intimate affair. It will be just Nan and Harding.

Right now, Nan is alone. She sits patiently in the lobby of the Imperial Hotel in Manhattan. She reads a newspaper while glancing regularly at the hotel's entrance. Eventually, she sees Harding enter through the revolving doors.

He heads directly to the registration desk to check in. Nan gets up and goes toward the elevator just as Harding leaves the front desk with the hotel key in hand. Their timing is impeccable. They arrive simultaneously as the elevator doors open. Neither acknowledges the other.

The two are among a half-dozen or so that board the same elevator. Nan and Harding have made no eye contact and only briefly glance at each other as they quietly ride the elevator. They have arranged this New York City rendezvous hoping to avoid prying glances from their Marion or D.C. acquaintances.

Nan is now a young woman. She is a very attractive, engaging and alluring 20-year-old woman. Though 30 years her senior, her companion is charming and handsome. Nan wears a short pink linen dress. She exits the elevator and looks back mischievously as Harding follows her.

Nan plays with the lapel of his coat as they stroll down the hallway. She takes the room key from him as they arrive at the door. Harding very much welcomes her flirtatiousness. He plays along and laughs lightly at her antics. Nan asks, "And what name did we check in under?" "Why," responds Harding, "We're Mr. Harvey and wife, tonight." Nan is delighted. "I get to play Mrs. Harvey then. What a pleasure." Nan opens the door and enters.

Nan gushes as she rushes to the window to admire the mesmerizing city view. Harding, having just closed the door, is similarly enthralled. He's beguiled, not by the city view, but by the contours of Nan's nubile figure. Nan looks back at him and motions suggestively to him to join her as she slowly unhooks and starts to unzip her dress.

Harding smiles and moves toward her. He stands behind her, gently massaging her shoulders and neck. Nan tilts her head back. She feels his erect penis against her butt and smiles. An ice bucket nearby holds a bottle of champagne. She takes a single ice cube from it, gently licks it, then reaches behind her and strokes it down his neck, then around her own neck so that her dress is now off her shoulders. She takes the ice cube to her chest and then drops it, swaying back to lift her firm breasts. Harding reaches over her shoulder and under her top to caress her breasts. She smiles, takes his hand, turns, and lovingly kisses him. The two kiss passionately as he unzips and takes off her dress. She wraps her legs around him and giggles as he carries her to the bed.

Some twenty minutes later, their lovemaking over, Nan lies naked in bed. She smiles softly as Harding, wearing a hotel robe, opens the champagne. Nan laughs joyfully as the cork pops. Simultaneously, the hotel door opens violently. Two members of the NYC Vice Squad, a police sergeant and an officer, burst in and proceed to handcuff Harding and the naked Nan.

"What's happening?!?" Nan exclaims. The police officer, matter of factly, responds, "You're being arrested." Harding interjects, "Let this poor little girl go. She's done nothing wrong. And you're embarrassing her. She's naked."

Truth be told, Nan is not the least bit embarrassed by her nakedness. She knows she has a good body and is not ashamed to show it off. She is, however, not thrilled about being handcuffed and arrested.

The police sergeant continues, unapologetically, "You're being arrested for adultery - sexual intercourse with another when there is a living spouse. Punishable by up to 90 days in jail and a $500 fine."

The accompanying police officer picks up Harding's wallet on the nightstand and peruses its contents. He is now alarmed and speaks to his superior. "Sarge, I think you should see this." The sergeant looks in the wallet just handed to him and then at Harding. "You're Senator Harding from Ohio?" Harding replies bluntly, "One and the same. Pleasure to make your acquaintance." The police officers hurriedly remove the handcuffs and hand Harding his wallet. Nan immediately puts on a robe.

The suddenly contrite sergeant is apologetic, "Our mistake Sir. Please forgive us." Harding is relieved and now in control. "No need to apologize, gentlemen. You were just doing your job and doing it well." The concerned officers make their way to the door, meekly uttering their appreciation, "Thank you, Sir."

"Hold on a second, gentlemen." The men stop and turn. "You two look like fine, understanding gentlemen. I imagine you've been in similar situations yourselves." The men nod vigorously, perhaps anticipating what is about to happen. Harding takes some cash from his wallet and hands it to them. "It'd probably be best to keep this under wraps." The sergeant quickly responds, "Of course, we understand, Sir. Mum's the word. We'll just be on our way."

Harding puts his arms around them as he walks them out. "Gentlemen, please come visit me if you're ever in D.C. Be great to see you again. I am impressed by your diligence." The police officer motions to Nan. "Sir, we're very impressed too." Harding laughs and winks at the officer as he closes the door after their departure. He sighs deeply, knowing he has just dodged a career-ending bullet. "Wow. That was exciting." Nan puts her arms around his neck, kisses him affectionately, and giggles, "Just one thrill after another tonight." The lovers laugh with abandon.

Chapter 13

The Most Important Diary Entry

It is the next morning, and Harding walks with Nan to Grand Central Station. Nan is on the platform, about to board the train to Ohio. She turns to Harding, "Back to Marion where it all began." Harding smiles. Nan continues, "You know, I'm seeing Daisy tomorrow - our book club. Should I say hello for you?" Harding is shocked. "My sister? Add fuel to that fire? She's already suspicious of us."

Nan laughs. "I'm just teasing. I know we're a secret for now, but won't it be great when we can tell everyone we're a couple." Harding exhales. "All in due course, my dear." The lovers embrace, and then Nan boards the train.

Now en route to Marion, Nan sits in the train car and writes the following entry in her diary:

July 30, 1917 - Imperial Hotel - NYC - The day and place I first gave myself to a man and to the man I love more than any I could ever love.

More magical and adventuresome than I even imagined. It was perfect. I love him so much.

She continues writing, with great explicitness, about their encounter. She smiles softly and sometimes slightly deviously. She re-reads what she has just written, sighs with the pleasure of the wonderful remembrance, and then closes her diary. She then takes out and reads her book, James Joyce's A Portrait of the Artist as a Young Man.

Chapter 14
Daisy's Book Club

It is afternoon, and the book club is having their monthly meeting in Daisy Harding's living room. Today's discussion is on James Joyce's novel, A *Portrait of the Artist as a Young Man*. The conversation about the book is now getting heated. It is no longer a discussion. It is a fierce debate about whether the novel is literature or base debauchery. The estranged friends, Nan and Daisy, monopolize the discourse and are clearly at loggerheads. It is awkward for all.

"I loved it. So full of life," Nan exclaims. "What?" Daisy retorts. "A life of debauchery. Prostitution, masturbation. You admire that?" Nan looks hard at Daisy, "The zest, yes. We are all human with carnal needs and desires. It's part of life. An important part. It's about life, Daisy, and how we should live life to the fullest."

Daisy is equally firm. "Absolutely not. The protagonist was completely shameless. He was depraved. Thank God, in the end, he overcame it. Intellect triumphed over his prurient desires." Nan is furious. "No. Not at all. That's not what Joyce is saying. He's telling us that intelligence allowed the protagonist, Dedalus, to embrace his sensuality. That is what this book is about; it's a guide for us all, telling us how to live our lives to the fullest and intellectually appreciate our own sexuality. We needn't be ashamed of our physical beings and the desires we all crave. These desires must be satisfied, not repressed, if we want a complete and fulfilled life."

Daisy breathes deeply and audibly. This conversation is going nowhere, so, as the leader, Daisy turns to another member: "Let's move on. Ruth, what did you think?" Before Ruth can respond, Joan, in an effort to ease the tension, interrupts. "I'd love some tea right about now. Daisy, can I brew some for you and the others?" The others jump at this welcome distraction. "Indeed," several say nearly in unison. "Tea time, it is!"

There is no further discussion of the book. Instead, the women chat about their everyday lives (recipes, town gossip, their children, pets, etc.). Eventually, the club breaks up and everyone starts to leave, and Daisy sees her guests out. Nan is the last to leave. "See any museums on your trip to N.Y.?" Daisy asks. Nan is embarrassed. "Didn't get a chance. Just visited a friend." Nan sheepishly smiles at Daisy, her expression confessing the truth. Daisy nods knowingly – the "friend" Nan refers to is her brother.

"Probably be the same for me when I visit Warren in D.C. next week. I'll just spend all my time with him." Daisy's tone turns a bit biting. "By the way, I heard Warren was also visiting N.Y. Coincidentally, just when you happened to be there. Interesting. You didn't, by chance, run into him?" Daisy is quite certain she knows the answer to this question, but she asks it just the same. She knows Nan won't lie. Nan can only smile awkwardly. "Daisy, given your feelings on the subject, I think it best we simply don't discuss your brother." "Enough said," says Daisy as she closes the door firmly behind Nan.

Chapter 15

A Sister's Counsel

It is a few days later. Nan and her sister, Liz Willits, are having lunch in an upscale Marion eatery. Nan cherishes her relationship with her older sister. They have always been quite close and have remained so even after Liz married Stuart Willits, a man Nan does not particularly like.

Nan proudly hands Liz her diary, opened to the entries about her recent tryst with Warren Harding. "Now, this is a secret and very private, Sis. You can't tell anyone." Nan looks on anxiously as Liz reads. Liz finishes, then looks up. She's not surprised by what she has read but far from happy either. She does a poor job trying to hide her disappointment from Nan. It makes no difference. Nan is just happy and oblivious to her sister's or anyone else's concerns. Nan then, with enthusiasm, asks, "Well?"

"Captivating story, well written. You've always been quite talented on that front." Nan quickly responds, "Thanks. That's nice of you to say, but aren't you happy for me?" Liz pauses. "It's what you always wanted," Liz says. Nan is gushing, "It's a dream come true."

Liz fakes a smile. "Well, it's nice we live in modern times." Liz reaches into her bag and hands Nan a book titled *Family Limitation*. "I have a present for you." Nan takes the gift. She knows of the book and is a big fan of its author, Margaret Sanger. Nan exclaims, "Margaret Sanger's book! I just love her." Liz is encouraged. "Good. Nan, you know this is for sexually active young women. It discusses birth control."

Nan laughs. "I know that. It's great, but it's not for me. It's for sexually active women that aren't in love." Liz is disappointed. Liz, well aware of Harding's reputation for philandering, broaches another topic, "Nan, do you think he loves you as you do him? As his one and only?"

Nan looks flabbergasted and motions to the entries in her diary. "Oh, Sis, he definitely does now!" Liz is exasperated but puts on a good face. "My little sister, I will always be here for you." Nan smiles, "I know that. Oh, and if you don't mind, I'll donate the book to the Women's Society. Plenty of others need it."

Chapter 16

Office Conception: February 1919

It is early in the evening, and Nan is paying a visit to D.C. She enters Harding's office as another leaves. Still thinking about his last meeting, Harding is slow to greet her and distracted when he does. "Oh, hello, Nan."

Nan is flirtatious. Harding is preoccupied. Having just learned his nickname, Nan says it laughingly, "Hello, Senator Good Fellow. I hear that's what they call you around here. You get along with everyone." Harding smiles slightly but is still thinking about his last meeting. "A penny for your thoughts?" she asks.

Harding sighs and then begins. "OK. That guy that just left, he's an economist—explained the Tax Bill to me. Smart fellow, but I didn't understand a word he said. I am not even certain if he thinks I should vote for or against the Bill."

Nan shrugs. "Well, what did you think when you read it? Do you think it's a good Bill?" Nan asks. Harding flips quickly through the pages of the Bill. "Reading won't help.

The words just kind of dance before my eyes. I fall asleep after reading just a paragraph or two."

"How will you vote, then?" Nan asks. Harding shoves the Bill aside, "I'll just skip the vote." Nan, partially teasing, partially scolding, responds. "Warren, do your homework, then vote! One way or the other." Nan then stands and moves coyly around the room. Harding rummages through a pile of mail on his desk and takes particular note of a letter from Carrie Phillips that is part of the pile. He opens and reads it.

> *My dearest Warren – You must vote against the Bill authorizing U.S. entry into the Great War. My love for Germany, my adopted homeland, is very strong. American money and lives should not be wasted in Europe fighting against Deutschland. I am sorry, but this is not a gentle request. Your action here is critical to me. And if you foolishly vote in favor of the resolution, I will publicly reveal things I am sure we'd both prefer were left unsaid. – Carrie.*

He is deeply concerned by Carrie's demand. Nan notes his upset, grabs the letter from him, and skim-reads it herself, unaware that it is a blackmail threat from another lover. "What, another issue? War this time. Serious stuff." She tosses the letter back on the desk. Harding shrugs and tries to deflect the reality from Nan. "Just a request from a constituent. Get lots of those."

Nan then approaches Harding seductively and unbuttons his shirt. "Let's see if I can't get your mind off those constituency problems. At least for a little bit." Nan then starts to undo her own blouse with one hand as she takes Harding's hand with the other. She leads him to the couch, lays down, and undoes her bra. Harding looks with delight at her naked breasts. The two then commence intimate foreplay that leads to full intercourse.

Chapter 17
Nan's News: April 1919

Nan watches an apprehensive Harding as he hurriedly moves through an out-of-the-way D.C. restaurant.

Nan has arranged this lunch and told Harding it was of the utmost urgency they meet. It was more an order than a request, and Harding diligently complies. She was anxious and precise on the telephone, telling him the exact time he was to arrive and the booth where she would be sitting. Harding fears bad news: terrible news.

He enters the restaurant at the appointed time, his head low, and, contrary to proper etiquette, leaves his hat on. He tugs on his hat and ducks his head as he walks quickly and directly to the back of the restaurant. His curious behavior, intended to avoid notice, does the opposite. Several patrons look curiously at the hurrying man with poor manners and bad posture. Fortunately, though he's noticed, he's not recognized.

He reaches the rear booth, where Nan awaits him. He enters and closes the curtains behind him, smiling nervously at Nan. "Nan, you look wonderful." She looks lovingly at him. "Am I glowing?" she asks. Harding is stunned and silent. His worst fears are realized. He is devastated and can only manage an uneasy and insincere smile as Nan takes his hand and puts it on her stomach. "Our child is in here," Nan says.

Harding struggles to respond. He has always performed poorly in confrontational situations. His concern is not only by the news but the fact that it is being relayed in a public place. If this leaks to the press, it could destroy his career, prestige, and marriage. The former two items are serious issues for him. The last matter, ending his marriage, would be a welcome relief.

As a well-known public figure who wants to remain so, he has few options. He must do his best to temper Nan's zeal and try to convince her to abort her pregnancy.

Harding manages a modicum of sincerity, "Wow, Nan, what exciting news." Nan gushes, "I knew you'd be pleased. What shall we name him?" Harding manages a nervous laugh. "We've got some time to decide on that." He pauses and looks at Nan with concern. He pats her hand and speaks softly, "You know, Nan, it's an interesting time to bring a child into the world." He takes a sip of water. "It's a bit scary right now." He takes another sip of water.

"I see all sorts of stuff the public doesn't. You get a real ringside seat to all the world's problems here in Washington, and I can tell you confidentially we are in for a very tough time in the coming years. The world economy is a mess, the flu pandemic is spreading, and there is other even worse stuff I'm not allowed to talk about." Nan again pats her stomach and tries to reassure Harding, "I'll keep him from harm. Your son will be protected so he can grow up and be as great as his father."

"Nan, I have every confidence in you. You'll be a great mother. Stupendous. But having a child, particularly in this crazy world, is a lot of responsibility. You need to be prepared to put your own life on hold." Nan laughs a bit, "I know that. I'm ready. I know I am. I've been reading books about childbirth and raising an infant." Harding nods, "That's great, Nan." He takes another sip of water and thinks hard.

He looks deeply into Nan's eyes and takes her hands. "No question, you'll be a great mom, but do you think now is the right time? I mean, you're so young; your whole life's ahead of you. Maybe we can do something."

Nan is confused and concerned, "What are you talking about?" Harding suggests in a hushed but serious tone, "Perhaps, given the awkward timing and, for your sake, that is, maybe we could undo it." "Undo it?" Nan asks in a state of shock. "You mean abort?"

Harding is determined and doesn't notice that Nan, in shock, is beginning to whimper. "It would probably be for the best, and I'd pay for it," Harding says. He is then silent as he now finally notices that Nan is crying. He responds cautiously, "Darling, are you OK?" Nan's now crying and proclaims loudly, "But I want to have our baby!"

Harding is now worried and desperate to avoid attention (which could lead to possible recognition). Harding decides to calm her with empty promises. "That's exactly what I was hoping you'd say. That's precisely what I want too!" Harding falsely proclaims. "Really?" says Nan. "Of course, my dear. I just wanted to present the options to you. You're the best thing that's ever happened to me - us having a child would be icing on the cake."

"Do you love me?" Nan asks. "Very much, my sweetie," Harding responds. Nan leans lovingly against Harding and speaks her mind, "I'd like for him to be a Harding. List you as his father on the birth certificate."

Harding abhors the idea. For political reasons, the child cannot have his name, and he must do anything he can to stop it. He must, however, be diplomatic. He lies, "Yes, perfect, but that would complicate things." This comment again takes Nan aback, and she looks at Harding curiously. "I mean my plans for us, my dear." "What plans?" Nan asks. With a false air of confidence, Harding says, "For us to marry, of course! That is if you'll have me. Then I could officially adopt the child and make him a proper Harding. We could raise him together as proud parents."

Nan is ecstatic. "Of course I'll marry you. You'll divorce your wife, then?" Harding nods as enthusiastically as he can muster in the circumstances. "Yes. After the Convention next year when the party bosses put me out to pasture." This added contingency now tempers Nan's enthusiasm. "So... we'll get married if they want you out of politics? Is that likely? You're still a Senator and a really good one."

Harding pats Nan on the knee. "Well, I appreciate your praise, but the party bosses may think otherwise. They've probably got a replacement lined up already." He pauses as Nan looks skeptical and questions this statement. "I find that hard to believe." Harding reassures her, "Look, it's the likely scenario, but it doesn't matter. We can get married even if I stay in politics." Nan's eyes widen. "Really? Will you divorce Florence anyhow? Even if you're still a Senator?"

Harding subtly shakes his head, looks lovingly at Nan and summons up his best tragic look. "Florence is five years older than me and not well. We'll just wait a bit until she passes." Nan, happy with this marriage proposal of sorts, cuddles up to him and kisses him softly. "Will you come to the hospital when I give birth to our son?" "Absolutely," Harding definitively replies.

Chapter 18
Hospital Room: October 22 1919

The maternity hospital waiting room is vacant, and Nan, very much alone, screams in pain as she gives birth to Senator Harding's child. A few moments later, the nurse hands Nan her baby daughter. Nan holds her baby and speaks to the nurse. "Has her father arrived yet?" The nurse responds sympathetically, "I'm sorry, honey. I haven't seen anyone." Nan is disappointed but lovingly holds her daughter and looks at her. "Well, welcome to the world Elizabeth Ann. You look just like your father. He is such an important and kind man. I can't wait until you meet him." The nurse, fearing this newborn will never meet its father, smiles all the same.

Chapter 19

Baby Going Home

Five days later, Nan is in a wheelchair outside the hospital with her infant daughter on her lap. Her concerned sister, Liz, stands beside her as the nurse holds the wheelchair. They wait for a taxi.

Liz tells her sister as gently as she can, "Nan, Stuart does not approve. I can only stay with you for a week. I'll come by though after as often as I can." "Thanks, Sis, and stop worrying so much. We'll be married by next summer." Liz looks at her sister and smiles. She knows Nan will almost certainly never marry Warren Harding.

A group of Suffragettes march down the street carrying signs and chanting their slogan. "Women work, women vote." One Suffragette peels off and hands flyers to Nan, Liz and the nurse. "Ladies, 17 states have ratified. We need 19 more. You can help. Write to key state legislators. Addresses are listed on the back." Nan returns the flyer. "I'd love to, but I can't. I just gave birth to my daughter five days ago. It's so exhausting."

The Suffragette laughs unsympathetically. "Little children, little problems. Big children, big problems. I have seven. I'm doing this for me, of course, but more importantly for my daughters." A car driving nearby screeches to a halt. A man jumps out, makes an obscene gesture and screams at the Suffragettes. "Stay home, bitches! Men rule the world!"

The Suffragettes return his insults as he quickly jumps back in the car, accelerates and leaves, gesturing obscenely as he goes. Nan, furious at the man's actions, re-takes the flyer from the Suffragette. "I am proud of all of you. I'll help. I will write to everyone on the list."

Chapter 20

The 1920 Republican Convention

The 1920 Republican convention is in full swing and not going well. Multiple votes and countless backroom negotiations have yielded nothing but anger. Not only is there no nominee, but there is also no plan to resolve the impasse. Delegates can't hide their disdain for one another. Security guards have had to intervene occasionally to break up outbursts that escalated into fisticuffs. Even Harding, who typically loves being the gregarious good old boy, is tiring of the protracted proceedings.

At this moment, though, Harding has little interest in politics. He's with Nan in his nearby hotel room. The two lay together in bed, having just completed their lovemaking. Harding looks at the clock and sighs, "It's nearly time for me to go. I'm afraid I need to re-enter the ugly fray." He shakes his head, "What a mess." He is clearly apprehensive, and Nan gently strokes his back, trying to ease his concern. "I wanted to show you something first," she says.

Harding looks at her curiously. He's not yet ready, nor does he have time for another sexual encounter. "What do you want to show me, Nan?" Nan smiles and reaches into her purse. She takes out a photo of Elizabeth Ann and hands it to Harding. "Look at your daughter. Isn't she beautiful?" Harding is indifferent but plays along, "Indeed, she looks just like you, Nan."

Nan raises her hand, trying to refuse Harding's attempt to return the photo. Nan implores him, "Keep it. It's for you." Harding smiles, "I'd love to Nan, but I might have to explain it to someone should another see it. Better if you hold on to it for me." Nan reluctantly takes the photo back. She turns her back to Harding, so he won't see her tears.

She gets out of bed and silently starts to dress. Harding is oblivious to Nan's pain. He reaches into his pocket, takes out an envelope, and hands it to Nan, "And here's this month's allowance." Nan takes it, saying nothing.

"So, are they putting you out to pasture?" Nan asks. Harding turns and looks at Nan. He's confused. "I'm sorry?" Nan is polite but firm. She's a bit put out that he doesn't remember. "Yes, you expected them to put you out to pasture during the Convention. And then you'd divorce Florence, and we'd marry. Remember, you said it in the restaurant when I told you I was pregnant."

Harding thinks a bit and nods. He's not particularly happy Nan took his empty promise so literally. In his mind, it wasn't a marriage proposal. Not really, anyhow. Rather, he said it to distract and calm her in her moment of emotional distress. He was just being compassionate, keeping her from what would have become an embarrassing, noisy and unsightly public exhibition of a woman's hysteria.

He doesn't take her comment too seriously and laughs, "Did I say that?" Harding doesn't wait for a response, "Well, they've not talked to me yet. They're preoccupied."

Harding puts on his tie and changes the subject. "It's going horrible, Nan. We can't agree on a nominee, and everyone is fighting." Fearing Harding might be the candidate, Nan asks, "Will it be you? I've heard you're on the ballot." Harding waves off the suggestion. "No, I'm just on the ballot to get Ohio stuff on the platform. I'm not getting many votes. Everyone knows I'm not the right guy for the job. I'm going to withdraw my name anyhow, put myself out to pasture."

Nan is delighted with this news. "Then, you can meet your daughter. I can start planning our wedding." Harding nods and says, "As soon as the Convention ends, yes. But you need to get out of here now. Florence arrives soon."

A happy Nan gets up, starts dressing, and sings out loud, "I'll be happy when the preacher makes you mine." Harding laughs, "OK, my dearie, start planning, but first get a move on." Harding opens the door, looks into the hallway, and sees no one. "OK, the coast is clear." Nan kisses him on the cheek as she hurries out the door. Harding gives her a light tap on the butt. Nan turns around and smiles at him as she scurries off.

Chapter 21

The Last Great Hope

Panic is setting in. There is no nominee, and the Convention is now just hours from its scheduled end. Dealmakers have spent days agonizing, cajoling, and negotiating. They've achieved nothing. On this, the scheduled final day of the Convention, they've avoided the fisticuffs of previous days. Verbal confrontations have, however, escalated. Exhaustion and exasperation have taken their toll, and all are rightfully suspicious of one another.

There have been eight failed votes. Harding has moved up in the balloting and is now in third place, albeit a very distant third. But Harding now has a chance. The two leading candidates' animosity has grown exponentially. They absolutely hate each other. Each now has the overriding goal that the other fail. Their desire for their competitor's failure is more important than anything, more important than their own success, and each is willing to fall on their own sword to deny the other.

Both Harding and Daugherty recognize this and the possibility that he could now win the nomination.

Harding is nervous. He does not want to be the nominee. Daugherty, however, is pleased and is cutting all sorts of underhanded deals to seize the opportunity.

Harding, completely unaware of Daugherty's shenanigans, catches up to him just before he enters the conference room where delegates will select the nominee. "Harvey, I need to speak with you." In a hushed but firm tone, he tells Daugherty. "Do me a favor, Harvey. Withdraw my name. I'm not fit for the office. Not smart enough."

Daugherty shrugs off Harding's concerns. "You've got nothing to worry about. Everyone knows you've not got the right constitution for the job. But we, Ohio, need you. Got to keep your name on the ballot to make sure Ohio's needs are part of the platform." Daugherty pats Harding on the shoulder, "Relax, you'll be fine. And you're still a very distant third. More importantly, you're nobody's second choice. You aren't going to win. No way."

Harding is unconvinced. "I hope you're right, Harvey." Daugherty again tries to ameliorate his concerns. "Look, you owe it to your home state. Stop worrying. Trust me. You're not going to be the nominee, no way."

Harding, not reassured, nonetheless sheepishly steps away as Daugherty enters the conference room. Harding shakes his head and speaks to himself. "It's not my enemies, I fear. It's my friends." Security guard Gaston Means overhears the comment and nods in agreement as he closes the door and stands guard outside the room.

Some two hours later, things are still going poorly. The weary and aggravated men are making no progress. They are exhausted. They agree on one thing. Further delay will hurt the chances of their eventual nominee winning the general election. For several minutes now, there has been a tense and awkward silence.

Daugherty breaks the silence, "Gentlemen, please. We have serious work to do here. We need to get behind someone. Our continued failure is making us look stupid." One delegate chimes in, "Stupid? Did someone say Harding?" The group laughs, easing some of the tension.

Daugherty is unapologetic. "Stupid or not, Harding's the perfect compromise. Our two top candidates hate each other. Harding is Senator Good Fellow, remember. Gets along with everyone." Most of the other delegates look at Daugherty aghast. "What?!" exclaims one opposition delegate. "Harding is a wishy-washy bore. Stands for nothing. Misses tons of votes."

Daugherty shrugs off the objection. "Less to criticize, then," he retorts. "And he's an Ohioan. He'd be going against another Ohioan. And we need that state. Critical state. Let's fight fire with fire. Meet them head-on. Harding's our man."

This suggestion leads to initial silence and surprise. Then one of two critical delegates that Daugherty has paid off handsomely shakes his head and reluctantly chimes in. "Like it or not, I'm afraid Daugherty might be right. Harding now probably is our man." The other critical delegate, similarly bribed, unenthusiastically concurs. "Don't love it either, but I must admit, we have no other choice right now. Harding's our best chance."

The room goes silent. No one in the room thinks Harding will be a good nominee. No one in the room thinks he will be a good President. And, except for Daugherty, no one favors his selection. They are nonetheless resigned to their fate. These two bribed delegates control enough votes to swing the election. Harding will be the nominee.

The formal vote, which, at this point, is just a perfunctory detail, is taken under a pall of gloom. The delegates reluctantly do their duty. They cast their votes under an unpalatable, regrettable and resigned acceptance of inevitable dread.

Chapter 22

Nan Gets the News

It is a lovely June morning, and Nan is in the process of juggling numerous tasks. She has her diary open at her last entry, she's jotted notes towards organizing her wedding, and she is writing, as promised, letters to the legislators urging them to support ratification of the 19th Amendment. Her progress on these tasks is significantly slowed by her child needing constant attention. Nan sits at the kitchen table, exhausted. She holds Elizabeth Ann and looks at her other, largely uncompleted, tasks strewn around. The nearby radio plays music. The broadcast is interrupted by a news bulletin.

News Flash - Republicans finally decide. On the tenth ballot, Senator Warren G. Harding of Ohio won the Republican nomination for President. Considered an affable and charming man, Harding's nomination for the highest office is nonetheless quite a surprise. He had done poorly on earlier ballots. Many within the party questioned his aptitude for complex

> *matters of the economy and world affairs. Nonetheless, this man, often considered a lightweight, is now their nominee. Now back to our regular programming.*

Nan is stunned. With mixed emotions, she speaks to herself. "He'll make a great president. He's plenty smart. I guess I can stop planning our wedding, though." She puts her child in the crib and then runs to her bedroom crying.

PART V
Women Win

Chapter 23
Mommy's Boy

Nan, with her daughter in a stroller, leaves the general store, where she has purchased a few items. It is an August evening. In fact, as Nan will soon learn, a momentous day in U.S. history. It is August 18, 1920, and the streets around her fill with Suffragettes. The seriousness they've previously exhibited is gone. They seem especially happy, joyful and spontaneous. She happens by a man angrily watching the Suffragettes with a newspaper in hand. "What's happening?" Nan asks. The man casts an evil glance at her, "Haven't you heard, lady? You got the vote now. Tennessee ratified, that put it over the top."

Nan is happy yet dumbfounded. "Really?" "Afraid so. By one vote. One snotty-nosed 24-year-old mommy's boy changed his mind at the last minute. He voted yes because his mother told him to. Jesus Christ, the guy's got no balls. Excuse my French, lady."

The man gestures angrily at the partying Suffragettes. "We're doomed. Wives will argue, want divorces, and kids will be delinquents. Women will think they're smart now." Nan looks squarely at the angry man. She smiles, motions to the celebrating women, then, with a hint of sarcasm, states matter of factly, "Well, we were smart enough to get this done."

Chapter 24
Nan Reads the News

Returning to her apartment, the afternoon newspaper awaits Nan (she subscribes to both the morning and afternoon editions). She grabs it, puts her baby in the crib, and eagerly devours the news, that reads as follows:

Women Get Vote!!!

One Vote Puts Amendment Over the Line

In an incredible turn of events, and by only one vote, Tennessee ratified the 19th Amendment yesterday. This is the 36th, and the last state needed to give women the right to vote.

The Amendment had seemed certain to go down to defeat. The opposition in the Tennessee house was loud and boisterous. They mocked the idea by wearing red noses to signify how silly they thought the Amendment was and their intention to vote against it. There were a lot of red noses worn by House members yesterday.

In fact, the state's youngest legislator, the 24-year-old Harry Burn, wore one.

The House Speaker, Seth Walker, had polled his colleagues carefully. The consummate vote counter, he knew it would fail. It would be a tie, 48 in favor and 48 opposed. He was certain this would be the result. A procedural nuance, an attempt to table ratification, had ended with this precise tie vote. Walker was sure the Amendment itself would get the identical vote. With no majority, the Amendment would fail. It was perfunctory, a fait accompli. At least, that's what Walker thought.

Just before the vote began, a legislative staffer approached the youngest representative, Harry Burn, giving him a letter. Burn, seeing it was from his mother, opened it immediately. The letter was a plea urging him to vote in favor of ratification, calling it a "moral obligation" to allow women the right to vote. In her mind, and she hoped her son would agree, women were every bit as capable as men in understanding politics, economics and history.

No one really noticed when it was time for Harry Burn to cast his vote. And few were paying attention when Burn removed his red nose and cast his vote in favor of ratification. In fact, it wasn't until all the votes were tallied and the outcome realized (49 in favor, 47 opposed) that the House began to murmur. A *re-count was done, and the surprised Speaker asked Harry Burn to confirm his vote in favor.*

His confirmation shocked all. Those in favor were elated; those opposed furious. Immediately, the opposition made several frantic, albeit futile, attempts to overturn the result. They asked for an additional re-count, looked for procedural discrepancies that might invalidate the result, and finally, they left the chamber in an attempt to prevent a quorum. All these attempts, conducted in absolute desperation, failed.

Tennessee's vote in favor of ratification means the Amendment is now the law of the land. After years of struggle, ridicule, and even violence, women have finally won the right to vote.

News of this result spread quickly, and an angry crowd gathered outside the State House. Harry Burn was vilified. The mob was determined to punish him. He hid in his office all night to avoid a certain lynching. When asked by reporters how she felt about her son's actions, Mrs. Burn simply said, "I'm the proudest mother in the world."

Nan looks at her daughter and smiles.

Chapter 25
Blood Pressures Rise

Congressman Tillman of Arkansas, the man who would become one of Nan's fiercest nemeses, read the same news. His reaction, though, was very different from Nan's.

It is the day after ratification, and a furious Congressman Tillman is in his office in Arkansas with a colleague, Jerry Higgins. Higgins, equally upset, cannot control his anger. As Tillman re-reads the Fayetteville Times lead story out loud, he lets loose several outbursts of expletives and guttural roars.

19th Amendment Ratified
- Tennessee Last State Needed

The state's youngest representative, the 24-year-old Harry Burn, unexpectedly changed his vote at the last minute. His shocking vote in favor of the Amendment broke a certain deadlock, a deadlock that would have doomed the Amendment. Representative Burn told colleagues that he had a change of heart

> *after getting a letter from his mother. After the vote, fearing for his life, Burn camped out all night in his office. Outside the capital, a large and angry mob marched, chanting, "Hang Harry." A few carried nooses.*

Higgins shakes his head angrily as Tillman reads the article and pounds his fist on the table. "Our Southern brethren let us down! The Tennessee Rats ratified the women's vote. Those creeps." Still looking at the newspaper, Tillman is equally furious. "And it was some lily-livered kid. That Harry Burn changed his vote because his mother told him to. Some are calling this mama's boy a hero." Higgins is beside himself. "Hero? He's a sniveling creep. Jesus, his mother probably helps him put on his big boy pants too."

Tillman reads another part of the article out loud, "His mother called the opposition bitter, misleading, fearmongering, hateful name-callers." He puts down the paper, slams his desk, then pauses to excoriate Burn's mother, "What a goddam bitch! What the hell could she possibly know?"

Higgins's anger boils over. "Mark my words. This will lead to chaos. Women won't listen at all now. They'll argue and want to go out to work." Tillman shakes his head in agreement and astonishment. "Probably want to get paid too – where will it end?" "And what about the kids?" Higgins asks and then answers his own question: "They'll end up living in the sewers." "Tillman jumps in, all I know is chickens need to stay home and sit on them eggs. Otherwise, we got no children, no future, no nothing. We're goners."

The two men silently stew in anger. Eventually, Higgins adds to their indignation by bringing up the race issue. "It's the end of the world, subversion of the proper order. Even negro women can vote now." Tillman shakes his head in bewilderment. "We're under attack. White men are under attack. They're cutting off our balls."

Chapter 26
Front Porch Campaign

Harding was a remarkably unremarkable man: a lazy, inept and ineffective public servant who understood almost nothing and accomplished less. His colleagues paid him no attention, and he made little impression on them.

When reminded of Harding's attendance at a meeting the day earlier, one fellow Senator once remarked, "Was Harding in that meeting? I don't remember him being there but nor do I recall any of the other furniture in the room."

With his nomination, though, Harding has a new and false belief in his own abilities. The reservations he had expressed just hours earlier immediately evaporated when he won the nomination. His insecurities gone, his ego restored, he's refreshed and hideously, mistakenly confident.

Being blissfully delusional is a horrifying trait for any leader, but it serves Candidate Harding well. It makes him an effective politician. He is good at getting elected. He's just awful at everything that comes after the election.

And he was born with genuine political assets. He is quite affable, tall, good-looking, and, as a newspaperman, he knows how to work the media of the day. This Presidential election is perfect for him too. Ohio, his home state, is critical, so he can minimize travel and effort and campaign from home, literally from home, not just his home state, but from his personal residence. He has organized what will become the last great front porch campaign.

Eager to get as much attention as possible, he built a luxurious and well-appointed structure for the press. He constructed a deluxe building on his property to accommodate newspapermen. He dubs this elegant structure "The Reporters' Shack" and spends much of his time there, schmoozing the press. It is a comfortable building with lounge chairs, working areas, nearby telephones, desks, and refrigerators. It has all the modern amenities. Cleverly, through his connections, he ensures that only supportive reporters from the most influential newspapers are invited to the The Reporters' Shack.

On this particular summer's day, a crowd has gathered outside his porch for one of his scheduled speeches. Harding's team is, as usual, preparing for the event. His press entourage is briefing reporters; the kitchen is abuzz with staff preparing hors d'oeuvres, and a string quartet is playing as the crowd arrives. The candidate though is nowhere in sight.

Daugherty, who is now Harding's campaign manager, is worried. He looks out the living room window at the crowd moving about, anxiously waiting to see their candidate, Harding. Daugherty then runs into the kitchen where he sees Florence Harding. She is about to head out to the Reporters' Shack with a pitcher of freshly made lemonade. Following her is their negro assistant carrying popcorn. Florence turns to her assistant. "Now this is just for the Press. We must keep them watered and fed." "Yes, Ma'am," the assistant replies.

Daugherty, still unable to find Harding, blurts out frantically, "Where's Warren? The crowd is getting restless." Trying to ease the tension, Florence reassures him, "Oh he's just upstairs working on his speech." "Working on what?" A frantic Daugherty retorts in response, "He's given that speech a million times. Get him down here. I'll go out there and stall." Florence dutifully changes direction and marches upstairs as Daugherty heads outside to the porch and begins speaking to the crowd.

Now on the veranda, Daugherty raises his arms to quiet the crowd. The string quartet stops playing. Daugherty suddenly gets a sinking feeling in his stomach. He now remembers what he arranged for Harding, has a good idea why he is missing and what Florence will soon encounter. It is too late though; he can only hope his fears are not realized and at this point can only play to the crowd.

"Ladies and Gentlemen. I am not Warren Harding." The crowd laughs. "The President "to-be" though will be here shortly. He's upstairs studying some confidential memorandums just received from D.C." The impressed crowd Ooo's and Ah's. "Though not yet officially President, he's working hard to ensure every Americans' right to life, liberty and the pursuit of happiness." The crowd cheers.

At that moment, Harding is upstairs sitting in a chair with his pants down. He is very much enjoying a most creative erotic encounter he is having with a young prostitute. Florence enters the study. Upon seeing her husband in this compromising position, she screams and drops the pitcher. It smashes, lemonade spilling everywhere. This noisy interruption brings an unwelcome, abrupt and premature end to Harding's liaison.

The young dalliance quickly gets up, gathers her clothes and scurries from the room. Harding, annoyed, looks at Florence and the broken glass and spilled lemonade. "God damn it woman, you made a mess." Florence, gesturing angrily in the direction the naked woman just exited, responds, "I made a mess?!?"

"How many times have I told you?" Harding says. "Politics is stressful. I need tension releases. That's all." Florence approaches Harding and grabs him hard by the balls. "Zip it up. And go down there and give your goddam tautological self-serving blather of a speech." Harding looks confused. "What are you talking about?" He feels belittled. "You know I don't understand big words."

He then goes silent. Now concerned, he looks at Florence knowing his candidacy depends on the public's belief that he has a happy marriage and a loyal wife. This is especially true as women will for the first time vote in a Presidential election. "What will you do?" Harding asks. "I need you by me. The image of a devoted wife." Florence scoffs at him, "You're an asshole but I'll pretend I'm fawning over my brilliant and dedicated public servant husband." Harding, in sincerity, replies, "Isn't that what I am?" Florence, about to leave, turns and looks angrily at her husband. "No. You're just an idiot."

Chapter 27
The Stump Speech

A few minutes later, Candidate Harding is delivering his stump speech. It's boring, devoid of passion or commitment and utterly unmemorable. He drones on emphatically, offering nothing of substance and no meaningful commitments. The crowd reacts mostly as desired, occasionally cheering although often just applauding politely, without enthusiasm.

Florence, as promised, stands nearby feigning pride in him. Behind him is a poster with his principal, utterly meaningless, campaign slogan, "Return to Normalcy." Florence smiles vacantly as Harding continues.

"Businesses make the country run. They can get America back on track if we can get them back on track so we must level the playing field. I have a two-fold solution."

"First, lower taxes on business." The crowd cheers. Florence looks out at the crowd, and smiles. Her smile disappears immediately though when she sees Nan, in the crowd, looking at her husband with adoring eyes.

Harding waits for the cheering to subside, and then continues with his speech. "First, lower taxes on business. And second, more tariffs. So, less taxes, more tariffs," Harding implores. Just then one heckler yells out, "Yeah. Tax the other guy!" The heckler points, "Yeah, tax the guy from over there but don't call it a tax. Call it a tariff."

Quite a few in the crowd laugh rather robustly at the comment. Harding is knocked off balance by the cynical comment. He laughs nervously but then continues with his prepared remarks. "Less government in business; more business in government." The crowd cheers again. The heckler sarcastically responds, "Less is more, sounds right to me." This elicits more laughs from the crowd. The heckler is one-upping Harding, and he is noticeably uncomfortable.

In the audience, Nan, oblivious to the heckler's criticism, turns to a nearby stranger. "He's such a dream boat. Harding will be the best President ever." The stranger looks curiously at Nan, one eyebrow raised in surprise, "Lady, we got prohibition now. You ain't supposed to be drinking." "What?" Nan asks angrily. "I don't drink."

Undeterred by Nan's visible anger, the man continues, "And your hero there - Casanova; you know he's got colored blood in him." Now Nan is livid. "What?!?" Nan exclaims, incredulously. "You heard me lady; he's had plenty of ladies and worse, there's some darky in his family tree. Not too distant darky too, I suspect." Nan is now furious, and repeatedly strikes the larger man with both hands and screams at him. "Those are all lies! Damn lies!"

A nearby onlooker separates the two. He had been eavesdropping on the conversation. And though he stops the physical fight, he jumps into the verbal conflict himself, "Calm down lady. What are you so upset about?

Are you his bastard daughter or something? You colored too, then?"

Nan is furious at all these insults. They're far more personal to her than these men know. The idea that she's his daughter is upsetting. Nan has become oblivious to her and Harding's age difference. As far as she's concerned, they're soul mates and, though entirely irrational, that makes them the same age. And she knows the rumors of his cavorting are false. She knows that, because she looked into his eyes and saw his soul. She is Harding's only lover.

But the worst and vilest allegation (in her mind) is that he has colored blood. She has heard this falsehood before; a common slur at the time, often used against public figures if anyone in the family had been a supporter of abolition. Abolitionists, the argument went, had to have colored blood; why else would they have supported such a degenerate cause?

Because Harding's uncle was a known abolitionist, Harding was often falsely labeled colored. This charge infuriated Nan beyond words as it implied Elizabeth Ann, their daughter, was colored. She breathes hard, thinking about this insult but is speechless and unable to even muster a response.

Harding, on stage, is still speaking. He reiterates one of his campaign slogans, "America First, I say." He then points to the "Return to Normalcy" poster behind him. "Ladies and gentlemen, I promise you a return to normalcy." The crowd cheers as Harding leaves the stage. The heckler and his friend loudly engage in conversation. "Return to normalcy? What the hell does that mean?" the friend asks. "Whatever you want," the heckler responds.

The heckler then applauds sarcastically and cheers. He calls out to where Harding just left. "Hey, greatest speech about nothing I ever heard. You're the best windbag of meaningless slogans ever to run for office." Some in the crowd laugh. Noting the commotion, Harding's henchmen hustle the heckler and his friend away.

PART VII
Starting on a Downswing

Chapter 28
A Dream Come True

It is early morning, Wednesday November 3rd 1920, before sunrise. Harvey Daugherty, in Chicago for business, wakes early and rushes to the hotel lobby just as the morning papers arrive. He breaks into a sinister smile when he sees the headline in this morning's Chicago Tribune.

> ELECTION OF 1920 - REPUBLICAN SWEEP - HARDING WINS IN LANDSLIDE; BOTH SENATE AND HOUSE RIDE HIS COAT TAILS. ALL BRANCHES CONTROLLED BY REPUBLICANS. HARDING FIRST PRESIDENT ELECTED WITH WOMEN VOTING.

A delighted Daugherty hands the man at the newsstand a dime. Daugherty declines the vendor's offer of a nickel in change. "Keep it," Daugherty says. The vendor is happily surprised, "Wow, thanks mister." He smiles broadly as he looks at Daugherty, "By jingo, my pockets will jingle." As he walks away, Daugherty holds up the newspaper and smiles back, "Mine certainly will."

In New York, Nan opens her apartment door and picks up the New York Times. She reads the headline with mixed emotions, then turns to her daughter. "Well Elizabeth Ann, it's probably going to be at least four more years before mommy becomes a proper wife." She pauses briefly, thinks, and then says, "Maybe though, I could marry the President when he becomes a widower. Maybe have a White House wedding! You could be the flower girl. That would be wonderful."

In Marion, Ohio, Florence prepares breakfast for the President-elect. She is silent as Warren reads about his victory in the Marion Times. "Well, who would have ever dreamed that a small-town newspaper man could become President of the United States of America?" Florence serves him his eggs, turns to leave the room, and then looks back at her husband, offering some parting words, "Sometimes there's nothing worse than a dream come true."

Chapter 29
Inauguration

There is huge excitement and anticipation in Washington D.C. this day, 4th March 1921. It is inauguration day. And the popular and affable new President is about to take the oath of office. Harding is relatively charismatic and, as such, a huge and welcome contrast from his taciturn predecessor, Woodrow Wilson.

Senator Philander C. Knox of Pennsylvania is at the podium delivering a long-winded speech introducing the new President. Harding, seated nearby, listens politely and waits patiently. The superstitious Florence, by his side, is looking frantically at her pocket watch. It reads 10:58 AM.

Knox rambles on endlessly, "So from a small town in Ohio, a man who bought a failing newspaper and turned it profitable." The crowd cheers: none louder than Nan who is in the crowd, looking adoringly at the new President. On stage, Florence leans toward her husband and speaks to him in hushed tones. "You must commence immediately while the clock is on the upswing. You only have two minutes." Harding shakes his head as he gently pats Florence's hand. "Florence, you and your superstitions."

Much to Florence's consternation Knox continues speaking, "What worked in Ohio, will work in D.C. and for the nation." Florence again implores her husband to begin. "Just start. Interrupt him if need be. Good things happen when they commence while the clock is on the upswing. Bad when they are on the downswing." Harding shakes his head at Florence, puts his finger to his pursed lips and quietly makes the "shush" sound.

Knox, still at the podium, seems to very much enjoy the sound of his own voice. "The kind of entrepreneurship he exhibited in Ohio will carry on here. His work and Senatorial experience make him the perfect man to lead us now. The Great War is finally behind us, but we must now navigate the Great Peace. No human being is better suited to this task than your President, President Warren G. Harding." Harding stands and tips his hat to the cheering crowd. Knox motions Harding to come to the podium. Florence looks down at her pocket watch. It reads 11:01 AM. She is beside herself, looks to the heavens and mutters to herself, "Oh no. He's going to start on the downswing."

Knox pats Harding on the back. "Ladies and gentlemen, I give you Warren G. Harding. A man who will undoubtedly go down in history as one of our..." Knox coughs making his next word, the adjective "greatest", inaudible, though the following word "Presidents" is heard clearly. So, Knox has inadvertently stated Harding "will go down in history as one of our Presidents." Indeed, an accurate prediction if ever there was one.

Harding and Knox shake hands and exchange pleasantries as the crowd cheers. Harding waves to the crowd as Florence looks up and sees a dark cloud overhead. This increases her anxiety. As the crowd settles down, Harding steps up to the podium to begin his speech. Florence looks at her watch. It is 11:04 AM. She crosses herself and silently prays.

Harding begins his speech, an unmemorable babble that begins,

> My Countrymen: When one surveys the world about him after the great storm, noting the marks of destruction and yet rejoicing in the ruggedness of the things which withstood it, if he is an American, he breathes the clarified atmosphere with a strange mingling of regret and new hope.

Harding drones on to an underwhelmed crowd. Some ten minutes later, President Harding, still at the podium, is nearing the end of his inaugural speech. The audience is rightly bored by his wordy and meaningless discourse. It is broadcast over loudspeakers (the first ever for a Presidential inauguration).

Harding finishes up, "I have taken the solemn oath of office." At this point the sound system malfunctions, and the President's speech is inaudible as the speakers buzz annoyingly with static. The crowd cringes and Florence believes it is yet another bad omen. Florence looks at the speakers, covers her ears and speaks again to the heavens, "Oh dear." The static finally dissipates, and the President's last few words can be heard, "to God and Country."

There is some polite applause, but most are just relieved the speech is over. Nan alone applauds enthusiastically.

Chapter 30
The After Party

With his dreary speech finally over, Harding could do what he does best: party, schmooze and glad-hand. Being incredibly adept at masking his insincerity, he comes off as a genuine and most affable host. These were Harding's true skills.

The party starts off with the President and First Lady heading to the White House gates in a motor vehicle! Harding is the first US President to use a horseless carriage to do so. He and the First Lady wave enthusiastically to the receptive crowd as they drive down Pennsylvania Avenue proudly ushering in a new era for America: an era of peace replete with new modern conveniences that will change the world.

The automobile and radio are no longer just fancy inventions for the wealthy. Ordinary working folks were acquiring them in increasing numbers and these new technologies are rapidly becoming part of the fabric of American life. With the Great War now over and a new, more engaging President in office, the future looks incredibly bright. Harding is at the helm of a brand-new ship and the American citizenry are confident.

The car stops in front of the White House gates. Military men open the car doors for the President and First Lady who smile and wave to the crowd as they approach the gates. It's the ceremonial opening of the White House grounds and the crowd cheers as he casts open the gates. He proudly announces, "My first proclamation as President. We are re-opening the White House. It's the people's house, everyone's welcome."

Floods of folks enter enthusiastically though they have limited access. There is a relatively small area of the outside lawn of the White House cordoned off for the public. Harding proclaims, "Main Street moves into the White House!" The crowd lets out a mighty roar.

Daugherty stands near Harding, smiling broadly. Daugherty watches with a hint of smugness as ordinary folks enthusiastically enter the White House grounds. For Daugherty he delights in the ironies of his accomplishments. The turtle he pushed off the log years ago is in deeper water than he ever expected. Daugherty has not only fooled Harding but also the poor masses that voted for a guy who will be loyal to the rich and powerful. Daugherty relishes his role as the secret power broker. He looks forward to becoming the weak President's puppeteer. Daugherty will make sure it all inures to his own benefit.

Meanwhile, the President graciously moves about the crowd, greeting the public. A young and pretty reporter, Mary Campbell, approaches him, catching the President's eye. He is clearly attracted to her and delighted she is coming toward him.

She hands him her business card. "Mr. President, I'm Mary Campbell, with the Columbus Times." He takes her card willingly and shakes her extended hand. "What are your goals for the first 100 days, Mr. President?" Harding smiles broadly, "Well, well, well, a girl reporter. How do you like that?" Harding laughs. Undeterred, Mary repeats her question, "And your goals, Sir?"

"My little dearie. Today we celebrate. Work starts tomorrow, sweetheart." "I see," says Mary, "Then may I come by the White House tomorrow and meet you at three?" Harding smiles with a leer, "Of course, be delighted." Mary responds professionally, "I'll see you tomorrow at three. Thank you. I am looking forward to it." Harding smiles, "Me too." He looks lustfully at Mary's nicely shaped derriere as she walks away.

Daugherty, the soon-to-be Attorney General, is now outside the gate and approaches Nan who's about to enter. He discreetly tries to hand her an envelope and sternly tells her to leave. She rejects his offer and vigorously objects to his order to leave. Instead, she tries to enter anyhow; physically and rudely pushing her way through the crowd. Daugherty motions for security and they forcefully remove her. Those nearby, upset with her attempts to cut the line, look disapprovingly and mutter concern as the struggling Nan is hauled away. "Crazy lady," yells one. "Good riddance," cries another.

Meanwhile, the President and First Lady are now together greeting and shaking the hands of their innumerable guests. Florence is particularly moved when meeting a group of wounded war veterans (in wheelchairs, on crutches, etc.). She is overcome with emotion at the horrible plight of these men. "Thank you so much for your sacrifices. We owe you so much and will do everything we possibly can to help you." Harding is oblivious and smiles vacantly at the men. Finally, Florence nudges him, and he responds on cue, "Absolutely, we'll do all we can."

A few moments later, Daugherty, now near the President and First Lady, looks over the crowd. He is quite pleased at the extent of the revelry and public affection for the President. "Great day, Warren. You exude warmth. Folks love it. Huge contrast with your predecessor."

Harding nods appreciatively and then asks, "How was my speech? Did it go over well?" Daugherty changes the subject, as the speech was abysmal. "It's a great party Warren. People will remember that." Florence, overhearing Daugherty, chimes in, "The party started on the upswing."

Harding is feeling a bit annoyed and impatient. There is only so much glad-handing he can take. Florence greets nearby guests. Daugherty speaks to the President, falsely believing Florence is out of earshot. "Sir, if you need some refuge, the Oval Office is off limits to all but you. A Secret Service man is guarding the door."

Harding nods as Daugherty continues, "A couple of your supporters are there and I think you might very much enjoy their company." Daugherty speaks softly but not quietly enough, as Florence overhears him. "I think they'll offer you a nice respite from the rigors of matrimony, Sir." Harding gets the hint, "I see." Florence glares at Harding as she watches him head to the Oval Office.

A few minutes later, Gaston Means, now the White House security officer, opens the Oval Office door, allowing Harding to enter. Inside, two young prostitutes dressed in negligees giggle as they slyly greet him. Harding is delighted. He starts removing his coat and tie as he enters. Means sneaks a peak as the encounter commences, then closes the door behind the President. He hears laughter and intimacy as he stands guard in the hallway, outside the Oval Office.

Chapter 31
Day One

Staff and reporters scurry around the White House on the morning of 5th March 1921, preparing for the first day of the Harding administration. Later that day will be Harding's first meeting with the men that have been appointed cabinet positions (with a Republican majority in the Senate, their confirmation is all but assured).

Harvey Daugherty will be Attorney General, and his friends and cronies will take other key roles in the cabinet and White House. Ultimately, this group will become known infamously as "The Ohio Gang". Today though, their date with infamy is some years off. Today the future looks rosy (at least it does to Harding and to others of similar naïveté).

Initially, there are some first-day jitters. These soon give way though to a wave of excitement and the false bravado of the "can-do" attitude of the blissfully ignorant.

Of particular interest to the onlookers is the proud strutting of Dr. Charles Elmer Sawyer, a doctor appointed to the newly created position of Brigadier General in the U.S. Army. He marches up and down the hallway in a military uniform to the delight of the press. Dr. Sawyer, a 64-year-old homeopathic physician, is Florence's favorite doctor. He is an odd yet charismatic doctor with limited formal training (he's a bit of a quack) and zero military experience.

The photojournalists eagerly snap his picture as he poses with a fanciful air of false bravado. "Oh, please, gentlemen. You're wasting your film on me. Save it for the President," he says with a specious demure as he continues to pose for the photographers. "Maybe you should be President," one photographer blurts to Sawyer as he snaps his picture. This elicits laughs from the crowd, including Sawyer himself.

A couple of newsmen comment discreetly on Sawyer as they walk away. "What's with that guy's uniform?" "Beats me," his friend replies. "I guess it adds panache to the made-up title they gave him, Brigadier General in the Army Medical Corps." The first reporter shakes his head in disbelief, "Is everyone in this White House as kooky as that old man?" His friend responds, "He's Florence's favorite doctor. She had to have him. Word is Dr. Joel Boone, who is a proper medic, was hired to keep an eye on the crazy General here."

The reporter nods, acknowledging the rationality of this comment, as a photographer snaps yet another picture of Sawyer as he exaggeratedly poses. The reporter then leans into the photographer and speaks to him softly, "Hey, the wacky General there has got a point, though. Why waste film on him?" The photographer quietly opens the back of the camera, revealing there is no film. "What film? I'm saving it for a picture of the new cabinet."

An announcement is made that the cabinet meeting is about to begin, and the reporters dutifully scurry down the hall. A few minutes later, the President and his cabinet pose for what seems like innumerable photos. After some ten minutes or so, Harding, tired of the photo session, chimes in, "Well, thank you all."

Daugherty then adds, "Yes, thank you. We're always happy to accommodate the press. So, do reach out to us if you need something. Unfortunately, we need to begin our meeting now. We have a very tight schedule with many pressing issues on our agenda." Daugherty then motions for them to exit, "Thank you again, gentlemen." The photographers exit, and Gaston Means closes the door behind them.

The men of the yet-unconfirmed cabinet take their seats and settle in. A moment passes without anyone speaking. They look at each other, not quite sure what to do. Finally, Harding, realizing he should initiate things, addresses his cabinet. "Well, gentlemen, that was a hell of a party yesterday. Should we start planning the next?" The cabinet members laugh. The laughter dies down and is followed by another awkward silence. The President looks around at all the cabinet members, and they at him. Finally, Harding again recognizes they are expecting him to speak and lead the meeting. He looks at them and does his best to speak firmly.

"Well, let's get down to business, shall we? We've got a country to run, Gentlemen!" Some cabinet members chime in, "Here, here!" Others say, "Agreed!" The group then comes to attention and is once again briefly silent. They again look to Harding, who looks back at them. There is more awkward silence. Finally, Harding speaks. "Now, who wants to start?"

PART VIII
Keeping Busy

Chapter 32

A Welcome Distraction

The first cabinet meeting has gone on for nearly two hours, and Harding is visibly bored. He fidgets, occasionally taps his pencil, and every now and then smiles vacantly at whoever is currently speaking. He says nothing, is unable to focus on the discussion, and is simply uninterested. Daugherty, capitalizing as planned on the President's limited attention span and profound lack of knowledge, leads the meeting.

There is a knock on the door. Means enters and hands Daugherty a note. He reads it and then whispers to Harding, "Mr. President, a reporter, Mary Campbell, is here to see you. Says she has an appointment." Harding, with delight, recalls the attractive Miss Campbell and whispers to Daugherty, "I hate to disappoint her." Daugherty is more than happy to have the President leave the meeting. He can't say that, of course, so instead bluffs and responds diplomatically, "Mr. President, if it's important, we can try to carry on here without you."

Harding nods and then speaks out loud to the group, "Gentlemen, I'm most impressed. I have to run to another meeting but am comfortable leaving the country's business in your capable hands." Some cabinet members reply, "Thank you, Mr. President." Harding gets up and speaks to the group as he leaves, "Please have Mr. Daugherty contact me should you need me for anything."

Moments later, Harding enters the Oval Office. He smiles at the attractive Miss Campbell who sits in the visitor's chair by his desk. Harding leers in her direction and motions to the sofa as he reaches into the liquor cabinet. "Why not make yourself comfortable over here on the sofa?" After preparing two high balls, he sets them on the table near the sofa, "Here, join me here on the couch. Relax, you're in good hands." He pats the sofa next to him, "Join me."

"Sir, I'm already set up here," Mary motions to her pad of paper she has taken out and laid on the visitor side of his desk. "It's easier for me to write and do the interview at a desk." She motions to his empty chair behind the desk, "And you look so distinguished seated behind the Oval Office desk." A disappointed Harding reluctantly accedes to her wishes and sits behind his desk. "Very well, as you wish, I guess."

Miss Campbell proceeds with her interview, "Our readers want to know about your agenda and what it means for them. With majorities in both houses, how soon should Americans expect to see the economic success you promised during the campaign?" Harding doesn't like the question and is still unhappy that Miss Campbell was unreceptive to his advances. He shakes his head in frustration and disbelief, "Now, why would a pretty girl like you care about politics?"

Chapter 33
Nan's Invite

It is now day two of the Harding administration, and what little interest the President may have had in governing has already gone. He's looking for ways to occupy himself, and his overactive libido is distracting him.

He would very much welcome Nan visiting him. She'd suit his needs nicely, and after all, she is just a short train ride away in her New York City apartment. Today, as he puts her childcare money in an envelope, he decides to add a bit more and calls for Gaston Means.

The next morning, Nan is dancing around her apartment, holding her daughter, and singing Al Jolson's song 'Swanee'. On her kitchen table is a newspaper photo of Harding and his new cabinet. She looks at it as she dances. She still sings, but now with revised lyrics, "Warren, How I love you, How I love you, My dear old Warren." She is so engaged in her song that she barely hears the knock on her door. She opens the door to find Mr. Means. He hands her his card – Gaston Means, Security Officer – White House. "The President sent me." Nan, still holding her daughter, motions him in, "Of course."

Means enters and reaches into his pocket, handing Nan an envelope. "He asked me to personally deliver this to you this month. It's your childcare money." Nan smiles, thanks him, and takes the envelope.

Means continues, "There's a little extra this time. The President would like you to use it to come to Washington next Tuesday for a private tour of the White House." Nan is ecstatic. "Wow. That would be swell. He probably wants to meet his daughter." Means pauses, and there is a brief awkward silence.

Means knows that it is important to clarify the President's wishes. "Yes, he'd love that, but discretion is, of course, of the utmost importance. He fears a child, especially one so young, might create a scene. Unfortunately, we need to be very clandestine. The White House is full of gossiping reporters and staff." Nan begrudgingly nods understandingly. Means continues, "He feels it is only safe if you visit alone. He was hoping you could arrange for a sitter for your daughter."

Nan is deeply disappointed. She sighs, "I understand. He'll have to meet Elizabeth Ann another time. I can arrange for my sister to look after her." Means puts on his hat as he leaves. "The President looks forward to your visit."

Chapter 34
The Coat Closet

It is the day of Nan's visit and her private White House tour. She was shuttled through a back door and is waiting downstairs in an empty room near the basement. She has seen nothing of the living quarters or offices. She has, as instructed, remained silent and out of sight. She waits nearly an hour and Means comes to get her. He ushers her through a workman's hallway and lets her into a kitchen, where she is told to wait.

It is early morning, and the halls of the White House are deserted. A few minutes later, Harding and Nan secretly enter the hallway from a service door and run down the hall giggling quietly like love-struck teenagers. Gaston Means holds open a door nearby. He closes the door as the two lovers quickly enter the room, which will provide them seclusion for their illicit tryst.

Harding looks at a surprised Nan, "Sorry, not exactly the Taj Mahal but kind of quaint." A disappointed Nan looks at Harding, "It's a coat closet!" Harding shrugs, "Kind of kinky, huh?" Nan shrugs, "I guess."

After they enter, Mr. Means stands outside. A few minutes later, the sounds of lovemaking can be heard inside. Means' job is to discreetly knock on the closet door should someone approach. And indeed, the knock becomes necessary when Means sees Florence approaching.

Means knocks lightly while still looking stoically ahead. The sounds within the closet cease, but not before Nan and Harding mischievously laugh from within. Soon Florence walks by. Means is unflinching as Florence passes. "Morning, Mrs. Harding." Florence looks suspiciously at Means as she walks by and mutters to him sarcastically, "Guarding a closet door? Americans really can sleep soundly tonight, can't they?"

Chapter 35
The Letter

It is now a month into his Presidency, and Harding has little to do. White House business and the executive branch are entirely in the hands of his Attorney General, Harvey Daugherty. Daugherty involves Harding only when absolutely necessary. It is a mutually agreeable arrangement.

Harding has little interest in much, other than the Presidential pomp, circumstance, and glad-handing. Daugherty is intoxicated, being secretly in control. He has all the power he needs to exploit ruthlessly for his own ends. For Daugherty, it is extremely lucrative, exciting and addictive.

On this day, Harding is alone in the Oval Office. He has set up a movie projector and screen and is rather enjoying watching a pornographic film. It stimulates him to both masturbate and simultaneously write an explicit letter to his buxom mistress, Carrie Phillips. He writes, sharing with her his private misdeeds. He especially likes to remind her of some of their intimacies and to use their personal code word "Jerry" (a term they alone use to refer to his penis).

> *Carrie, my dearest concubine, as I watch explicit images of nude women actively engaged in various delightful acts, I have remembrances of you and your exquisite nakedness. This excites me to the point where I have lost all self-control and, without you here, must resort to self-stimulation. We must watch these together and jointly enjoy their pleasures. It will undoubtedly lead us to an ecstasy beyond. Your friend "Jerry" can HARD-ly wait to visit.*

He then takes out another piece of paper and writes a nearly identical letter to Nan.

A few days later, Carrie Phillips is on the steps of her home, accepting the mail from the busybody mailman. "Mrs. Phillips, looks like you got another letter from the White House." She gives the mailman a dirty look. "Mrs. Harding is a good friend of yours, right?" Carrie Phillips, annoyed by the meddling, grabs the mail. "Thanks for the mail."

She steps inside, opens it, and blushes as she reads the letter. She says to herself, "Warren, I told you to stop this nonsense. In your position, you really shouldn't be doing this!" She pauses and then thinks to herself as if an idea has come to her. "Really, Warren! You really shouldn't have. I am not letting you off the hook this time." Carrie immediately sits down at her writing table, takes out a pen and paper, and begins composing a letter.

Chapter 36
Blackmail for Real This Time

A week later, Daugherty, following his normal morning routine, stops in the White House business office to pick up the President's mail. He quickly sifts through it, looking at the return addresses. He stops and is concerned when he sees the letter from Carrie Phillips. He knows her well and knows about her and the President's intimacy. He also knows she is smart and cunning. His concern turns out to be well-founded.

Daugherty also knows that the already 'not-very-smart' President shifts into a higher gear of stupidity when his libido is aroused. Harding's uncontrollable sexual urges, combined with his obliviousness to the political damage that might ensue if his sexual escapades came to light, make him an easy target for exploitation.

Daugherty, pleased with the empire he has built for himself, has one major concern - Harding's idiocy. In his view, it, and it alone, could jeopardize all he has built for himself.

Daugherty opens Carrie's letter with great trepidation. His fears are realized. Mrs. Phillips is blackmailing the President and has attached a copy of the smutty letter Harding sent her. Daugherty is furious.

He immediately marches into the Oval Office with Harding's letter to Carrie in hand. He thrusts it in the President's face, interrupting him as he reads the comic strips in today's newspaper. Harding looks up, quite surprised as Daugherty exclaims, "You want to tell me what this is all about?"

Harding looks at the letter, then looks sheepishly upward at Daugherty, "She was supposed to rip those up and return the scraps to me. I asked her to. Nan does so with her letters." He reaches into his drawer and pulls out an envelope from Nan and turns it upside down. Scraps of paper fall out.

Daugherty shakes his head in disbelief, astounded that he would admit to writing such letters to yet another woman. He responds sarcastically, "Mr. President, I guess Mrs. Phillips isn't quite as good as Nan at ripping up paper." "Well," Harding says, "Is there a problem?"

Daugherty holds up the blackmail note included in the letter, "She wants two first-class ocean liner tickets to Japan for her and her husband." Harding inadvertently interrupts and, though he's not quite sure why, feels he must express similar anger as Daugherty. "That's outrageous!" A dumbfounded Daugherty replies, "I'll gladly pay to get her out of town. That's the part I like." Harding asks sheepishly, "There's another part?"

"She wants a lot of money too." Harding pauses a bit. "Well, what do we do?" Daugherty blurts out, "We pay it unless you've got a better idea." Harding pauses, then shrugs innocently, "No, that sounds good."

Daugherty looks at Harding as he leaves. "Now that you're President, you need to do a better job of controlling your pecker and your pen." Harding, looking witless, nods in agreement. He ignores the first part of Daugherty's advice but concedes somewhat on the second item, "I guess I could write fewer letters." Daugherty is astonished. "Not fewer. None. And just bonk the women I bring you. I know I can keep them quiet." Daugherty puts the letter and note back in the envelope and storms out of the Oval Office with the incriminating documents in hand.

Moments later, Daugherty tracks down Gaston Means in the hallway and hands him the envelope. "Destroy this crap but write down the address." Daugherty points out the return address. "We need to pay off Mrs. Phillips. Get her a couple of first-class ocean liner trips to Japan, plus a one-time $25,000 payment and arrange for another $5,000 a month." Dutifully, Means accepts the assignment, "Yes, Sir. Will do."

Means heads off with the envelope and enters the White House business office. As instructed, he jots down the return address. Contrary to Daugherty's instruction, he, however, does not destroy the documents.

Means sees a golden opportunity here to exploit the situation and decides to take advantage of it. Seeing no one in the office, he makes a photostatic copy of the smutty letter and puts it in his pocket. He returns the original to the envelope and puts it in Mrs. Harding's mailbox.

A few days later, Florence, letter in hand, marches into the Oval Office. She slams the door shut and immediately excoriates the President. Fuming, she confronts her serially unfaithful husband. "And with my friend Carrie! I thought that ended years ago! How many others, Warren?

How could you still be doing this to me?" Harding shrugs it off. "Florence, you and your goddam detective work."

Florence, even though all too well aware of Warren's inability to grasp even the blindingly obvious, is astounded by this display of sheer ignorance. "Detective work? You fool. One of the many lowlifes you have working in your White House put this letter in my mailbox. Whoever did this wanted me to find it, and I am sure I am giving them their desired result. And I'll do better than that." Florence turns toward the closed door (assuming the culprit is behind it listening) and says in a theatrical voice, "And do you think I don't know about Nan?"

Outside the door, Means is eavesdropping. As Florence intends, he hears her comments and smiles. Inside the room, Harding not only sees nothing wrong with his actions but believes Florence is not being adequately appreciative. "Woman, you should be thanking me. You've been riding my coattails for a long time." Florence is steaming and looks Warren directly in the eye. "I ran the business, not you. I made the money. I pretended to be the devoted wife so you could get the women's vote. It was me that put you in office."

Harding waves Florence off. To him all this is just another example of irrational female hysteria. Worse, he believes he has done no wrong. "You're delusional, woman. Look, I just have manly urges. I'm sure even Jesus had manly urges." "I'm sure Jesus was better able to control his," Florence angrily responds. Then, in a distraught and resigned tone, and more to herself than to Warren, she wonders aloud, "What will become of me?"

Harding, now believing he has won the argument, replies, "I don't care. You can do what you damn well please. You ran me down, Florence. Ruined me." Florence is astounded. "Ruined you. What about my legacy?"

Means, outside the Oval Office's closed doors, is still eavesdropping on the argument between Harding and Florence. He is pleased by it. He smiles and quietly walks away.

Chapter 37
Surprise Veto

The newspaper headlines on this day, September 19th, 1922, report unfavorable news about President Harding. He has vetoed a bill that would have made good on his pledge to help war veterans. He's broken a campaign promise to America's finest, and it is costing him politically. The news is met with strong and universal disapproval. The public is hugely disappointed. This is viewed as a grave betrayal to those who sacrificed so much for their country.

Nan is in her apartment. She is acutely aware of the public's upset and is very concerned. With great apprehension, she reads the story in the NY Times.

HARDING SURPRISE - VETOES WAR BONUS BILL - *Turning his back on a campaign pledge to help veterans, the President says "No" to a bonus for them. Though expressing his sympathy for the plight of veterans, the President declared that it was simply unfair to add to the national debt for fewer than 5*

> **million veterans at the expense of 110 million Americans.**

Nan's initial anxiety evaporates as she reads Harding's stated reason for his action. She very much accepts his rationalization. He did it for the greater good. He made a difficult yet rational and appropriate decision. Sometimes the public misunderstands. They don't understand the nuances. The decision has been unfairly characterized by the public. It is unpopular, but only because people fail to see how the President was really working for the benefit of the American citizenry.

A good President must work for the greater good even if there is a political cost. That's what brilliant and compassionate leaders like Harding must do – sacrifice themselves for their people. He is such a brave man. She stands proudly, looks at the article, and declares, "Strong, courageous decision, Mr. President. As one of the 110 million, I thank you."

At the same time, Florence reads a similar article in the Washington Post and is furious. She marches into the Oval Office and slams the newspaper on the President's desk. "How could you? We shook hands with those veterans and promised them. They put their lives on the line for their country, many are forever ruined, and you're worried about money?"

Harding defends his decision, deflecting like the politician he is. "It was a tough decision. I would have loved to sign the bill, but budgetary constraints got in the way. We just had to make a choice to do other good work. And we're doing lots of other things for the veterans. We're building new hospitals." Florence finds this explanation less than adequate. "You should have given them the bonus *and* built the hospitals. And how is the hospital construction going anyhow?"

Harding doesn't have a clue how the hospital projects are going. He shrugs, "I guess OK." Florence is outraged. "You guess!?!" Harding stammers in response, "Well, yes, Charles Forbes is in charge. He's a fine fellow." Florence raises her eyebrows, "You guess? He's a fine fellow? Do more! Find out for sure! Don't disappoint me again! Get Hoover!"

Harding, perplexed and angry, responds, "Hoover? Are you nuts, woman? We were talking about Forbes." "I said Hoover, and I mean Hoover!" Florence yells. "He may be the only honest one you've got here and the only one that might be able to figure out what's going on... Get him to look into this!"

A flabbergasted Harding shakes his head. "I'm in charge. I call the shots. I know what's going on." "The hell you do. The leeches you've hired are eating you alive." Florence then reminds him of the advice he often gives himself. "It's your friends you should fear, remember?" Florence storms out of the office. Harding thinks for a moment and listens as Florence's footsteps fade away. As soon as she is well out of earshot, he picks up the phone and calls Hoover.

Chapter 38
Breakdown

After some six months of investigation, Hoover has walked Harding through the initial findings of his investigation, and it is scathing. There are numerous proven and serious scandals. And Hoover is still investigating other anomalies potentially as bad.

Harding is a wreck as he looks over the report. He's depressed and ashamed. Under his command, the grand projects he had promised the American people will not now come to fruition. Instead, a few of his men (men he trusted) have illicitly gotten rich, very rich. Harding shakes his head in disgust as he throws down the report. "Behind every great fortune is a great crime."

One of the proven scandals involves Charles Forbes, head of Veterans Affairs and the hospital project. A project that has wrongly enriched Forbes at the expense of American heroes (wounded American soldiers). Herbert Hoover, Secretary of Commerce, has provided Harding with incontrovertible evidence documenting Forbes's theft of funds destined for the construction of the hospitals: he stole a huge amount of money.

The hospitals will never be built. Worse, Hoover has explained that Forbes is one of many in the White House stealing money. The malfeasances are widespread. They are very costly and will likely be politically crippling, as these stories are nearly certain to become public, and their release will be a reputational disaster.

Harding is devastated. He's been caught completely off guard and is furious. He just passed the two-year mark in a Presidency he now knows has come completely off the rails. Particularly painful is the sickening knowledge that he has been exploited by men he trusted. He should have seen this coming. Daugherty and his "Ohio Gang" played him like a fiddle. And the worst truth for Harding is that Florence had it right all along – the lowlife leeches he hired have eaten him alive. Harding is beyond angry.

Forbes has been called and now enters the Oval Office. Harding angrily waves Hoover's report at him and explains the findings. Soon the two men are arguing ferociously. It is a colossal fight.

Forbes is the first object of his ire: not an enviable position. Harding is a large imposing man. As their argument continues, Forbes's feeble excuses cause Harding to become increasingly manic. Forbes falsely maintains his innocence. "It was uncontrollable events, unforeseen overruns, all beyond human control that caused," as he called it, "a most unfortunate but sadly unavoidable circumstance. No man, or even God, could have foreseen or prevented it." These lies send the already infuriated Harding into a monstrous rage.

Harding is uncontrollable. He stands, grabs Forbes by the throat and starts shaking him. He screams his contempt while choking him to death. "You yellow rat, you double-crossing bastard!" The men struggle, knocking over chairs and lamps. Forbes, barely able to speak, blurts out, "But Mr. President, cost overruns happen." Harding screams at him while still shaking his victim. "Cost overruns, my ass! You're a despicable lowlife thief. Stealing money from sick and needy veterans! You are the most absolutely depraved human being to have ever lived. You are the scum of the earth!"

Harding shakes Forbes violently as the two tussle around the Oval Office, slamming into a bookcase. On hearing the commotion, Gaston Means and Herbert Hoover rush into the room. In shock, they struggle to separate the two men and do so just in time to spare Forbes' life. All are now breathing heavily. Harding stares madly at Forbes. Forbes, in shock, pauses briefly, then hurries out of the Oval Office.

Harding prances around wildly. He looks to Hoover, "And Jess Smith, too. He was stealing, taking bribes. Where is he? I want to fire him too!" Hoover looks with grave concern at the distressed President and tries to respond calmly. "He was told to come to your office, Mr. President, but apparently, he went home early today." Harding replies angrily, "Well, go get him." "Yes, Mr. President," Hoover says and then nods to Means, who leaves quickly, in search of Smith.

Harding looks at Hoover. "How do we replace the stolen money?" "We don't know yet, Mr. President. We may have to propose a tax hike." Harding moans in desperation. "This will be the end of my Presidency. I'm fucked." Hoover nods sympathetically and tries to ease the President's pain. "That's not a given, Mr. President." Harding ignores him and continues, "So, Forbes and Smith. Who are the others?" Hoover matter-of-factly responds, "Mr. President, we're still looking into that, need to confirm a few things." "Daugherty?" Harding asks, "Was he part of this?" Hoover grimaces a bit, then nods affirmatively.

Harding is distraught and begins to whimper. "So, it's already really bad, and it'll get worse," he laments. "I didn't want this job. I should never have been President. I'm not smart enough." The anguished President storms out of the office and walks quickly and erratically on the White House lawn. His arms flare in the air as he bemoans his ill fortune.

Hoover follows cautiously behind the President. Two nearby Secret Service agents, seeing the hysterical President, follow Hoover. Harding whimpers as he aimlessly zigzags on the lawn. Eventually, he falls to his knees and cries. His crying subsides a bit, but he is still crazed as Hoover approaches slowly. Hoover looks back at one of the Secret Service agents, "Get Dr. Sawyer!" The agent runs off. Hoover looks at the distraught Harding as he kneels on the lawn, lamenting his fate.

"No legacy is as rich as honesty, and they've taken that from me." Harding turns toward Hoover. "Perfection eludes all men, does it not?" Hoover nods, "Indeed, it does, Mr. President." Harding continues, "Have I done no good?" Hoover tries to reassure him, "There have been accomplishments, Mr. President. Unemployment is quite low."

Harding laughs cynically, "Yes, unemployment is low. Thank me? And while we are at it, can we thank the rooster's crow for making the sun come up each morning? What hogwash! Have I done nothing?"

Harding laughs maniacally and then blurts out possible achievements. "The Bureau of the Budget, improving the highways. Those were my doing. Those were good, weren't they?" Hoover encouragingly responds, "Yes, Mr.

President. They were good." Harding, now crying, blurts out, "But the good is oft interred with the bones. It is the evil that lives on. Isn't that right?"

Sawyer and Florence arrive. Sawyer kneels beside Harding. Florence, who is near Sawyer, looks at her husband with grave concern. Sawyer reaches to help the President get up. "We need to get you inside, Mr. President." Florence chimes in, "Warren, we're here to help you."

With Sawyer's help, the President slowly makes his way back on his feet. Harding sees Means returning. He's a bit confused, not quite sure who he is or what he wants. "And what do you want?" Means replies, matter of factly, "Mr. President, I was asked to fetch Jess Smith." Harding smiles, "Oh, yes, good. I want to fire his ass. Is he here?" Means stiffens, "No, Mr. President." Harding, upset that his orders were disobeyed, angrily asks Means, "What? Why not?" Means takes a deep breath, "Mr. President, he's dead."

Harding is shocked. "What? How?" Means shrugs, "Mr. President, they're still investigating, but it looks like he shot himself." Harding initially has no reaction whatsoever, but then he starts to laugh. "Shot himself. Yes, of course. Not a bad exit under the circumstances. I should be so lucky."

Hoover and Sawyer guide the President back into the White House. Harding looks at Hoover. "You're trustworthy. What do you advise?" Hoover has already thought about a resolution, "Well, Mr. President, these issues are bound to be found out sooner or later. Perhaps you should expose them yourself right now."

Harding looks at him, perplexed, "What?" "Yes, Mr. President, admit and apologize. Claim credit for at least your integrity. Tell them your shortcoming was only that you trusted people too much." Harding is befuddled, "Huh?" Harding now ignores Hoover. The terms "admit and apologize" are simply not in his vocabulary.

Undeterred, Hoover continues, "Note your corrective action - the firing of Forbes and the planned firing of the late Jess Smith. Then clean up the White House, fire everyone, and start afresh." Harding, focusing on Hoover's strange suggestion to confess wrongdoing, puts up his hand, motioning Hoover to stop speaking. Harding looks at him as if he's looking at a man from another planet, "Admit my own mistakes? No one does that, certainly no politician." "But, Mr. President," Hoover implores.

Harding waves him off mid-sentence. He looks at Florence. "Well, Duchess, what now?" Florence offers her standard solution for every intractable problem: run from them. She looks confidently into her husband's eyes, "A long trip is in order. We must put some perspective on our problems."

PART IX
Getting Out of Dodge

Chapter 39

Voyage of Understanding

It is a late May morning in 1923, and The White House Press Room is abuzz. Reporters grab their seats as the Press Secretary heads to the podium to address the overflowing room. They are announcing the President's upcoming trip titled the Voyage of Understanding. It has been in the planning for months.

As part of the announcement, assistants pass out the itinerary for the President's sojourn west. It will be a nearly two-month excursion commencing June 22nd and take the President all the way across the country, to the westernmost states, and even to the Alaskan territory. Traveling during the hot summer months will be arduous.

The Press Secretary addresses the reporters. "Thank you all for coming. We wanted you all to be aware of the President's plans. He will be absent from Washington during the summer months on a working trip west." A reporter blurts out a question, "Why in the middle of the hot summer?"

"As you know, it is a working trip. Congress will also be out of town on summer recess, so, despite the heat, the President felt this was the best time to go. No regular business will be going on in Washington anyhow." One reporter comments sarcastically, "Well, that's a relief." This comment elicits some laughter. The Press Secretary appreciates neither the comment nor the laughter.

Another reporter jumps in. "But it's a 46-day trip. There must be some business going on in the White House?" "The President will be in touch with all that is going on here but feels it's time to get reacquainted with the ordinary folks of America that elected him. He's their President too."

A third reporter asks, "Why visit Alaska? It's just a territory. No President has ever done that." "The President wants to better understand their vast resources and help create new policies that will properly protect them." The same reporter asks yet another question, "He's also going to San Francisco. Is he worried about another earthquake?" The Press Secretary smiles and shakes his head, "The President is very much looking forward to seeing San Francisco. We understand it's been magnificently rebuilt. He's sure everything will be just fine there."

Chapter 40
At the Movies

Having secured a babysitter for Elizabeth Ann, Nan has arranged a free afternoon and is delighted to be spending it with her sister. She breathes deeply with relief as the two walk down the street. It is now late afternoon; the sisters are heading to the movie theatre. "I'm so glad I found a babysitter. I love my daughter but needed a break. This afternoon off is a nice diversion. Thanks for joining me, Sis." "Delighted," Liz responds, "Let me get the tickets. My treat."

Liz purchases two tickets, and the women head inside. The marquee reads "Rudolph Valentino - *Blood and Sand.*" "It's supposed to be quite good, and I just love Valentino," Liz exclaims. Nan nods in agreement, "Who doesn't? But Elizabeth Ann keeps me so busy I haven't kept up with the latest movie gossip. I know nothing about this film."

"Oh," responds Liz enthusiastically, "It's supposed to be quite the story. Love triangle. Valentino's a dashing matador and tormented. He's trying to choose between his wife and his mistress." Nan immediately replies, "Oh,

I know what he should do." The two women laugh and enter the theater.

They take their seats, and in a short time, the theater darkens. The organist plays along dramatically to the opening newsreel. Images of President Harding waving from a train appear on screen with the title "Voyage of Understanding - President Harding embarks on a 46-day western journey." The screen shows footage of the President's travels as the subtitles read, "A rigorous trip that will take him all the way west. He will be the first President to visit Alaska." Liz whispers to her sister, "Did you see him before he left?" Nan shakes her head. "No. But he sent me two monthly allowances and said he'd see me as soon as he returned."

Chapter 41
An Upset Stomach

In the following weeks, Nan scours every newspaper she can get her hands on, reading all the articles she can find about The Voyage of Understanding. She especially likes looking at the photographs accompanying the articles that show her lover in such a wonderful light. His images are so striking and impressive. He looks almost regal as he greets the adoring and appreciative people of this great country.

One article, at the beginning of the trip, has a photo of the President waving to onlookers from the train. A few weeks later, there's a photo of him boarding a ship in Seattle for the trip to Alaska. And another of him visiting native Alaskans.

On July 29th, she reads an article that makes her a bit uneasy. The President, having returned from Alaska, was in Seattle giving a speech. According to the article, he appeared a bit disoriented, stumbled at one point, and dropped his notes. He raised his arms to ward off the concerns of the crowd. He then downplayed the incident and laughed it off, declaring that he was just intoxicated by the natural beauty of Seattle.

On July 30th, Nan is further concerned as she reads the lead story in the N.Y. Times.

> *President Harding is ill. Activities postponed as he recuperates in San Francisco - Dr. Sawyer orders President to rest after he was stricken with food poisoning in Seattle. A tired President smiled and waved but did not speak to reporters upon entering the Palace Hotel in San Francisco yesterday. He looked a bit gaunt as he moved briskly through the lobby and boarded the elevator to the Presidential suite.*

She picks up her crying daughter and sits her on her lap at the kitchen table. She calms her while continuing to read the article.

> *As he boarded the elevator to the Presidential Suite, the President gestured to his stomach. A few hours later, his staff told reporters that the President took a much-needed nap. They reported that the President was now refreshed and feeling much better. The worst symptoms had subsided though he still had a lingering yet mild stomach ache.*

> *The staff elaborated that, to be on the safe side, Dr. Sawyer had prescribed more rest. The President was well enough and did, in fact, attend to some pressing matters. They said his health was expected to improve*

> *significantly and that he planned to resume his travel schedule in the next 48 hours. His staff was busy rescheduling meetings. At the date of publication of this article, the President's new itinerary was still a work in progress.*

Nan sighs with relief, looks at her daughter, and says, "Daddy just has a little tummy ache."

Chapter 42
Getting Better

It is 7:15 PM, August 2nd 1923, and inside the Presidential Suite of the Palace Hotel in San Francisco, the tension is beginning to ease. It has been a long day, particularly for Dr. Joel T. Boone, the 34-year-old US Naval Officer and Medal of Honor winner. He is a White House physician, and though ostensibly Dr. Sawyer is his boss, this is in name only. It is common knowledge that Boone is the far superior physician, and even Sawyer looks up to him. Sawyer is an old, out-of-date country doctor and nowhere near as skilled as the meticulous and traditionally trained Boone.

President Harding lies in bed in the bedroom where Sawyer takes his temperature and blood pressure. Mrs. Harding escorts a very tired Dr. Boone to the door. "Thank you, Dr. Boone. He's improved marvelously these last couple of days." The President chimes in from the other room, "Yes, I'm feeling much better."

Boone smiles and looks at Florence. "I am going to step out for a breath of fresh air. I'll return shortly." Boone clandestinely motions to Florence that she should follow him. Responding to his gesture, Florence looks at him, "Of course." Florence then follows Boone into the hallway.

At the same time, Nan is in her New York City apartment, lovingly looking over her sleeping three-and-a-half-year-old daughter. She looks at that evening's New York Evening Post headline.

> **PRESIDENT'S HEALTH MARKEDLY IMPROVED.** *Harding resting at the Palace Hotel in San Francisco – Dr. Sawyer says he is recovering well from his bout of food poisoning. Should be fully recovered soon and will resume an abbreviated schedule of his trip and then return to D.C. as planned next week.*

Nan smiles, kisses her daughter good night and speaks to her, "Everything is going to be just fine, Elizabeth Ann. Returning to normalcy."

On the other side of the country, Florence follows Dr. Boone into the hallway outside the Presidential Suite. They walk away from Gaston Means, who alone stands guard outside the door. Boone and Florence speak in whispered tones.

"Look, Florence. I have a heart specialist, Dr. Wilbur, coming from Stanford. I am, frankly, skeptical of Dr. Sawyer's diagnosis and even more of his treatment." Florence is perplexed. "But Dr. Sawyer's such a dear friend." Boone shakes his head a bit, "He's charming, but his medicine is not up to date. He may be doing more harm than good. Let the President be - do nothing until Dr. Wilbur arrives." Florence takes Boone's hands and looks him in the eye, "I understand. Now you take your much-needed break."

Chapter 43

Turn for the Worse, Much Worse

Florence watches as the doors shut on the elevator Boone has just boarded. She then heads back into the suite where, in a few moments, the world will change. It will be brief and tragic. And it will mark the beginning of a saga that will become an indelible and sordid part of American lore. There were no independent witnesses, recordings or evidence of any kind but the minutes that follow will, for decades to come, spawn endless rumors, rampant speculation, and sickening exploitation.

On the other side of the country, Nan Britton is in New York, getting ready for bed. She smiles and sings happily to herself. She is relieved at the news of her lover's markedly improved health and happy in the knowledge that she will see him in a couple of weeks when he returns to D.C.

Nan's dreams will soon be shattered. She will never see Harding again. The events about to unfold some 3,000 miles away in San Francisco - the place where Harding's Press Secretary, just a few months earlier, had assured reporters would be benign ("Everything will be just fine there", he said) - will forever and unalterably change many lives. No one's life though will change more dramatically than Nan Britton's.

Back in the hotel suite, Sawyer, syringe in hand, is standing over the President as he lies in bed. Sawyer nods to Florence as she enters the suite. She returns the nod and walks over to the bedside table where there is a half-filled glass of water and a newspaper. She looks at the water glass and then her watch. She picks up the newspaper and notices an article favorably reporting on the Voyage of Understanding. "Warren," she says, "Let me read this nice article to you." She reads the headline:

Marvelously   Successful   Voyage   of Understanding to Resume Soon

Florence stops reading and smiles at her husband. Harding looks back at her and utters what will be his last words: "Good, go on." Harding's eyes then open wide, he looks directly at Florence and begins to shake uncontrollably, a shake that quickly turns into violent spasms. Florence gasps loudly.

Outside, Gaston Means, the sole agent still guarding the door, raises his eyebrows when he hears Florence's gasp. Seconds later, Florence abruptly opens the doors and frantically addresses Means, "Go find Dr. Boone. Immediately!" Means looks stoically at the First Lady, "Sorry, Mrs. Harding, I cannot leave my post." The First Lady grabs him by his lapels and screams at him, "Immediately means NOW!" Means, shocked by the First Lady's aggressiveness, complies instantly and runs down the hall.

Boone is just stepping away from the hotel when he hears his name being called. He turns as he hears and sees Means rushing toward him with urgency. "Dr. Boone. You're needed at once!" Together they rush back into the hotel and up to the Presidential suite.

Boone hurriedly enters the suite. Sawyer is attending to what is now the President's lifeless body. Florence is beside him, and she looks at Boone as he enters. "Bring him back!" Boone approaches the dead President, looks at his pupils and then closes the President's eyes. He slowly shakes his head and looks at Sawyer, "What happened? He seemed to be improving when I left."

Sawyer is speechless. There is a moment of silence, which Florence breaks by saying, "I was reading to him from the newspaper, an article he found of interest. I paused, and he said, 'Go on.' Then he suddenly shook violently and keeled over." Boone again looks at the dead President as Florence nods and gestures to Sawyer. She mouths to him that he should corroborate her story. Sawyer finally gets the hint, "Yes, that's what happened."

Boone, still looking at the deceased President, speaks in medical terms. "Looks like an apoplectic stroke, but we should know for sure after the autopsy." Sawyer looks at Florence with grave concern. Florence nods back and then speaks up, stating firmly, "There will be no autopsy."

Boone is shocked, "What? But he's the President of the United States! The world will want to know. I mean, it's not like he's Jewish." Florence queries Boone, "So Jews don't believe in autopsies?" A still-angry Boone replies, "That's my understanding." Without emotion, Florence looks at her dead husband. "Well then, I guess he just converted." Boone continues his plea, "But for the sake of his and all our reputations." Florence breathes deeply and looks firmly at Boone: "No means no. No autopsy."

Chapter 44
Nan's Bad Morning

It is the morning of August 3, 1923, and Nan wakes abruptly from a bad dream. She gets out of bed and picks up her daughter. With daughter in her arms, she opens the front door. She immediately sees the New York Times' horrific headline. She grabs the paper from her doorstep and screams out, "No!" She stops breathing momentarily, clenches a fist and thrusts it back and forth in the air, and shrieks over and over, "No. No. No." She is too stunned to cry, though. She is immobilized by the shocking news. She manages to get back into her apartment, closes the door, and falls to her knees to avoid fainting, only just managing to deposit Elizabeth Ann safely on the floor.

Tears eventually come, and she is now crying uncontrollably and whimpering. She strikes herself in madness, "No. No. This can't be." She remains hysterical and flings the newspaper down. She can only manage to read the first few words of the headline; the remainder of the newspaper is an incoherent blur. She gets up and is close to losing consciousness. She staggers to the couch and lies down, still unable to grasp the unfathomable news. The newspaper on the floor nearby tells the story, though, a truth she is not ready to accept.

PRESIDENT HARDING DIES SUDDENLY IN SAN FRANCISCO; STROKE OF APOPLEXY AT 7:30 PM; CALVIN COOLIDGE IS PRESIDENT.

DEATH STROKE CAME WITHOUT WARNING - *Mrs. Harding Was Reading to Her Husband When First Sign Appeared -- She Ran for A Doctor.*

NOTHING COULD BE DONE TO REVIVE PATIENT -- *News of Tragic End Shocks Everybody, Coming After Day Said to Have Been the Best Since His Illness Began a Week Ago.*

PUBLIC MEN VOICE TRIBUTES TO HARDING'S WORTH AND RECORD: *Hughes Says He Was a Brave and Strong Leader -- Marshall Calls Him a Great Human American - Honored a Martyr to His Duty -- Sympathy Goes Out to Mrs. Harding.*

Then, a distraught Nan turns to her daughter, "Elizabeth Ann!" She grabs a tissue and begins to cry, somewhat muted at first, then nearly uncontrollably. "Elizabeth Ann! Daddy is dead. Now Mommy needs to find a way to make the rent all by herself."

PART X
The Morning After

Chapter 45
All the News

It is the morning after the President's death. The stunned nation absorbs the news with grief and shock. This grief, though, would soon be replaced by troubling and nagging questions. The prurient interests of the general populace, as it often does, would gravitate to the more titillating aspects of death, sex, and corruption.

Even at the outset, though, there were glimmers of skepticism. How could the President, with all the advanced care he was afforded, die so abruptly? His diagnosis, just a mild case of food poisoning, shouldn't have yielded this result. Furthermore, just a day earlier, he was supposedly well on the road to recovery. Why the dramatic and abrupt change to this worst possible outcome? How could his medical team have gotten it so wrong? Was something, maybe something important and devious, being kept from the public?

Shortly, people would begin scouring the news for any morsel of information about Harding's shocking demise. There would be an insatiable appetite for base tidbits, scandalous rumors, and wild, blatant conjecture. For years to come, there would be a plethora of stories, innuendos, accusations and speculation about his death. It would become great fodder for magazines, books and newspapers (ironically, boosting sales of the President's former business).

On this morning, though, the nagging questions are back of mind, not yet at the forefront. They soon will be, though, as, the lobby of the Palace Hotel is now bustling with newspaper folks and politicians. A press conference is about to begin that will generate more questions than answers.

The ballroom itself has been hurriedly converted into a press room. A stage has been set up, and reporters eagerly enter the room. The Secretary of Commerce, Herbert Hoover, stands in the wings, preparing to address the reporters.

Hoover, with Mrs. Harding by his side, looks over his prepared remarks. He folds his notes, puts them in his interior coat pocket, and takes out some telegrams, showing them to the First Lady. "The world mourns your loss, Florence; remarkable tributes from friend and foe alike. He left a most distinguished legacy." Florence looks at him steely-eyed, "Let's hope it stays that way."

Hoover goes to the podium on the makeshift stage. Dr. Sawyer, Dr. Boone and other dignitaries enter and stand behind him. Mr. Hoover raises his hands to quiet the crowd. "Ladies and Gentlemen. We have a brief statement." The room quiets, Hoover looks at his notes and reads his statement: "As you know, we are all saddened by the news of President Harding's unfortunate passing. It was most unexpected and sudden. He expired last night at 7:30 PM. His wife and his physician, Dr. Sawyer, were by his side at the time. The cause of death was apoplexy stroke."

Some reporters busily scribble notes. One reporter tries to interject a question. "Mr. Hoover, Sir?" Hoover waves him off, ignores the query, and continues. "His family and friends appreciate the outpouring of sympathy. The President worked diligently for his country. Died a martyr. Like so many others, I was honored to have worked with him."

Numerous reporters' arms shoot up and they shout out, trying to ask questions. It is a cacophony of sound. Hoover again raises his hands, successfully silencing them. He continues with his prepared remarks. "Within the hour, the President's body will be placed in the drawing room here at the hotel. This afternoon his casket and the entire Presidential party will board the train and depart for Washington, D.C., where he will lie in state. Ultimately, he will be laid to rest in Marion, Ohio, the city where he married and spent his happiest years. Thank you. We will have a press release available for you all shortly."

Hoover gathers his notes as he prepares to leave. Undeterred, the reporters compete to ask questions. One reporter looks at his notes where he has written the word "autopsy" and shouts out above the others. "When will you release the autopsy?" Hoover glances uncomfortably at Florence backstage and then responds. "At the family's request, there will be no autopsy."

There is a murmur among many in the crowd. Some look suspiciously at one another. Another reporter has a follow-up query, "How then was the cause of death determined?" Hoover looks behind him at Dr. Sawyer.

Sawyer steps forward, falsely believing he is being given permission to address this query. Hoover motions him back and responds. "It was the unanimous conclusion of the President's medical team." Sawyer nods in agreement. Hoover makes what he hopes is his final comment, "Now, thank you, but we do need to prepare for our departure." Hoover then leaves the stage.

The Presidential party struggles to move through the throng of reporters who crowd around them, barraging the party with aggressive questions. A third reporter calls out to Sawyer as he is trying to move through the crowd: "Dr. Sawyer, did the food poisoning contribute to his death?" Sawyer instinctively replies, "It probably weakened him." Hoover tries to shout over the noise. "Ladies and Gentlemen, as mentioned, we will have a press release."

Another reporter calls out a question directed to Sawyer as the party leaves. "Did anyone else in the Presidential party suffer food poisoning?" Sawyer, shaken by the implications of the reporter's question (which he believes might put his diagnosis in doubt), shakes his head and softly utters, "No."

Hoover tries to usher Sawyer out of the noisy room. One reporter's question is heard over the roar. "Has the body already been embalmed?" A nervous Sawyer nods but says nothing. A few reporters manage to surround Sawyer as he moves through the lobby. "Dr. Sawyer, can you describe the President's last moments alive? His last words?" Sawyer, extremely shaken by this probing and contentious interrogation, now moves deliberately through the crowd and blurts out, "No! No, I can't."

The reporter follows up, "Was it then just Mrs. Harding that was with him at the last moment?" Sawyer tries not to react and hurries away. The reporter believes, however, that he detected an affirmative nod from Sawyer. The reporter frantically scribbles on his pad as he and others rush off.

Chapter 46
Spreading the Gospel

Harding's death, now just some 12 hours ago, is the lead story of every morning, evening, and special edition newspaper in the country. The public's appetite for news about what happened in San Francisco is now insatiable. Though Herbert Hoover did his best, he had sketchy facts, and the hastily called press conference at The Palace Hotel has started to sow doubts about the cause of the President's death.

One man in particular has his finger on the pulse of the public's base interests. That man is Mr. Charles Klunk, publisher of the Evening Graphic, an unapologetic tabloid. Klunk has been scouring every angle of the story. He will exploit the situation and feed the crowd with whatever will sell, be it truth, half-truth, or lie.

Klunk now sits in his office, musing over the many articles describing Harding's death. His head writer May Dixon Thacker is with him taking notes.

Klunk's wheels are turning as he motions to the newspapers. "This is the story of the century." Klunk looks to the heavens. "It's a godsend." Klunk shakes his head, still not believing his good fortune. "Harding, the goddam President of the whole United States of America, dies suddenly and his wife says no autopsy and has him embalmed in seconds flat. Jesus. I mean, what the fuck? Like no one is going to want to know how the most powerful man in the world dies unexpectedly on vacation."

Thacker clarifies, "It was a business trip. Voyage of Understanding, he called it." "Voyage of No Return if you ask me," Klunk responds. "Who planned this thing? In the middle of a hot summer. Why go at all? This thing stinks to high heaven." Thacker tries to calm him down, "Everyone dies somewhere. Maybe it was just a bad heart. After all, he wasn't the picture of health. He was a large, overweight man who drank, ate and smoked like there was no tomorrow."

Klunk laughs. "For him, there was no tomorrow." But he brushes off the suggestion. "Bad heart. I don't want to see those words in the Evening Graphic. That's too boring a cause of death. Look, the President dies unexpectedly while out of town, and we got no autopsy. This is great. There are an infinite number of unanswered questions here. Lots of holes to fill in. Your job is to fill those holes with as many innuendos as you can. Create holes if you like. Create conspiracies and suspicions. The whackier, the better. And we start with our next edition. This story's got legs."

Klunk continues, "And I think there might be an angle with that crackpot of a doctor, Dr. Sawyer, who's telling us he had food poisoning? Come on. No one else got food poisoning." Thacker smiles and counters, "Maybe it was food poisoning." Klunk looks disappointedly at her. She continues, "But maybe someone slipped the poison into his food. But who?" Klunk smiles broadly, "Now, you're off and running. Great. I love it. Let's dribble this thing out. There could be a ton of stories here."

Thacker asks, "Should we do any research?" Klunk shakes his head. "Eventually, maybe, but for now, just write. The more insidious the storyline, the better. Just has to have the thinnest thread of marginal plausibility. Our target audience is your below-average idiot, so that's a very, very thin thread; these numbskulls will believe anything."

Thacker continues, "I'll mention his philandering too. He was known to dip his pen in lots of ink wells." Klunk, perhaps surprisingly, is firmly opposed to this. "No. Sexual peccadillos are out of bounds. That's the rule. Everything else is fair game." Klunk responds to Thacker's look of curiosity. "It's the one rule I've kept from my days in real journalism."

Chapter 47
Something is Fishy

Nan too is obsessed with the news. Her interest, of course, is more personal. She can't focus on anything. She's in a constant fog and having difficulty remembering even basic things. For instance, she is now hurrying down the street, pushing Elizabeth Ann in her stroller. She knows she had a purpose when she left her apartment, but for the life of her can't recall it now. She stops dead in her tracks and is now simply frozen on the sidewalk, trying to remember why she left her home in the first place.

Nan keeps replaying in her mind all the interactions she shared with her now-dead lover. She fantasizes about how things were supposed to be - Florence would pass, and she would marry the President, move into the White House, and become First Lady. Harding would adopt Elizabeth Ann. Life would be perfect. This dream all went poof in a flash in San Francisco. Instead of being First Lady, she is now a penniless single mother. Her dream is now a nightmare.

A woman hurrying to a nearby newsstand accidentally bumps into Nan, shaking her from her daydream. The woman's friend, Gladys, exclaims, "Lorraine, be careful!" Lorraine apologizes to Nan, "Excuse me, Mrs. So sorry. But you shouldn't just be standing there. This is a busy sidewalk. Hope I didn't hurt you or your child."

Nan manages a faint smile and can only say, "It's OK, we're fine." Nan longs to tell her more, tell anyone, in fact, that she is not fine, not at all, and that her daughter is American royalty. The daughter of the late President. She wants to tell someone of her great loss, receive condolences, and share her feelings with someone just to help ease the terrible ache inside. Nan, of course, says nothing.

The two women each purchase the latest edition of the Evening Graphic and immediately gravitate to the headline articles discussing Harding's death. They read out loud the sensational stories, freely and openly expressing their opinions while Nan is well within earshot. "No one else got food poisoning. That's suspicious. And pray tell, why no autopsy?" Gladys adds her two bits, "You know they embalmed him before rigor mortis even set in. Seems someone was intent on not having the post mortem. Someone wants to cover up a pretty stinky can of worms, I think. Maybe it's that Dr. Sawyer. Did you see his photo? I don't trust that guy. It's all pretty fishy if you ask me."

Chapter 48

Clean Up

The ballroom of the Palace Hotel, except for the trash left behind, is now empty. Two maids charged with cleaning up the mess enter. One picks up a discarded copy of the morning tabloid, the Daily News. She starts reading the lead story about Harding's death and shakes her head. "This strange tale happened right here! There's something very odd, not quite right with that man's death."

The other maid nods in agreement, "I know. I was working the night shift. I was here when it happened." She winks at her colleague, "I know a thing or two." The first maid, eager to hear the gossip, implores her co-worker to spill the beans, "Ooh. Go on. Dish it out." The maid looks about and, certain no one is around, tells her story.

"Well, there was all sorts of scurrying around last night, so I knew something was up. And I knew it was really serious when Miss Johnston showed up. She was summoned here by someone, and she looked really upset. Didn't say a word as she ran through the front doors. I mean, how often does the owner of this place show up after hours in a tizzy like that."

"Anyhow, she went straight to the Presidential suite. And I followed her, took the next elevator, and quietly snuck out so no one knew I was there, and I stood outside and heard a terrible argument." The listening maid interjects, "Really?"

The storyteller nods her head. "I swear on my father's grave I am telling the truth, so help me God. Well, sparks started to fly. Miss Johnston was in the room, and the First Lady was in a rage, and she starts screaming at her, and all the while, the dead President was just lying there in bed. I mean, arguing while the President's corpse is in the room.

"Mrs. Harding yells at Miss Johnston that it was the hotel food that killed the President. 'The hotel killed him', she says. Well, Miss Johnston would have none of it and pointed out our A+ rating from the Health Department. We are, of course, a class establishment. Well, the two of them went back and forth for nearly 10 minutes. It was a terrible catfight."

"And then what?" the friend asks. "Well, the First Lady threatens her, says she'll sue her for everything, and that she will end up owning the hotel." The storyteller takes a deep breath. "Then there is a moment of silence, and I hear some footsteps inside the room, and the next words are Miss Johnston's. Apparently, she has picked up a glass on the President's nightstand, and she says, 'Oh really? This water glass smells awfully strange to me. Can't keep it to my nose for more than a second. I am going to have the chemists take a look at it. I suspect the contents of this glass, whatever it is, killed the President.'

"Then there is another moment of silence, and I hear more angry footsteps. This time I'm pretty sure it was the First Lady, and she says, 'Give me that!' Then I hear her footsteps going into the bathroom, and I hear liquid going down the toilet and then hear the flush sound. I am pretty sure the First Lady poured the glass's contents down the toilet. Anyhow, the next thing I hear, the First Lady says, 'Changed my mind. There will be no lawsuit.' And with that, I scurried out of there as fast as I could. I didn't want to get caught eavesdropping as I was pretty certain Miss Johnston would be coming my way." The storyteller nods knowingly at her astonished colleague.

Chapter 49

The Long Ride Home

After a simple religious service for the deceased, a priest leads a procession taking the President's casket, draped in an American flag, from the hotel. A large but quiet crowd watches outside as the casket is ceremoniously placed on a horse-drawn carriage for the procession down Market Street and ultimately to the train station. Mourners, still shocked by the news, line the street from the hotel to the station and pay their respects to the late President as the carriage goes by.

Upon its arrival at the station, Dr. Sawyer and Florence watch solemnly as the casket is placed in the last car of what is now the Presidential funeral train. Once it is on board, Sawyer and Florence, assisted by military personnel, climb the steps and board the train. Florence is dressed in a mourning gown and sits in a window seat draped with black curtains. Dr. Sawyer sits next to her and tries to offer some gentle comfort.

Without looking at him, Florence speaks, "You know, I didn't get the chance to choose his casket." Sawyer is silent and feeling uncomfortable. Florence continues,

"The mortuary said you gave them the one we were already traveling with." Sawyer begins to sweat as Florence glares at him. She continues by asking, "So, you decided we should take the unusual step of including a casket in our provisions when we left D.C.?"

Sawyer is now extremely uncomfortable. He stammers, turns red and is flummoxed as to how to respond. It was indeed his idea to travel with a casket. An awkward and long silence follows, and then Sawyer breathes deeply and does his best to explain.

"It was the middle of summer, a long rigorous journey. Many in our party weren't well to start with. Anything could have happened to anyone." Florence says nothing, making Sawyer even more uncomfortable. Truth be told, Sawyer was as concerned about Florence's health as the President's. Nonetheless, there's no denying that it was a strange, large and awkward item to include as part of one's traveling provisions. If any member of the President's entourage passed during the trip, they could have surely found a casket at the local mortuary where the deceased passed.

Florence looks dispassionately at Sawyer, then picks up the afternoon San Francisco Examiner. She becomes distressed as she reads articles about her husband's death. In New York, Nan is in her apartment reading similar articles in the New York Times.

BODY OF PRESIDENT HARDING LEAVES SAN FRANCISCO FOR WASHINGTON D.C. - PRESIDENTIAL PARTY TO BOARD FUNERAL TRAIN - VOYAGE OF UNDERSTANDING HAS AN UNEXPECTED END *Accompanied by the First Lady and the late President's* *entourage, President Harding's casket will make the long trip east, by rail, retracing the same route that took the living President on his ambitious cross-country tour. His Presidency and westward trip have both come to an abrupt end.*

FIRST LADY SAYS NO AUTOPSY - BODY EMBALMED JUST A FEW HOURS AFTER DEATH - The First Lady, who was alone with the President when he died, refused an autopsy. No reasons were offered, and officials have anonymously confirmed that this is not normal protocol. The mortuary has also reported that the President's body was embalmed last night at 10:15 in the evening, not quite 3 hours after his death, which, Secretary Hoover confirmed, occurred in the hotel at 7:30 PM.

ROLE OF FOOD POISONING STILL BEING INVESTIGATED - ONLY THE PRESIDENT STRICKEN WITH FOOD POISONING Curiously, it seems that it was only the President who suffered from food poisoning. Dr. Sawyer confirmed that no other in the party was stricken with the malady.

Florence is aware of the innuendo in these words and knows well that the tabloids are already suggesting that the President was murdered. Since she's been reported as being the last one with the living President, she will certainly be, at least in the public's eye, a suspect.

Florence puts down the newspaper, and speaking more to herself than to Sawyer, says, "The body's not yet cold, and the rumor mill is working full steam." Sawyer, well aware of these articles, tries to calm her. He pats her hand and says, as calmly as he can muster, "Florence, you're reading too much into this. It will soon pass anyhow." Florence gives him a steely look. "It will get worse!"

Nan is also upset reading these articles. She thinks about the conversation she overheard, questioning Harding's death, and wonders out loud, "Did she kill him? Because of me?"

PART XI
Tidying Up

Chapter 50
Switching Trains

A few hours later, while the train is en route, Gaston Means approaches Florence. "Mrs. Harding, we can, as you requested, get you back to Washington sooner." "Good," Florence says. She then looks at a surprised Dr. Sawyer. "I need to prepare for the funeral and tidy up a bit before." Means continues, "We can put you on a different train in Reno. We should probably be discreet. Let's go with the plan as discussed. I will accompany you." Florence nods appreciatively. "Very well." She then stands and heads toward a sleeping car.

A few hours later, Means, carrying a suitcase, approaches the now casually dressed Florence. Beside Means is a woman of nearly the same height and size as Florence, wearing the mourning outfit the First Lady had been wearing. Florence, to disguise her identity, has changed her attire. She has a large hat, scarf, and sunglasses. Means tips his hat, "Mrs. Harding, shall we? We need to exit trackside." Florence stands up and joins Means.

"Can you see well enough?" he asks as he points to the First Lady's sunglasses. "Sorry, those aren't prescription."

"I'll need to take your arm." Means offers his arm. "Fine. It's a helpful decoy." Florence takes Means' arm as they move toward the exit. Her double quickly sits in her place. Another agent lowers the black curtains next to the double and moves toward the back of the car. The train slows as it approaches Reno station and comes to a stop.

Mourners on the station stand solemnly. Some have their hands on their hearts, others have removed their hats in respect. A few in uniform salute. Some local press are there as well. None, however, notice as Means and Florence exit trackside and quickly board an awaiting train. Once on board that train, it speeds off towards D.C.

Chapter 51
Loose Ends

It is the morning of August 6th 1923, and upon their arrival in Washington D.C., Florence and Gaston Means head directly to the White House. Means has called ahead and made appropriate arrangements. He escorts Florence into an office where dozens upon dozens of storage boxes await her. They are strewn on the floor, stacked on desks and tables, and take up nearly the entire room.

Means announces his departure. "I will leave you to sort through all this. Is there anything else you need from me first, Mrs. Harding?" She shakes her head. "No, thank you. I just need time to go through these papers. I will need privacy." Means nods knowingly and announces his compliance, "Very well, I will leave you alone."

"Oh, Mr. Means," Mrs. Harding interrupts. "Before you go, would you please be so kind as to light the fireplace? I am not feeling well and am a bit chilled." It is the middle of summer and quite warm. Means raises his eyebrows but complies nonetheless. "Of course."

Means lights the fire and then, as he leaves, turns to Florence, "I'll be nearby, in the small side office, should you need anything." Means exits and Florence begins going through the papers. Florence spends the next several hours repeatedly gathering documents from the boxes, occasionally glancing at them before throwing them into the fireplace. At one point, Means peers secretly in at her through the keyhole. He smiles slyly when he sees her burning the papers, shakes his head, and walks away.

Chapter 52
A Very Bad Decision

It is now some hours later and Means sits alone in the small office. He reads some newspapers while listening to the radio. A few minutes later, he hears a knock on the door. He smiles, turns off the radio, and opens the door. His guests, as expected, are Nan and her daughter. He gestures for them to come in.

Nan initiates the conversation. "Thank you for agreeing to meet with me at such short notice. I'm sorry to bother you, but you're the only one I know of that's familiar with my situation." Means is gracious. "My pleasure. How may I help?" Nan's pent-up concerns come flooding out, "My rent is due the first of the month. I don't have enough. Do you, by chance, have my September money?" Means shakes his head, "I'm afraid not."

Nan is now even more anxious, "Do you know how he planned on providing for us after his death?" Means shakes his head. Nan asks again, "Surely, you must know." Means laughs sympathetically, "Sorry. I really don't. That's above my pay grade." A desperate Nan continues, "Is there someone in the Republican party I could maybe ask?" Means shrugs, "Probably, but off-hand, I'm not sure who. I can ask around."

Nan is grateful for even this tidbit of help. "I'd appreciate it. It's a delicate matter, so please be discreet." Means sits straight up, "I'm always discreet, Miss Britton."

Nan hesitates before asking her next question. "You know..." She pauses. Means remains silent, waiting for her to continue. Eventually, she does. "You know, I'd like to see him one last time. Will it be an open casket?" Means shakes his head. "No, not for the public."

A disappointed Nan gets up to leave. "I'll always have the memory." Means is silent but thinking as Nan heads to the door. He finally volunteers, "There's to be a family-only private viewing. You can't attend, of course, but perhaps before?" Nan lights up, "Could you arrange that?" Means again shakes his head. "Me, no. And I know it'd be awkward, but..." Means stops mid-sentence and then shakes his head as he thinks better of what he was about to say. "Oh, sorry, forget it. Not appropriate of me. I am sorry, Miss Britton, but good day."

Nan is frustrated. She wants to hear what Means was thinking. She turns, "No, complete your thought. Let me decide what's appropriate here. He was my lover and the father of my child." Means looks at her sternly, hesitates for a long while, and then finally continues. "Well, what I was going to say is that if you want to see the body, you could make an inquiry with Mrs. Harding. You could do it right now. She's in the next room."

Nan immediately responds with a loud "No!" Means nods sympathetically. "Silly idea of mine. Sorry. It's just that for several decades now, Mrs. Harding and the President have just had a business relationship, nothing more. And she knew." Nan perks up, "She knew about us?"

Means nods. "Oh, Mrs. Harding didn't approve, mind you, but was resigned to it."

Nan hesitates and thinks. Finally, she says, "No, I still can't ask her." Means nods in agreement, "Don't blame you. I wouldn't have the guts, either. Too bad, though, there won't be another chance. And nothing really to lose." Nan is nearly hysterical. "Mr. Means, I'm too emotional right now to make such a rash decision." Means plays along. He is rather enjoying watching her struggle, and continues, "Better not make any decision then." Nan openly discusses her dilemma, "Choosing not to ask is a decision, though. This is awful." Means acknowledges her issue, "Damned if you do, damned if you don't."

Nan breathes deeply. She can't help herself and knows she is about to make a very bad decision. She says more to herself than to Mr. Means, "There is, though, as you said, nothing to lose, I guess. A sin of omission or commission. Which do I choose?" Means smiles softly, "Nothing ventured, nothing gained." Nan stands up and takes a very deep breath. "Mr. Means, if you'd be so kind, please take me to see Mrs. Harding."

Chapter 53

An Unwelcome Visit

A few minutes later, Means knocks and then opens the door to the room Florence occupies. Florence is still at the fireplace burning documents and is upset by the intrusion. Her upset turns to anger when she sees Nan (holding her daughter's hand) just behind Means. Means profusely apologizes for the interruption, "I'm sorry, Ma'am. Miss Britton was most insistent. Said it was urgent that she speak with you." Mr. Means closes the door behind him, leaving Nan, her daughter and Florence alone in the room.

There is an awkward silence between the two women. Nan eventually offers her condolences, "Mrs. Harding. I am so sorry." Florence remains stony silent as she looks angrily at Nan. Nan continues, "It's a great loss." Nan pauses for what seems like an eternity, then continues, "For both of us. And the country." Florence breathes deeply and asks curtly, "What do you want?" Nan steels herself, "Elizabeth Ann never met her father. I was hoping there would be a private viewing of the body."

Florence finds the request an affront and an insult and shakes her head unsympathetically. Nan continues, "There won't be another chance, and I'd like a photo of Elizabeth Ann and her father, the dead President." Instead of replying Florence goes to the door, opens it, and calls out to Means, "Guard! Please come here now and escort our guest out!"

Nan looks at Florence as she heads to the door. "I didn't mean to upset you. It's just that I owe it to my daughter. She's your husband's daughter too." Florence holds the door open for her as Means approaches, and now finally says something. "My dear, you made your bed. You lie in it." Means is escorting Nan out when she turns toward Florence, "He spoke well of you. Said you helped in the business, were a good bookkeeper. And your family was of the right pedigree."

Florence is now furious. And it is because Nan's words ring true. She is quite certain her late husband did describe her as one with a pedigree who kept books well. In essence, he called her a dog while praising her as a bean counter. Hardly the affectionate comment or accolade one would hope to get from their spouse. Florence lets out a loud humph as she calls out to the departing Nan. "My naive little child. I'm quite certain you were truer to him than he was to you."

Nan is now upset and angry too. She manages to free herself from Means' arm and turns and stares at Florence. "Rest assured, I will do anything for our daughter." Florence smiles slyly, "Anything?" She pauses and then offers some advice: "I'd advise against breaking the law. Your daughter won't do well with her mother behind bars."

Florence addresses Means as he leaves. "Escort this young lady from the premises immediately". Means dutifully replies, "Yes, Ma'am," as he then walks Nan down the hall.

Chapter 54
The Not-So-Solemn Funeral Procession

A few days later, a horse-drawn carriage with the President's casket leads the funeral procession down Pennsylvania Avenue. Florence walks beside Dr. Sawyer just behind the casket. Beside them are the President's brother, Dr. Harding, and his sister, Daisy Harding. Other dignitaries walk behind the family.

Public mourners, including Nan with her daughter in her arms, line the street. Sawyer looks at the crowd and turns to Florence, "Florence, he was very much beloved." Florence somewhat cynically replies, "A good start to the end for him then."

Florence looks at the crowd and notices Nan with her daughter observing the procession. She tries to hide her upset as she glances in Sawyer's direction, "Good starts don't always end well, though, do they?" An angry man near Nan is among the public mourners. He holds up a copy of the Daily News. Its headline reads, 'No Autopsy?

- What is the First Lady Hiding?' He looks at Florence and screams, "Murderess!"

Nan looks at the man, thinking the claim may possibly be true. Sawyer finds the outburst most disconcerting. He tries to ignore it and hopes Florence has not heard it. Sawyer takes her arm as they continue in silence for a moment until Florence speaks to him quietly. "If I was going to kill him, and I probably should have, I would have done it years ago."

PART XII
Single Mom

Chapter 55
We Ain't No Charity

It is September 10 1923, and Nan is in her apartment in New York City. She is exhausted and, at the moment, very strained trying to take care of her nearly-four-year-old finicky daughter. There is a loud and repeated knocking on her door. Nan has been expecting this unwanted visit. She has no choice so opens the door for her gruff landlord.

He immediately gets to the point, "Rent was due ten days ago. You got the dough?" Nan is apologetic, "I'm sorry. I'm just waiting for the money. I'm sure it will be coming." The landlord rolls his eyes in disbelief and replies sarcastically, "Sure, Lady. Manna from heaven. Or maybe the deadbeat father's going to be sending you a pot of gold." Nan struggles but responds, "Not a pot of gold, but yes, I think the father will be sending me money. He always has." The landlord laughs, scornfully. "You think? I can't tell you how reassuring that is."

Nan begs him, "I'm doing my best. It's really, really difficult right now for me. Please have mercy." The unsympathetic landlord heads to the door, then turns, "We ain't no charity. Get me the money or get out. You got a week."

A distraught Nan sits paralyzed as he slams the door shut.

Chapter 56
Moving Day

It is one week later. No money has shown up, and Nan, forced to vacate her apartment, is moving her belongings. Her sister Liz is helping to take packed boxes to a waiting truck. Nan will, at least temporarily, move in with her sister and her brother-in-law, Stuart Willits. Elizabeth Ann is nearby looking on at the activity. A neighbor keeps an eye on the child.

Liz speaks to Nan, "Stuart is not at all happy about this." Nan quickly responds, "Nor am I. I'll move out as soon as I get back on my feet. What about the other part of our plan? What Warren suggested years ago. For Elizabeth Ann to take your last name - Willits?" Liz is silent. Nan implores her, "We must, though. To keep up appearances as she attends school. We're telling everyone you've adopted an orphan."

Liz is direct. "Nan, if you must know, Stuart hates the idea. Really hates it. But I pleaded with him, and he very reluctantly gave in. And I mean very reluctantly. Now he's really angry with me too."

Nan is ashamed. "I am so sorry, Liz, to have to put you through this… it is all my fault. Things haven't worked out at all as I had hoped. I was stupid and naïve." Liz looks at her sister. "You were in love. Not stupid. So, Nan, any job prospects?" Nan shakes her head. "Not yet."

A few hours later, the two women carry boxes into the modest apartment. Liz brings them to what is no more than a reasonably large closet. Stuart Willits, Liz's husband, looks on harshly, says nothing, and then leaves. Liz looks at her sister. "Sorry, Nan. We have no other place to put you. Stuart uses the other bedroom for his office, and he won't give it up. You can sleep with me, though, when he goes overseas. Until then, this will be your and Elizabeth Ann's bedroom." Liz leaves. Nan looks at the closet and starts to cry.

Chapter 57
Old Friends

It has been several months, and Nan hasn't heard from Gaston Means or anyone else that might have the funds Harding surely left her. She is still living with her sister and becoming increasingly desperate by the day. How could she, and more importantly, the President's daughter, find themselves in such dire circumstances? It is unfathomable to her, and she seeks to radically improve her situation.

She is now in the lobby of an upscale Marion restaurant, anxiously awaiting the arrival of her estranged friend, the President's sister, Daisy Harding. She must try to resurrect, at least to some degree, their former friendship. She greets Daisy nervously when she enters. "Hello, Daisy." Daisy looks at Nan sympathetically, "Hello, old friend."

This is their first meeting in years. They have, however, corresponded in writing since Harding's death. And Daisy, in response to Nan's request, was gracious enough to forward Nan money to help her raise her child. Nan and Daisy are now seated in the restaurant. It is awkward, and their conversation is strained.

Nan is the first to speak. "Daisy, thank you for all you've done. And sorry for imposing on you again, but I'm desperate." Daisy acknowledges the obvious. "I gathered that from your letters. But I've sent you all I could. School teachers only make a pittance." A reassuring Nan continues, "I'm not asking more from you, but Warren must have left us something?" Daisy shakes her head, "Not that I know of."

Nan reiterates her case. "His lover? His only child? He was so generous to us in life. He just had to have provided for us." Daisy shrugs, "Our brother is handling the estate. He's not mentioned anything." "Daisy," she asks, "would you mind asking him?" Daisy shakes her head, "I can't butt into his business." Nan pleads, "Then let me ask him. Just arrange a meeting. Please."

Daisy is taken aback by this request and shakes her head. "I'm sorry." Nan won't give up, though. "Please, just a meeting. I'm asking for my little daughter. For your brother's daughter. Your niece. Please." Daisy is worn down and offers a shred of hope. "I'll try. No promises."

Chapter 58

Off to the Doctor

It is a month later, and Daisy has managed to arrange the meeting. In relaying the information, she had to severely damp down Nan's optimism. She was careful to warn Nan that her brother, Dr. George Tryon Harding II, did not look kindly on her request. He agreed, according to Daisy's telling, to the meeting only as a courtesy to a fellow Marionite. Daisy bluntly told Nan that in the absence of compelling and verifiable documentation regarding Elizabeth Ann's parentage, Dr. Harding would give her nothing.

Nan has no such evidence, but she has no other options. She has as much chance of getting in a spaceship and visiting the moon as she has of getting money from Dr. Harding. But there is no alternative. She will proceed with the meeting and is now in Grand Central Station in New York, about to embark on her trip to visit Dr. Harding in Marion. Nan is in the train station bookstore. She is about to purchase Virginia Woolf's novel *Jacob's Room*. Some patrons nearby are reading the latest headlines in the tabloids and talking out loud to one another.

"The Harding scandals keep coming. Teapot Dome, now. A cabinet member is off to jail. What a Presidency! Maybe the worst mess ever," says one woman. Another patron looks in the direction of that woman, "All those crooks around. I still think that man was murdered." Nan overhears this and is upset by their chatter. She speaks to the proprietor as she is about to purchase her book. Nan offers her view: "He was a good President. Can't they just leave him alone?"

The proprietor rings up Nan's purchase. "Lady, those stories sell. People eat 'em up. That is, everyone but the bigwigs in the G-O-P. They hate 'em." Nan stops to think, then grabs one of the tabloids. "I'll buy this too."

Chapter 59
Bad Bedside Manners

Nan's taxi arrives at Dr. Harding's home. The driver is familiar with the home and with Dr. Harding. "Oh, Dr. Hyde's home. Good luck, Lady. He's the meanest SOB in the county. And his brother was actually a really nice guy. Go figure." Nan pays the fare. She gets out of the car. Nan takes a deep breath.

She replays in her mind the reason for the visit. The President has been dead more than eight months now, and Nan is anxious. She has been patiently waiting for the money she is certain the President left her and his daughter. She understands that the President's post-death arrangements for her would have been discreet. That's a given. Even in death, no one was to know of their love and their child.

Harding was a kind and thoughtful man, though, and he undoubtedly put aside a generous sum for her and their daughter. They would be well cared for; it would be just as it was during his lifetime. But where were the men that delivered the funds so regularly when the President was alive? Why hadn't they yet shown up with the money?

It was unfathomable to her that it had now been over eight months, and no one had yet even contacted her. She ran out of money months ago, and it is now impossible for her to support her daughter. She has so few options at this point and has decided to take her case to the Harding family itself.

The Harding family, though not admitting it publicly, certainly was well aware of her relationship with Warren. His sister Daisy has always known of their affair, as it caused her relationship with Nan to become strained. The once good friends have been estranged for years. An estrangement just broken recently by a few tense and awkward encounters.

Nonetheless, Daisy had proved to be sympathetic to Nan's situation. She absolutely believes her brother fathered Nan's child, so when requested she sent what little money she could. Nan needs more, much more, and so has taken this courageous decision to reach out to others in the family.

So, here is a nervous Nan, knocking on the door of Dr. Harding's home for the scheduled appointment. Daisy Harding, in recognition of their past friendship, has decided to be present, and composes herself so she can do her best to greet Nan graciously at the door. "Come in. Have a seat." She motions Nan to the living room, where, to her surprise, Florence Harding is also a guest. Florence says nothing; she just sits there stone-faced.

Daisy continues, "My brother will be here in a minute." Then the room goes dead silent. They all just sit uncomfortably, awkwardly awaiting Dr. Harding's arrival. After what seems like an eternity, Dr. Harding enters. He says nothing and ignores Nan.

Daisy motions to Nan, who breaks the silence by saying, nervously, "Thank you for meeting with me." Dr. Harding appears annoyed. He says nothing. At best, he appears to maybe nod in Nan's direction, but it is an almost imperceptible nod. Nan turns to Daisy. "And Daisy, I appreciate what you have given me, but the President had to have left something for his daughter and me." Dr. Harding raises an eyebrow and scoffs in disbelief, "His daughter?"

Nan had intended to try to stay calm, but this makes her angry. "Yes! His daughter! Your niece." "Right," responds Dr. Harding sarcastically, "If you say so. I can assure you, though, Miss Britton, he left nothing for you or *your daughter*." Nan screams back, "That can't be true. He was so generous to us throughout. He sent substantial sums regularly."

"Have you proof of that?" asks Dr. Harding. "No, the money was given to me in cash. He was an important public figure, you know that, and cash was the only way to keep it discreet." Dr. Harding smiles. "No proof then?" He's pleased but wants to double-check. Nan shakes her head. She pauses, thinks, and then blurts out, "The Secret Service men would know. They delivered the cash."

Dr. Harding, though outwardly calm, is now inwardly ecstatic. He knows well that Secret Service men are sworn to secrecy and will not, under any circumstance, break their oath. "I see." Dr. Harding has gotten the assurances he wants. There is no proof that his brother fathered her child. This was the outcome he had sought when he agreed to the meeting. So, it is now time to send Nan on her way empty-handed.

Dr. Harding responds curtly, "Miss Britton, my brother's affairs were arranged meticulously by the finest attorneys in the land, and his Trust and Will provided nothing for either you or your daughter."

Nan shakes her head in disbelief and her anger now turns to despair. Her voice begins to shake. "I understand he would not have put it in the official documents. I know that he would have made clandestine arrangements, though." Dr. Harding retorts, "So now you think there were secret papers. Your imagination is running wild." Nan does her best to be polite but firm, "Maybe you just haven't found them yet."

Dr. Harding responds, "I can assure you that the President of the United States' papers were in fine order and his affairs looked after flawlessly. There are no secret papers." Nan is now beside herself and blurts out, "Maybe Mrs. Harding..." Nan stops mid-sentence. She was about to suggest that perhaps Mrs. Harding burned them, but realizes, at this point, that would be counterproductive.

She resumes, looks knowingly at Florence, and completes a different point. "Maybe Mrs. Harding has them in her possession, as they would have been part of his personal, not official, documents." The two women look silently at one another.

Dr. Harding, now confident in how this is going to be concluded, is patronizing. "I'm afraid not." Nan continues, "He had to have left us something!" "My dear," replies Dr. Harding, "If your story were true, surely he would have given you the secret documents you now seek, and you'd have then been able to present them to us to claim your rightful inheritance."

Nan is speechless. The President should have done exactly as Dr. Harding suggested. Why hadn't he given her something? Nan can say nothing. Dr. Harding feels this is the coup de grace. "He apparently didn't give you anything in writing either. Interesting."

Nan is left with no option but to beg. "I cannot provide for her by myself." An unsympathetic Dr. Harding asks, "Are you trying?" "Of course," Nan says. "I just took a proofreading job at the Bible Corporation of America. But it pays so little." Dr. Harding scoffs, "It's not our fault you can't find suitable employment." Nan replies firmly, "I'm a woman. There aren't many options."

"Well," responds Dr. Harding, "Maybe you should have thought about that before you decided to have a child out of wedlock." Daisy, trying to ease the tension, jumps in. "I'm glad you're working, Nan. Who takes care of Elizabeth then?" Nan replies, "My sister." Daisy smiles as Nan continues, "But I must provide for her. She's my daughter. The President's daughter, too! Elizabeth Ann is a Harding!"

"He even said Elizabeth Ann would legally become a Harding when we married!" Nan, angry, speaks as if Florence is not in the room. "After Mrs. Harding's passing, that is, he expected that, as she was so much older than him and not well." Florence, now also beside herself at this revelation, exclaims, "Please!" Dr. Harding jumps in, "Stop already. You're upsetting Mrs. Harding. It's time for you to leave." He stands up and opens the kitchen door, speaking to an unseen servant. "Please call for a cab for our guest. She is leaving."

Nan is now sobbing. "I am $2,500 in debt on account of Elizabeth Ann and need another $50,000 for her future costs." Dr. Harding is flabbergasted but tries to keep his cool. He ignores Nan's request and instead looks at Florence, "Look, Mrs. Harding is fragile, and this isn't helping. She is under Dr. Sawyer's care at the sanatorium.

I need to take her home." He moves toward Florence to help her up.

Undeterred, Nan continues, "Will Elizabeth Ann get the support she needs and deserves?" Dr. Harding, ignoring Nan, continues to help Florence get up. Realizing the meeting is over, Nan gathers her belongings and heads to the door ahead of Florence and Dr. Harding. Daisy opens the door for her. As Nan is about to step out, she turns to Daisy and says, "When can I expect to hear from you?" Daisy looks back at her brother and Florence as they, too, are approaching the front door on their way out, "We need to chat amongst ourselves first. Good day."

Nan is about to leave but has one desperate card left to play. She turns and says, "Oh, you should know, I've kept a diary." She takes it out of her purse. As she does, the Evening Graphic (the tabloid newspaper she picked up at the train station) falls from her purse. She quickly retrieves the newspaper, but not before all see the head-line – 'Harding's Death - Only Florence Knows, and She's Not Talking - Why?' Nan continues, while holding up her diary. "I am planning on turning my diary into a manu-script for a book." Nan looks at Daisy, clearly the most sympathetic of the family members and the one most familiar with her writing skills. "I don't want to tarnish his reputation. I still love him, and I always will, you know that, but I'll do anything for Elizabeth Ann. Good day."

Nan leaves, and Daisy shuts the door behind her and looks at her brother. "How much do we give her?" Dr. Harding waves off the question. "Nothing. She'll come back for more regardless." "That's going to be an uncom-fortable conversation," Daisy says. "Don't bother calling," Dr. Harding says. "She's a contemptible lying tramp."

Florence looks straight ahead as she walks toward the door while holding on to Dr. Harding's arm. She responds cynically, "Contemptible lying tramps are particularly contemptible when they're telling the truth. Aren't they?" She pauses, then continues, "Maybe we should give her something. What if that diary of hers makes it into print?" Dr. Harding responds, "I will contact all of Warren's political and publishing friends. I will personally make sure that crap of a memoir of hers never sees the light of day."

PART XIII
The Last Resort

Chapter 60

Kitchen Table: Last Resort

Nan, still residing in Liz's apartment, puts her daughter to bed and then goes to the kitchen table. She opens her diary and begins typing her manuscript. This has been her routine since the Harding meeting some seven months ago.

She has maintained her job at the Bible Corporation, but her salary is insufficient to even cover her food and clothing needs. She runs out of money by each month's end. Were it not for her sister's generosity, she'd be living on the streets. There is no prospect of her being able to improve her situation.

Gaston Means, her only contact with connections to the Republican Party, has not gotten back to her. He had promised to try to find someone within the Party that Harding might have confided in and that might have her money. And she's heard nothing from the Harding family. Nothing at all, not even from Daisy. Accordingly, Nan is desperate.

Her last-ditch effort is to convert her diary into a manuscript, and that is what she is working on. She thinks it will sell, and sell well. And if not, at least the exercise is cathartic. She's reliving all the wonderful moments she had with the deceased President. She escapes her current living hell by letting her mind drift to a real and imagined past.

The radio plays in the background as Nan works on her manuscript. Her ears perk up as she hears the broadcast interrupted by a news bulletin.

NEWS BULLETIN

Breaking news - Florence Harding is now dead. On this day, November 22 1924, a little more than a year after her husband's death, the former First Lady is now gone too. The Sawyer Sanatorium reported her passing. She resided there for the past year. Dr. Sawyer himself, who had also been President Harding's attending physician, was caring for her until his demise just two months earlier. Now all those who were with President Harding at the moment of his death are themselves gone.

Nan turns off the radio and speaks to a photo she keeps of the late President. "Warren, we would have now married. If only you were still alive." She sighs, begins to cry, and then heads off to bed.

Chapter 61
Klunk Slump

The Evening Graphic is in a bit of a slump. Its circulation during the past month is well off its peak, and Klunk knows why. There haven't been any new Harding stories during that period. His wheels spin, looking for a Harding angle, but no ideas spring to mind.

A restless Klunk decides to walk to May Thacker's desk. He looks over May's shoulder, reading the piece in her typewriter. He shrugs. "No new Harding stories?" Thacker shakes her head. "But I am working on a pretty good piece. Some banker committed suicide after he could not repay the money he stole from the bank." Klunk is disappointed. "Huh, just another white-collar graft suicide story. Murder's better. Gotta be some new Harding story?" Thacker shakes her head, "Sorry."

Klunk picks up a copy of Bram Stoker's *Dracula* from Thacker's desk. "You read this shit?" Thacker smiles, "Sure, it's fun. Everyone loves it." "Just the idiot masses, I reckon," Klunk retorts. He pauses, thinks, and then looks wide-eyed. He has an idea.

One week later, the Evening Graphic hits the news-stands with the following front-page splash.

HARDING DEATH - THE VAMPIRE CONNECTION - *Alaskan vampire bite metamorphosed the President. He became one himself. He was put out of his misery as he screamed for blood that fateful evening.*

The beginning of the end came in Alaska a week or so before the President's reported death. And truth-be-told he may not have been humanly alive for that entire week.

The horrific and dastardly attack that led to the end happened, as these things often do, in the middle of the night while the President was sleeping on the ship touring Alaska. A Secret Service agent was outside his room. He was supposed to be guarding our most revered public servant, but the imbecile had himself fallen asleep.

Our President was sleeping peacefully at the time, having retired to bed under the false belief that he was absolutely safe. And why shouldn't he have felt that way? He had a guard right outside his door. Unfortunately, his safety was far from assured. Unbeknownst to him, he was in huge peril and would shortly suffer a fate no man should have to endure. The evil forces were there nearby; they knew the weak link, saw an opportunity, and the bastards took unfair advantage of the situation.

Disgusting as it sounds, a devious vampire tiptoed past the sleeping agent and stealthily entered the President's bedroom. He looked cravenly at his sleeping prey, let out a sinister laugh, and then viciously bit Harding on the neck. It was a fierce and most dishonorable sneak attack from a cold-blooded enemy.

The attack, of course, woke the President. Our gallant President, still a strong man and a powerful leader, put up a most ferocious fight. But in the end, he had no chance. The initial sneak attack had left him too debilitated to overcome his wicked assailant. And sadly, with just a little help, he most certainly would have prevailed over this repulsive foe, but the help that should have come did not.

The cowardly guard, awoken by the President's struggles, was paralyzed with fright when he laid eyes on the vampire. So, rather than help the President as was his charge, the scaredy-cat, terrified for his own safety, abandoned his post and ran on deck, giving himself the sign of the cross while muttering to himself, "God help us; God help us all."

After that, the President was under the vampire's power for the rest of his remaining, albeit brief existence. He was one of them, just as they had planned. They wanted a vampire to be President. And for a week or so, that is what we had – a Vampire President. Remember how he dropped his notes when speaking in Seattle? Well, that was a direct result of the weakness he suffered because he needed human blood.

And things got worse. He could barely keep himself up during the day. Remember how he struggled when entering the Palace Hotel? Vampires do poorly in daylight. Well, by this time, his death was pre-ordained.

And that final evening was a sad and sorry scene in the Palace Hotel. With nighttime approaching and the President starting to wake, he began frantically searching for a victim as he so craved blood, human blood.

He, of course, wasn't alone. Dr. Sawyer and the First Lady stood over the bed watching the writhing President with vampire fang scars on his neck. He was gaining strength with every minute as darkness came across the city. And as is true with all vampires, they are particularly motivated and violent as their hunger grows. Two nurses and half a dozen Secret Service agents struggled mightily to hold the President down as he writhed to and fro in his bed.

It was clear they couldn't hold him for long. His strength would escalate exponentially as the sky darkened and the evening turned to night. Soon his power would be overwhelming, and even the might of a hundred strong men would be insufficient to restrain him. He was now madly blathering and trying to bite the necks of those holding him down. "Blood! I need blood! Human blood. Now!" There was little time and fewer options.

Dr. Sawyer looked at the President, shook his head, and turned to Florence. "We need to put him out of his misery." Florence reluctantly nodded in agreement, "The sooner, the better. Sad to say, he is no longer fit to be President." Dr. Sawyer grabbed a huge syringe, one designed for an elephant, and filled it with cyanide. "There's enough cyanide in here to kill three hippopotami." Florence looked first at her husband lovingly, then at Sawyer and, with concern, said, "Do you think it will be enough?" "It should do the trick. Let's keep our fingers crossed."

Then Dr. Sawyer did the most merciful act both for the President and the Country and administered the injection. The President immediately calmed down. He looked straight into his wife's eyes, seemed to nod appreciatively, then turned his head to look out the window. He smiled peacefully as *he looked to the heavens, closing his eyes. Seconds later, he had left this world.*

The issue flies off the shelves.

Chapter 62

Start Pounding the Pavement

Some five more months have gone by, and Nan's predicament is unchanged. She has now completed her book and is proud of her work. She has read it over and over. Oh, how she wishes she could share it with her former teacher Daisy Harding, but that is impossible. Given the subject matter, Daisy would have nothing good to say. She'd want the book destroyed.

Nan's initial trepidation, that it might sully the reputation of the man she loved, has faded. The more she reads her work, the clearer it becomes. The book is a beautiful love story, her love story. The President, a warm, kind, smart, and generous man, was in love with her, and she was with him. Uncontrollable circumstances kept them from marrying, but their love was real.

Her book isn't scandalous. It is beautiful. She is certain the public, once they read her story, will understand that their affair was not at all illicit. Rather, it was true love, a modern fairy tale that spawned a beautiful child. She has convinced herself it would help not hurt his reputation.

She also believes her book will sell well and is happy she lives in New York City - home of America's publishing business. This morning, she will be late to work but not too late. She's arranged for a 9:00 AM appointment, the first appointment of the morning, with Harper Collins, one of the largest publishing companies in the city. With the manuscript in hand, she arrives some 30 minutes early. As directed by the receptionist, she sits and waits in the reception area for her meeting with Mr. Stewart.

Nan sits patiently at first but gets increasingly impatient as the time for her scheduled appointment passes. She looks regularly and nervously at the clock as the minutes tick by. She was to be Mr. Stewart's first appointment, so the delay perplexes her.

She will now certainly be quite late to work, and this could jeopardize her standing at the company. She is well acquainted with business etiquette, and at 9:20 AM, exactly twenty minutes past the appointment time, she again approaches the receptionist.

"Sorry to disturb you, but I'm just wondering how much longer it might be so I can plan the rest of my day." The receptionist gets up. "Just a moment. I'll check in with Mr. Stewart." A minute or so later, the receptionist returns with bad news. "I am sorry, but Mr. Stewart said we're pretty committed right now. You say it's a first draft of a personal memoir?"

"Yes," Nan replies. "It's about my daughter. About her father, a prominent man, and me." The receptionist looks at Nan's wedding finger. "You're not wearing a wedding ring." Nan, upset by the implication of her statement, stands up straight. "I am single. We never married, though we were planning to," Nan says. The receptionist turns curt. "A book about a child born out of wedlock! I'm sorry, we're looking for things of higher morality." Nan, now angry, responds, "There is nothing immoral about a child born to a mother that deeply loved her father and he her." The receptionist is dismissive. "Well, we don't deal in sleaze. Try the Evening Graphic. Good day."

Chapter 63

A Clue

For the next few months, Nan spends a morning or two a week trying different publishing houses and gets similar results. She shows up for a scheduled appointment and is told, "Something's come up, and you'll have to reschedule." A similar excuse awaits her on the rescheduled date. She's treated coldly, always rudely dispatched, and often just by the receptionist, as she rarely even gets into the publisher's office.

The rejections make her despondent, but she continues on all the same. One day she stops by Viking Press, a newly formed publishing company, and meets with the junior editor, Mr. Olsen. She tells him her story and shows him the manuscript. He reads the first page and then flicks around a bit in the book. "Where's the hot stuff, lady?" "There's no hot stuff! There are, though, portions of the book where we demonstrate physically our love for one another, if that's what you mean."

She grabs the manuscript and turns the pages. She finds what she is looking for and returns the open manuscript to Olsen. "Here is the passage describing our first intimate encounter. Perhaps that's what you are looking for." Olsen reads the passage with some excitement. Nan then takes out the picture taken long ago of her and Mr. Harding. "See, here is a picture of the two of us." Olsen looks at the photo and is ecstatic.

Nan continues, "And it's all true." "It doesn't matter. This would sell, regardless," Olsen says. "Maybe we can put that picture of you two on the cover." Nan, thrilled with this idea and by Mr. Olsen's enthusiasm, responds, "I'd love that." Olsen stands and says, "Wait here one second."

The junior editor goes into the next room. Nan sees him speaking with his boss through the glass wall. Their conversation appears to be getting increasingly agitated. After some ten minutes, Olsen returns dejected and returns the manuscript. "I am sorry, Miss Britton; we can't take this."

Olsen escorts an extremely disappointed Nan to the door. He is also upset and steps into the hallway with Nan. In a hushed and sincere tone, he warns her, "Miss Britton, some powerful forces are trying to keep your book from being published. Be careful. Watch your back." Though not quite sure what to make of this warning, Nan is nonetheless extremely concerned.

Chapter 64
Reacquainting

It is the next morning, and Nan leaves her apartment, heading to work. She is in a hurry. Her off-and-on tardiness the past month has caught the eye of others in the office, particularly her boss. She fears she will be dismissed. She is heading to the subway just down the block from her apartment building. She is apprehensive and feels something is wrong.

Many people are on the street, so she believes it is safe, but she nonetheless is fearful. She senses someone following her but dares not look back. She thinks of Mr. Olsen's warning yesterday and quickens her pace. She begins to descend the steps to the subway when she hears a man call her name, "Miss Britton?" Nan turns around, startled. She does not immediately recognize the man calling her name.

The man approaches, speaking gently. "Miss Britton, it is me, Gaston Means. I have a new position now." Mr. Means hands Nan his card. She looks at it, puts it in her purse, and then carefully looks again at Means. "Of course, yes. How are you, Mr. Means?"

"Miss Britton, would you be so kind as to allow me the pleasure of buying you a cup of coffee?" Nan hesitates a bit, not being sure what Means wants. Will he perhaps harm her? She politely declines the offer, "I am sorry, I'll be late for work." Means continues, "It will just take a minute, I promise."

Means continues his pitch, "And I have some information I think will greatly interest you. I have a money proposition for you." Nan is now relieved. She had given up hope. This is finally the news she has been longing for - the money the President surely left her has finally arrived.

This will end her financial woes and allow her to raise the President's daughter properly. Her book can remain her private remembrance; she can forgo the now seemingly impossible goal of trying to get it published.

Nan now wants to meet with Means but tries not to look too anxious. "Well, if it will just take a minute." Means smiles. "Oh, I promise, it won't take long, and I think you'll welcome what I want to share with you."

The two sit in a booth, and the waitress pours them coffee. Means starts with some brief chitchat. "Good to see you again. You're looking well." "Thank you." Nan pauses, then looks at her watch, "So you have some news for me?"

Means smiles. "Indeed I do. It's about your book." Nan is surprised, disappointed and scared. How did he know of her book? Is Means the one Olsen warned her about yesterday?

And even if he intends no harm, she certainly does not want to talk to him about her book. She is cautious and queries Means, "My book?" "Yes," Means says, "I understand you're trying to get a book published." Nan is puzzled, "Yes, but how did you know?" Means waves her off. "Doesn't matter. Suffice it to say, it ain't getting published. Your failure has been pre-ordained."

Nan is now visibly angry. Means continues, "Oh, not be me. By folks a lot more powerful than me. You see, they don't want the President's reputation sullied further. Nan Britton is not going to be able to get any publisher to bite." Nan is angry and perplexed. "How do you know, and why are you telling me this?" Means smiles slyly, "Calm down. I can help." "How?" Nan asks.

Means takes out and lights a cigarette. "Make *me* the author. You'd be my ghostwriter, so to speak, and I'll peddle it under my name. It'll get published, and we split the profits."

Nan looks suspiciously at Means as he waxes on, "I can even add some tidbits about some other Harding philandering you may not know about." This is more unwelcome news Nan does not want to hear or believe. She responds sternly, "Mr. Means, our love was pure. We were true to one another."

Means laughs. "Look at this." He takes out the copy of the lewd letter Harding wrote years ago to Carrie Phillips. Nan had received a virtually identical letter, and her initial understanding, albeit false, is that this was one written to her. She is now bewildered and furious that Means has a copy.

"Where did you get this? I destroyed all his letters." Means immediately realizes Nan's confusion and points to the salutation on the letter. "This one wasn't written to you! He wrote it to another of his lovers, Carrie Phillips – a confirmed German spy. Kind of kinky if you ask me. Doing it with a German spy. I get that part of it. But she was also his best friend's wife." Means shakes his head in disgust at the idea. "You can have an affair. Even better if it's with a German spy but not with your best friend's wife. That's really scummy."

Even with the evidence right under her nose, Nan refuses to believe that Harding had an affair with another. "Another woman? What? I don't believe it." Means scoffs, "Oh honey, you can believe it. Everyone knew how overwhelmingly horny he was; he couldn't control himself. Harding had tons of extracurricular activities. Kept him busy. Being so busy made it tough for a guy as dumb as him to really be much of a President. Probably contributed to his failure."

Nan is now furious. How dare he insult her lover and falsely call such a great man a dumb failure? She stands up to leave. "It's my book, Mr. Means! Not yours." Nan gathers her belongings. "Mr. Means, you can take your ideas and put them in a place where the sun doesn't shine." She slams a nickel on the table, "And here's money for my coffee. You can put this nickel in the same place!"

Means watches Nan storm out the door. He sips his coffee, picks up the nickel Nan left and puts it in his pocket. He says to himself, "A woman with spirit. I like that."

Chapter 65

Words Never Heard in The Bible

After her meeting with Means, Nan is once again late to work. She rushes off to her job at the Bible Corporation of America, a company dedicated to publishing religious journals. It is a curious work environment. The company was founded by Richard Wightman, a man who hates religion. Mr. Wightman is a self-proclaimed entrepreneurial heathen who makes a good living by, as he puts it, exploiting the weaknesses in the human condition.

Nan is unique amongst his employees. She did well in school and even completed high school. She is well-educated, immensely competent, and a great proofreader with superior language skills. Her co-workers are largely uneducated, generally mediocre at their jobs, and, unlike Nan, religious zealots (or at least pretend to be).

Nan's co-workers find their boss to be a disgusting, crude and vulgar oaf. They have willingly though, cut this deal with the devil as it allows them to achieve their higher purpose. The Bibles they publish help them bring

God to the masses. The arrangement is equally accept-able to Mr. Wightman, as it has allowed him to amass a small fortune.

Nan's late arrival is particularly conspicuous this morning. The entire office now knows of her frequent tardiness. Today there are more and harder stares than usual. The burning contempt of her co-workers is partic-ularly unpalatable, and she feels especially vulnerable. One worker gets up and surreptitiously knocks on Mr. Wightman's door as Nan puts her bag down and sits at her desk. All eyes are focused on Nan.

Nan is very concerned, and with good reason. No sooner is she seated than Richard Wightman himself pops his head out of his office and, in an angry tone, instructs her to come to his office immediately. Nan's very bad day is about to get worse. She is certain she will be fired.

She trudges, head down, into the office. She closes the door behind her, sits, and waits for the blow she knows is coming. And indeed, it does come. Mr. Wightman delivers the news she expects, "Nan, I am sorry, but you've been late too often these past couple of months. I am going to have to let you go." Nan starts to cry. Mr. Wightman hands her a tissue, but her tears are unrelenting. "Nan, I like you. I really do, and you are an excellent employee, at least you can be, but you're just not pulling your weight anymore, and it is not fair to the company or your co-workers, sorry."

Nan, through her tears, responds, "I'm sorry. I know it's my fault, but it's just..." Nan is now crying so hard that it is difficult for her to speak. Eventually she calms down. "It's so difficult being a single mother, and I was late only because I am trying so hard to raise my daughter." "Nan, that's no excuse. Just get out of here.

Leave now so we can get on with our work. We have a business to run." Nan continues crying. "I know. Again, I am so sorry. I will pack up my things and go immediately." She stands to leave.

Wightman follows Nan as she leaves his office. "I will see you out. You needn't stop at your desk. If you have personal belongings here, we will send them to you. You must simply leave the premises." Nan looks at him with disdain and, contrary to Wightman's order, heads to her desk and angrily grabs her bag. Wightman, equally upset, follows her. The entire office watches them.

Wightman grabs the bag from Nan. "Nan, I need to ensure you haven't stolen any company property." Nan grabs her bag back from Wightman and screams at him, "The hell, you will." The Bible company employees gasp upon hearing such a vulgar term and uttered by a woman no less.

Nan and Wightman each now have a hold of her bag and tussle over it in an angry tug-of-war. Nan, realizing she has nothing to hide and that Wightman is much stronger, eventually relents and shoves the bag in his face, "Here asshole, look all you want."

Wightman scours through the bag, eventually pulling out Nan's manuscript. He glares at her. "Are you stealing our material? That's more than just theft. It's a copyright violation." Nan screams back, "I am doing no such thing, and I can assure you I wouldn't even think of copying a word of your drivel." Wightman is now perusing the manuscript. "What is this, Nan? What are you reading? This is salacious. You are sicker than I thought. This is pornography!" The employees again gasp loudly.

Nan grabs the manuscript from him. "I'm not reading! I'm writing! It's a manuscript for my book. My story. My love story: the love I shared with Elizabeth Ann's father."

"Love story, with whom?" Wightman asks, scornfully. "You heard me, my love story with Elizabeth Ann's father." Wightman laughs sarcastically, "Father? Oh, you mean some drifter alcoholic that banged you one night when you were probably as drunk as he was." The employees look on in horror. Swearing and arguing about alcohol, sex and bastard children is all too much for their delicate ears.

Nan looks pointedly at Wightman and slaps him hard in the face. "You prick! You don't know anything about me. And if you must know, her father was Warren Harding, the President of the United States." Wightman goes silent. He is stunned but skeptical. He laughs disbelievingly. "What, don't believe me?" Nan says, as she takes out the photo of her and Harding and shoves it in his face. "See, here's a photo of me and the President."

Wightman looks at the photo and then at Nan. He is astounded, immediately calms down, and then is silent for a minute. He says, in a half-whisper, "President Harding is the father of your child?" He is in a bit of a daze. He looks at the manuscript, and his tone changes completely. "This would sell." "Yeah, lame brain," Nan responds. "That's why they're trying to censor it."

Nan grabs the photo and the manuscript from him and starts toward the door. She looks back furiously at Wightman as she leaves, "And fuck you!" And then she looks at all her supposedly pious co-workers staring at her wide-eyed. "Fuck you all!" She slams the door behind her.

Wightman's entrepreneurial wheels are spinning fast. He knows a good story when he sees it and knows what will sell. To hell with Bible stories. A salacious tale about the former President's illicit sex life could make him a million. Whether true or not. He gets an excited look in his eyes and runs after Nan. He catches up with her as she hurries down the street. He is nearly out of breath. "Nan, let's go back to the office, the conference room. We got a business deal to discuss."

Chapter 66

The Deal

A little later, Nan and Wightman are suddenly on terrific terms. Their acrimony of a few minutes ago is long forgotten. They now have a common goal. They want to publish her book. They both believe it will sell well and provide them each with commensurate financial remuneration.

Nan also believes that America will be as smitten as she is with her love story and with the great man that fathered her child. America will fall in love with her and the man they elected as the 29th President. Nan's thinking on this score does not even cross Wightman's mind.

Right now, though, Nan and Wightman are speaking the same language, and a deal is about to be consummated. Wightman has skim-read about half of Nan's manuscript and is thrilled and excited by what he has read. "Great job, as always. Well written and captivating, Nan." "It better be. This is at least the 250th version," Nan confesses.

"You know, though," Wightman continues, "It still needs some work. I'll give you some suggestions. Live with us for a while, it's quiet there, and you can edit it at our house." Nan, though happy that she has a book deal, is not looking forward to yet more editing. "I'm in re-write hell."

Wightman reassures her. "Nan, this is hot! It'll sell." Nan shakes her head, "No. It's a love story, a real-life love story."

Wightman says, "Look, this is a bit beyond our normal fare around here and a much bigger proposition, but I'm willing to give it a go." "Me too," Nan responds, eagerly. Wightman is thinking now of the business angle. "The Bible Corporation can't publish this... it's got words in it never heard in the Bible."

"We'll start a new company, you and me, our own publishing company. I'll provide the capital and arrange for publicity and distribution. You provide the material." He holds up the manuscript. "All proceeds firstly need to cover costs plus 10%, but then the balance we split, a 20% commission for us, 80% for you." Wightman holds up the manuscript. "This is terrific work, Nan." Nan is thrilled and agrees, ecstatic she finally has a publishing deal. "Fine with me."

Wightman looks again at the manuscript, "We may have to sell it door-to-door with brown wrapping, like pornography." Nan objects. "It's not pornography! Not at all." Wightman is unconcerned. "We'll do what we have to. Have we got a deal?" Nan and Wightman seal their deal with a handshake. "Can we name the new company after Elizabeth Ann?" Nan asks. Wightman's eyes light up and he holds up his hands, as if spelling out a billboard: "The Elizabeth Ann Publishing Company. Perfect. Great publicity trick. I'll work with the PR folks to get more up-front buzz."

Chapter 67
Gaston Reports In

A dejected Gaston Means sits in Charles Klunk's office. He is next to May Thacker. Klunk is behind the desk. Means shrugs, "Sorry, Charles, it was a great idea, but Britton wouldn't budge. Doesn't want a co-author for her book. Even if it is the only way to get it published."

Klunk shakes his head. "Naïve as a kitten, that one." Means nods, "Yeah. She still thinks Harding was true to her. In her mind, she was his one and only. Put Harding's smutty letter to Carrie right under her nose too. Talk about the willing suspension of disbelief. Man, that lady is in never-never land."

Klunk ruminates, "Doesn't she get it? The most powerful folks in the country are blackballing her and her book. She doesn't have a chance." Means replies, "She might get that, but she just doesn't seem to want to look at alternatives." Klunk looks astounded. "Maybe she'll eventually come to her senses. Any chance she'll come around on this?"

Means shakes his head. "Don't think so." Klunk continues, "You sure? I mean, how did you wrap up the meeting?" Means laughs. "I didn't wrap up anything. She did. I don't recall her exact words, but it was something about me shoving something up in a place where the sun don't shine." Klunk laughs and shakes his head. "Very eloquent. Anyway, too bad. Yeah, too bad for all of us. Now that book of hers will never get published. Nobody will make a dime." Klunk shakes his head. "We could have all made a fortune from her story. Shit happens. Bad shit sometimes."

Means tries a different angle. "Look, I got so many other stories for you. I was part of the Harding White House. I heard and saw stuff you wouldn't believe." Thacker's ears prick up and she takes out her notepad to start writing. Means continues, "Of course, I'll need to be properly compensated."

Klunk motions to Thacker, gesturing to her to stop taking notes. "Thank you for your offer, Mr. Means, but we have plenty of sources for Harding stories." Means nods and stands to leave. He shakes Klunk's hand. "I understand. Let me know if you change your mind. I'll always make myself available to you."

Chapter 68
Setting the Table

The re-write of the book worked out exactly as Wightman planned. Nan spent the next nine months living and working in Wightman's home. She re-wrote and re-edited ad nauseam until both she and Wightman agreed *The President's Daughter* was ready for publication. Wightman is now preparing for production and creating the printing plates needed to reproduce the book. It won't be too long now, and knowing the release date is in sight, he is working on drumming up publicity.

Wightman's skills in PR were in fact quite good. This would prove to be, however, a pretty easy book to publicize. He kicked things off, but after that, the book soon took on a life of its own. The Harding scandals, real and fictitious, were still selling. In particular, the public had an insatiable appetite for Harding's failures and flaws, especially ones dealing with his erotic proclivities.

Contrary to Nan's fantasy, the early indications were soon obvious - the public would find this to be a sleazy affair, and love reading about it as a result. It was seen as pornography (or nearly) and not at all the innocent love story Nan still had in her head. Wightman tried unsuccessfully to alter Nan's firm belief on this score. Nan's explicit prose, written, in her mind, in the spirit of setting out the truth about her affair with Harding, in fact offered the most detailed, lurid and titillating view yet of some of the most sordid details of the now disgraced President. The public would eat this up because to them it was sleaze, and sleaze they could all-too-easily believe.

A good sex scandal by his young concubine would not change the public's low opinion of the late President. Instead, it would have the reverse effect, adding further infamy on top of the incredible fall from grace Harding's reputation had already suffered. Schadenfreude sells and sells well. This is the much sought-after comfort the average loser craves, especially when the misfortune is piled onto the formerly privileged and distinguished. Wightman put it succinctly: "People might want good news, but it's bad news that sells. Especially bad news about rich assholes."

So, months before its release, the public was already well aware of the book and its author. A book written by a woman detailing the intimacies of her illicit affair with the President of the United States. An affair that resulted in the President's illegitimate child. The American public would devour it, and all Wightman had to do was to make sure the table was set. And Wightman was excellent at setting tables.

Chapter 69
Vice Pays a Visit

With the printing plates complete, Wightman sets up the presses to mass-produce the book. It is nearly evening, and he and Nan are alone in the print shop as the first copy of *The President's Daughter* comes off the press. He hands it to Nan. "You should have the first copy." Nan smiles, holds the book proudly, and says, "Finally!"

They are overjoyed. The fruits of all their hard work, particularly Nan's, is in their hands. Nan is relieved and proud. Her bliss, though, is short-lived as it is interrupted by the sound of an arriving fleet of police cars with their sirens blaring. The vehicles stop outside the shop, and the officers get out and knock loudly on the door. Wightman looks at Nan and smiles, "Perfect timing." Wightman opens the door and greets the officers, "Welcome, gentlemen."

Half a dozen New York police officers enter. The sergeant speaks to Wightman and Nan. "Mr. Wightman, Miss Britton, we are here on orders from John J. Sumner, head of the New York Society for the Suppression of Vice." Nan is upset; Wightman though is delighted by the visit.

Wightman replies, "Mr. Sumner? I'm afraid I've never had the pleasure."

The sergeant continues, "Mr. Sumner has filed a complaint against your organization and your publication. He and the New York Society he represents have declared officially that your work here and the book you are now producing is obscene, lewd and indecent." Nan immediately responds, "It's none of those things. It's a love story. True love. And how would he know, he's not read it? No one has."

Ignoring Nan, the sergeant proceeds, "As required by law, we are obligated to halt all publication activity. Therefore, we must immediately seize the printing plates." "Don't you need a Court order for that?" asks Wightman. The sergeant doesn't know and certainly doesn't have a Court order. "Good question. Ask the judge. In the interim, we'll take the printing plates." The other officers go to the presses and remove the plates.

"And we'll need all copies of the book produced so far." Nan looks at the sergeant and hands him her copy. "Here's the only copy." The sergeant starts flipping through the pages of the book. Nan notices his seemingly intense interest and anticipates what he seeks to find. "I think page 72 might be what you're looking for. It's the passage where I lose my virginity." "Thanks," the sergeant says, matter-of-factly, as he quickly turns to page 72.

Much to Nan's puzzlement, Wightman looks quite pleased. As the officers leave, he waves to them and calls out, "We'll see you in Court." The sergeant replies, "It will be a pleasure."

Chapter 70

Dr. Harding's Desperation

Dr. Harding is in his attorney's office. "Any chance the raid will be traced back to us?" Dr. Harding asks. The attorney shakes his head. "Very unlikely. Sumner just needed a little reminding, and he's got an ego. He'll want to take credit for it himself." Dr. Harding smiles, "Good, then things are going as planned."

The attorney looks wearily at Dr. Harding, pauses, and then offers a sobering assessment. "Look, don't kid yourself. The cat's now out of the bag. The story is already in the public domain. Everyone knows about Nan and your brother. And that's without a published book." He pauses and continues, "At best, this is a temporary pause. The book will likely still get published, and you just gave them some incredible publicity."

Dr. Harding reluctantly takes in this information. He looks hard at his attorney. "You're saying this thing will backfire?" The attorney nods, "Certainly could. Likely, in fact. And I really can't see how it will make anything better." Dr. Harding asks, "Well, what do you advise?" The attorney says firmly, "Do nothing. Lay low. You're making things worse by poking the hornet's nest." He pauses and then looks at the doctor, "Frankly, my friend, you've lost."

Dr. Harding stands and looks angrily at his attorney. "Maybe it was just bad lawyering." He then turns and leaves.

Chapter 71

Kangaroo Court

A few weeks later, the hearing to rectify the wrong Wightman believes was committed by the Vice Squad is about to begin.

Judge Brown initiates the largely perfunctory hearing. Nan joins Wightman in the courtroom. The judge addresses Wightman. "You are suing for the right to publish your book and for the return of company property, in this case some printing plates. Is that correct?" Wightman responds, "Yes, your honor."

The judge addresses the defense attorney. "And the plates were taken pursuant to an order by some unofficial group called the Society for the Suppression of Vice, which claims the book cannot be published because it violates morality standards and therefore isn't protected by free press laws?" The defense attorney nods, "Yes, your honor."

The judge shakes his head and continues. "Has the state legislature granted this Society the authority to interpret laws or given it policing power?" The attorney responds weakly, "No, your honor. But they are very concerned citizens." The judge is to the point. "So are vigilantes, but that doesn't make it legal or right."

The judge continues, "And what statute, regulation or other authority creates a morality exception to our free press laws?" The defense attorney looks the judge in the eye. "We would like you to create that authority by so ruling in this case. You would set the precedent."

The judge rolls his eyes. "The most polite response I can offer is – are you out of your fricken mind?" There is some giggling in the courtroom. Finally, the judge bangs his gavel. "Motion denied. The book can be published."

The judge again addresses the defense attorney. "And in addition, said Society, your client, is countersuing for damages of $2,500, with the argument that they held the property safely in storage for a couple of weeks. So, this constitutes a rent charge, I guess."

Nan blurts out, "Extortion." The Judge looks angrily at her, so she apologizes. "Sorry. I meant to say 'Extortion, your honor.'" The few in the courtroom laugh. Even the judge chuckles a bit as he bangs his gavel. "Quiet in the court!"

The judge offers his solution. "Why don't we try to make things easy on everyone? I will grant the defense's motion for payment of the $2,500 and also grant the plaintiff's motion for the return of the plates. Mr. Wightman, you get the plates, and you pay the $2,500." Nan looks at the judge, still angry. "They stole our stuff! We shouldn't have to pay anything." She has forgotten procedure again, but then corrects herself, "Your honor."

The judge smiles and nods. "I know, Miss, but if they get the money they want, they're unlikely to appeal, so it's probably over now, and you get your plates. This is cheaper and quicker in the long run." Nan jumps at the opportunity. "We'll pay the damages... your honor, thanks." The judge smiles. "Sounds prudent to me. It is hereby ordered. Case dismissed. And Miss Britton, I very much look forward to reading your book." Nan smiles broadly. "Thank you, your honor."

The judge pounds his gavel. Wightman says to Nan, "2,500 bucks. What a bargain! A million dollars of advertisements wouldn't buy us this kind of publicity."

PART XV
Beating the Odds

Chapter 72
The Release

It is summer 1927, and Nan's book, *The President's Daughter*, is about to hit the bookstands (or a few bookstores, anyhow). Its release has now been extremely well publicized. Many stores have refused to carry it. Its notoriety has preceded it, and some, fearing a backlash from their clientele, have refused to stock it.

Even before its release, a vocal and violent segment of the population made clear that they believe the book to be a sacrilege and its author a sinner. It is a bawdy false tale of and by a woman who reveled in her adulterous sin. She had no shame. No shame at all in having a child out of wedlock. Rather, she flaunted this fact.

And worse, without proof, she has now claimed her intimacy was with the late President of the United States. She has claimed that Harding impregnated her. The fact that the late President's reputation was already on thin ice was irrelevant. Nan had defiled proper mores most flagrantly. She has done so by sullying the integrity of the country's most cherished institution – the head of state, the Commander-in-Chief.

The buzz that Wightman had started about the book some months earlier quickly took on a life of its own. The tabloids, mainstream newspapers and even radio talk shows had been discussing the upcoming book for months.

And the public, though claiming to hate and not believe the story, was addicted to it. And not just the affair and the President's purported illegitimate child but also by the shunning from the Republican Party, the President's family, and well-known publishing houses. And even without reading the book, they are eager to condemn Nan's explicit descriptions of her body and the intimacies which she claims took place.

Few, if any, believe this is the love story Nan thinks it is. Some are angry, very angry. Even though not yet released, they call her story a lie, an unwarranted blasphemous attack on a dead statesman by a cheap conniving tart who first attempted to blackmail the family. It's seen as an unprecedented assault on the country's moral fabric.

It is indeed unprecedented. Nan has written America's first tell-all memoir. And it will go on to sell incredibly well. By November 1927, just three months after its release, it had sold more than 42,000 copies. By July 1931, that will rise to more than 110,000 copies.

The book's price was $5, very high at a time when books were usually selling for half that amount. Its notoriety made advertising largely unnecessary, and since many sales were direct to the reader, bookstores siphoned off less. So it proved to be highly lucrative for Wightman and Nan. For Nan, though, the notoriety would take a terrible toll on her. She gained the financial security she needed but would forever wonder if it was worth the price.

On this day, though, the day of its release, crowds gather in Mosk's bookstore – on Fourth Avenue's Book Row in New York City - one of the few around the country carrying the book. Purchasers and protestors (holding signs and screaming slogans decrying the book) have gathered outside long before dawn. The protestors shout angrily at customers as they rush inside as the store opens.

Posters at the store usher in its release with this headline: 'Now Available – *The President's Daughter* - President's Young Mistress Tells All!' This lurid summary is printed: 'Her intimate affair is revealed in explicit detail, including their illicit romps in his Senate Office and even in the White House. She sets out in detail her painful labor and the birth of the President's daughter, the illegitimate child he supported financially but never met.' Newspaper headlines nearby also describe the release of Nan's book and what are seen as her sordid claims.

Few accept the claim that Harding was the father, and many are fuming. They nonetheless hurry to buy the book. One woman reads the dedication out loud: "Dedicated to all unwed mothers and their innocent children whose fathers are usually not known to the world." A man nearby shakes his head, "Blasphemous. Cheap lying whore trying to make a buck off a great dead man." Another woman holds up the book proclaiming, "He must be spinning in his grave. Is there no dignity for the office, the man? These days, anyone can lie about anything and get away with it. Where's the proof?"

There is a moment of silence; these prospective customers look at each other sheepishly. Even with their guilt and outrage, they each rush to get in line to purchase the book. A woman, already with one book in hand, runs back to grab another copy. "I need to get a copy for my friend." She purchases the two books. As she leaves the store, she discreetly hands the second copy to her friend (one of the protestors). She winks at her as she walks away, "This really shouldn't be legal."

Chapter 73

Ban the Book

It is a few months later, and Nan is in the Capitol building in Washington, D.C. She is there to witness the introduction of legislation spawned by the publication of her book. The legislation, if passed, would create a Board charged with reviewing books, magazines and newspapers, and censoring those that fail to meet appropriate standards of decency.

For the first time, she will confront her most public and vocal nemesis, the bill's author, Congressman John Tillman. Nan and Wightman sit together in the gallery and are part of a fairly large crowd watching the proceedings.

Tillman is on the floor and begins.

Mr. Speaker, I come before this body to introduce much-needed legislation. We need to nip a problem in the bud before it gets worse. The rampant lies and falsehoods that are promulgated today are degrading our society and confusing the public. People cannot distinguish between right and wrong. And how could they be expected to?

It is impossible for them to know the truth these days. There is so much false and misleading information bombarding people daily. The lies outnumber the truth by a hundred to one, and the bigger the lie, the more it is believed. It is a terrible, uncontrollable situation, and if we let it be, it will be the end of us.

We need to protect the people. In fact, that is our job. As elected officials, we are charged with protecting the public from everything bad, and that includes from this insidious brainwashing I am about to discuss. And how will we do this? The solution, my friends, is for us to make sure the truth and only the truth is spoken, and to do so, I propose creating a National Board of Magazine and Book Censorship.

Cheers and boos come from the gallery, and one person screams, "What about free press?" The Speaker pounds his gavel. "Order, order. Mr. Tillman, please proceed." Tillman continues,

And this Board's first order of business should be to ban any future publications of a book I am sure you all know of; maybe some of you, God forbid, have even read it.

Tillman holds up a copy of *The President's Daughter.*

The most sordid tale and grossest attack ever launched against any man, living or dead. Page after page of pornography, brazen description, sickening details, monstrous charges. I know, I've read it. Twice. Some parts where I couldn't believe my eyes, I have read dozens of times. And these lies are ruining a great man's reputation. A great man unable to defend himself.

Nan, in the gallery, is unimpressed. She turns and speaks softly to Wightman. "We've heard all this before." Wightman nods in agreement as the Congressman continues.

Let me be perfectly clear. I make no war with women, as many claim. In fact, though the purported author is a woman, I know better. I'm sure this was not written by a woman but rather a lowlife man who did it for the vilest of reasons - money and greed!

This comment is too much for Nan; she stands and screams at Tillman. "Liar. I wrote that book! Every word! Mr. Tillman, why can't you believe the truth?"

The Speaker pounds his gavel. "Order, order." Nan, undeterred, continues, "Mr. Tillman! Stop making things up! I wrote every word of that book, and I *am* a woman." Tillman looks angrily at Nan and says deprecatingly, "If you say so."

Nan looks down steely-eyed at Tillman and challenges him. "And I will make you a wager, Sir; I will donate $1,000 to any charity you choose if you can prove a man wrote it. Do you accept my offer?" Tillman is silent. Nan glares at him, "What? Don't have the balls?"

Tillman shuffles uncomfortably and gets quite embarrassed as many in the gallery laugh and applaud. He is silent and does not accept the challenge. Still angry, Nan, nonetheless, manages to nod appreciatively to her supporters as she storms out of the gallery.

Chapter 74
Moving Day

It has been some six months since the book's release, and, with its success, Nan's financial situation has been transformed. She is now a reasonably wealthy woman. It is time for her to move out on her own. Today, she, her sister and Wightman are carrying moving boxes into Nan's new apartment, a brownstone in New York.

Wightman brings one last box into Nan's new home office as Nan puts her typewriter on her desk. Nearby is the current edition of the N.Y. Times, whose headline reads:

**Saint Francis Dam Collapse
– Hundreds Dead**

Worst Man-Made Disaster in U.S. History. The dam failed spectacularly just 12 hours after esteemed engineer William Mulholland signed off on its safety. Hundreds are dead. Thousands of homes have been lost. A despondent Mulholland takes all the blame;

says he wishes it was his life instead, he envies the dead.

Wightman looks at the headline and shakes his head. "Terrible tragedy." He then puts the last box on Nan's desk. It is full of letters, mostly all extremely angry letters, decrying Nan's work. He picks up some letters in the box and states sarcastically, "Here's your fan mail, Nan." Nan shrugs. Wightman grimaces, "Are they still bullying you?" Nan shakes her head, "No, these are mainly old letters. The public seems to have forgotten." Wightman sighs. "Americans aren't known for their memories," he pauses, "nor their smarts either."

Wightman nods at the headline about the dam collapse. "And they've got a new villain now. A real one this time. A guy who has killed hundreds." Nan responds, "Oh, he's just the current flavor. And my crime's worse." Wightman looks quizzically again, gesturing to the headline about hundreds dead, "I'm sorry. Worse?" Nan continues, "Of course, he's a he. I'm a she."

Wightman tries to reassure her. "Americans are fickle. They've moved on. They don't care about you anymore." Nan breathes deeply. "Let's hope the indifference lasts." There is a brief silence, and Nan continues, "One thing I've learned this last year is that there are a lot of assholes out there that like to stir up dirt." Wightman laughs, "Shit disturbers." She pauses, "Yeah. That type. And the last thing I need is for one of them to remind the public of me."

Chapter 75
Klunk At It Again

May Dixon Thacker is in Klunk's office at the Evening Graphic. Klunk holds up a copy of Nan's book. "How'd you like the gumption of that lady? Got this thing published after all. All the big shots in the world tried to stop it, good lord, the President's people wanted to kill it, and she did it anyway. Amazing. Kudos, lady."

Thacker nods in agreement and chimes in, "And the reaction is bizarre. People hated the story. They hated her. But they just couldn't get enough of it. It's the car accident people can't look away from." "Exactly," Klunk agrees. Thacker continues, "And I can see why. It's quite the read. Kept me captivated. It's actually pretty good."

Klunk shrugs, "Good or bad, I don't care. What's got my attention is that it's still selling like hotcakes. And we got ourselves a new villain, Nan Britton—a woman. People love to hate women. The problem is, folks are starting to forget about her." Thacker looks quizzically, "Why's that a problem?"

Klunk leans forward, "Oh, don't get me wrong. I love the problem. It's a problem I am uniquely able to solve.

What we need to do is to resurrect the devil, exploit the bitch and ride her coattails." Klunk speaks more to himself than to Thacker. "I was born for this moment. I ain't proud. Let's oil and grease the wheels and then piggyback off this thing. Make Nan Britton, once again, the most hated woman in America."

"What are you thinking?" asks Thacker. Klunk leans forward. "Look, we re-work the Harding death stories. Expand the mystery. Get Nan in there as the devious deviant. Her insatiable need for the nasty made her crazy and irrational. So much so that it killed the elderly President." Thacker is confused. "So you want Nan to be the murderess?" Klunk is quick to respond. "No! Absolutely not. Just the catalyst for his death. Maybe he died of a heart attack while performing a kinky sex act the young trollop insisted they try?"

Thacker speaks bittingly. "That's going to be a hard one to pull off. She was 3,000 miles away on the other coast at the time of his death. I don't think Harding's penis was that long." She laughs at her own joke and continues. "And I thought you said the philandering angle was off-limits." Klunk waves his hand in dismissal. "I was just being sarcastic." Klunk holds up Nan's book. "And with Nan's pornography here, that door is now wide open."

Klunk looks at Thacker. "Maybe we can get help from that Gaston Means fellow. I understand he works at very reasonable rates these days, given his circumstances. Remember Means?" Thacker nods, "Sure, he was memorable. He even out-sleazed you." Klunk smiles, "I actually take that as a bit of an insult. Anyhow, why don't you pay him a visit?" Thacker interjects, "But can't you just invite him to come see us?" Klunk shakes his head, "You're going to have to make a personal visit." Klunk hands her a note. "Here's his new address."

Thacker looks at the address and raises her eyebrows. "OK," she says as she heads out the door. Klunk calls to her as she leaves, "And remember, Florence is dead now too. And so is Sawyer. Lots of dead people all around. That's got to be good for something."

Chapter 76
A Page from Nan's Book

May Dixon Thacker enters Atlanta's Federal Penitentiary a few days later. She hands the guard her card. "I have an appointment with Mr. Gaston Means." The guard nods and leads her to the visiting room, where she waits patiently for her incarcerated interviewee, Mr. Means.

She is curious to hear what Means has to say, notwithstanding his credibility issues and criminal conviction. He didn't play a significant role in the White House, but he certainly knew both the late President and Nan, and often served as their go-between. And given his circumstances, another Harding confidant to end up in jail, he's likely willing to talk, albeit who knows how truthfully.

Thacker researched him before paying her visit. Means in fact gained a level of infamy following his testimony before Congress: it was a testimony that backfired spectacularly. He tried to finger former Attorney General Daugherty, saying that Daugherty had asked him personally to handle his bribes. Daugherty gave him the money, he said. And Means, as instructed by Daugherty, doled the cash out to one crony after another.

Means may have been telling the truth and probably was, but ultimately the charge blew up when it was determined that he forged the documents he said proved his claim. And that led to Means himself being convicted of perjury.

The Feds then decided to investigate the devious Mr. Means further, and what they found wasn't good. He had personally benefited from issuing Prohibition-era liquor permits to unworthy recipients. It turns out Means was overly generous in issuing 'alcohol pharmacy medical exemptions.' These exemptions allowed pharmacies to sell alcohol for medicinal purposes. Most of the certificates Means distributed went to well-known bootleggers who, in turn, put money in Means' pocket.

So, Thacker now waits for Means in the penitentiary waiting room.

Means enters and smiles, "Nice to see you again." He sits down and lights a cigarette. "I see Miss Britton got her book published after all. Would that have anything to do with your visit today?" Thacker nods knowingly, "You're clairvoyant, Mr. Means. Actually, Mr. Klunk thought you might be able to help us with a story we're planning about Harding's mysterious death, his late wife, and the shrewd Miss Britton."

Means smiles and nods, "Happy to help, Miss Thacker. I got nothing but time on my hands right now, and I've got some scores to settle. Goddam Harding is why I'm in here. So, let's work on your story, but I've got bigger ideas. I think we can do a whole book." "Interesting, a whole book," says Thacker. "Let's start with the article first, but

I'll come back another time for the book." Means smiles and looks at Thacker. "OK. Maybe there will be a book in our future, Miss Thacker. I can assure you it would be in our mutual interest," says Means as he rubs his thumb with his fingers, symbolizing money.

Chapter 77
A Very Noble Animal

A few days later, Thacker is again in Klunk's office. He has just finished reading the draft article she has written with the help of Means. It is titled, *Sex and Death – What Really Killed President Harding*. Klunk is silent and smiles broadly.

Thacker has had plenty of second thoughts about her piece. "I don't know about this. Harding frequented prostitutes, had gambler and bootlegger friends and surrounded himself with other lowlifes. And none of these sleazeballs did him in? Instead, we're making a 27-year-old girl who worked at a Bible company the impetus for his death. No one is going to believe that. We must be underestimating the intelligence of the American public?" Klunk scoffs, "Impossible; Americans are certifiable idiots."

Thacker challenges this assumption. "There's got to be some sort of baseline one might cross. You can't fool all of them all the time." Klunk shakes his head. "Don't have to fool all of them, just enough. And nearly 100% of our readers will eat this shit up." Thacker complains, "People can't be that gullible!" Klunk shakes his head. "Sure they can. Look at the idiots we elect; that's proof of American stupidity." Thacker shrugs, still uncertain.

Klunk continues, "Listen, no one has ever gone broke underestimating American intelligence." Thacker is also somewhat ashamed. "I feel guilty, though. We're not just dragging Nan Britton through the mud but also Harding, Florence and Sawyer. Three dead people. I feel like a vulture."

Klunk sits up in his chair. "My dear, the vulture is a very noble animal. It never kills its prey."

Chapter 78

Sex and Death

A few days later, the latest issue of the Evening Graphic is on the newsstands with the lurid headline, now embellished by Klunk: "*Sex and Death – What Really Killed President Harding – With New Evidence Should Body Be Exhumed?*" A crowd, attracted by the tabloid, gathers around.

One man shakes his head and grabs the newspaper. "Another Harding scandal. I gotta read this!" Nearby, a woman reads a passage out loud:

Mrs. Harding was with the President. She looked back at Dr. Sawyer, showing him the dosage she planned to administer. Sawyer nodded approvingly. She put it in the water glass, then tilted the President's head and forcefully made him drink the entire glass. Moments later, his eyes bulged in a state of shock. Mrs. Harding looked at him dispassionately and then back at Sawyer, who was smiling slightly. Sawyer motioned to the door. Florence then ran out to ask for the help she knew would achieve nothing.

The woman and man look at each other in shock. "Good God!" The woman pauses for a moment and then continues reading:

Heartless, right? Actually, not really. What was in the glass? Medicine or poison? Even if it was poison, was it heartless? We think not. When one hears the back story, one can almost sympathize with the woman.

Nan Britton is in her apartment a few days later, with the same edition. She's read the above and is now on to the remainder of the article.

Mrs. Harding was tormented for years by Harding's rampant philandering. He had hundreds, if not thousands, of women and did so right under her nose. That would drive any wife crazy. Worse, he was even having an affair with her former friend turned German spy - the well-endowed Mrs. Phillips.

Nan screams out, "Liar!" and then continues reading.

But she put up with it for so long. What finally pushed her over the top? The young trollop Nan Britton - she was the final straw.

Nan exclaims, "What!?!" She storms around her apartment, still reading.

Britton's ceaseless obsession and stalking of the President sent Florence over the edge. Britton wouldn't stop. She couldn't be stopped. So, it was time. Florence knew the only way to stop Britton was to take away the bait. She needed Harding himself to disappear to make Britton disappear. Her solution: get rid of him. She needed her husband dead. That would end the philandering and leave Britton heart-broken and forever denied. She'd kill two birds with one stone. The one she had despised for years would really be dead. And the young hussy would get the cumuppance she so deserved. She'd be left crushed and penniless. The appropriate retribution for them both. And the perfect moment to administer the punishment came in San Francisco.

Nan is beside herself, "Oh no!"

Chapter 79
Dr. Harding Strikes Back

A few weeks later, Dr. Harding, still furious about Nan's book, pays a visit to the Evening Graphic. He passionately hates the Evening Graphic. Their ceaseless exploitation of his deceased brother and sister-in-law enrages him.

The tabloid, though, has a vast circulation, and their utter lack of scruples, their turning a blind eye to even minimal journalistic rigor, suits his purpose well. He is in the office of its publisher, Charles Klunk.

"Well," Klunk says, "I never thought I'd see a Harding in my office." Dr. Harding is blunt. "I never thought I'd be here." He then takes out the *Sex and Death* article just published. "This is why I am here."

Klunk asks sheepishly, "Did you like it?" "I hated it," Harding responds. "You implied my late sister-in-law killed my brother and you made him an uncontrollable womanizer." Klunk is defensive. "We're just a tabloid. Checking facts and printing the truth ain't our forte." Dr. Harding nods, "I know, and that's why I am here. The one part of the article I did like is where you slam Britton and call her an obsessed stalker." Klunk smiles, "That was a nice tidbit. My idea." Harding continues, "Obsessed stalker. Yeah. Nice tidbit but not enough. You can make up a lot worse shit about her than that."

Harding holds up a copy of Nan's book. "This was not supposed to happen. It was not supposed ever to be published!" Klunk shrugs. "I know. Pretty gutsy of that lady. And her book is selling well. Real well. You gotta admire that, pal." Dr. Harding won't let it go. He holds up Nan's book again. "We've got to undo this thing." Klunk laughs. "So, put the genie back in the bottle." "Exactly," says Harding. "And you can do it."

Klunk laughs again. "Sorry, pal. I ain't Aladdin. And Houdini didn't give me his powers when he died so I can't help you," Klunk responds while shaking his head. "Yes you can," says Harding. "Tell the world she's a lying whore. Look for holes in her story. Make shit up. Slander her any way you can and do it over and over again. Truth be dammed. Repetition makes things believable."

"I see. Maybe I was too quick to turn you down. That is our line of work, but what's in it for me?" Klunk asks. Dr. Harding smiles. "We need to resurrect the reputation of the Republican Party too. So, I thought you'd want to do it just to help out the Grand Old Party."

Klunk is surprised. "For free?" he asks. "Yes," Harding continues. "Oh, and by the way, the Party records show you overpaid your dues." He winks at Klunk and hands him an envelope with dozens of $100 bills. "Here's the refund we owe you." Klunk looks in the envelope and smiles. "Well, happy to help the Old Party out."

Harding heads to the door. He turns and addresses Klunk, "Destroy Britton, destroy her book. Call her whatever evil names you want, make her a deviant, a criminal, a half-human devil, and repeat it ad nausea. The more you repeat the lies, the more believable they'll sound." Klunk looks at Harding. "Truer words were never spoken." He is pleased, very pleased. He holds up the money Dr. Harding has just handed him and smiles at him. "Now, before you go, just tell me, what exactly would you like us to say?"

Chapter 80
Special Delivery

Three days later, the Evening Graphic is on the newsstands featuring the first article Dr. Harding has surreptitiously commissioned. The headline and first paragraph read as follows:

NAN BRITTON'S FICTION - How a small-town deviant and known sex pervert lied and ruined the legacy of a great man and great President. In our weeklong exposé, we will examine the numerous and provable lies in Nan Britton's book, The President's Daughter. How the President couldn't have fathered a child, and Britton's unquenchable desire from a very early age for sex, tons of sex, including perverse sex with multiple partners, alcohol, and drugs. Why did this lowlife lie about the President? To make money, of course. The money she needed to feed her drug and sex addictions. The only question is, does anyone believe her?

Klunk is in his office reading the same headline. He is pleased with himself and laughs at the absurdity of it all. He's exploited the Harding mystery for years. They hate him for it. Now, to get even with their adversary, Nan Britton, they've hired him. For him, it's just business. He'll switch teams on a dime.

And though he doesn't care, he's certain Nan's story is true. Harding's sexual escapades were well known, and it's clear he had some relationship with Nan. Look at the photo of the two of them. It's frankly unimaginable that a powerful man as horny as he was wouldn't have taken advantage of the pretty young girl's infatuation.

Nan Britton is in her apartment, also reading the same article. She's furious. She throws down the newspaper and screams at her empty apartment, "A lowlife sex and drug addict! Is this the crap you're making up about me now!"

She is beside herself with anger. She hears an automobile stop abruptly outside and then screams as a brick crashes through her window. She is shaken by the sound of the shattered glass and the words written on the brick: "Die Deviant." This is just the start. Over the next few weeks and months, Nan will again become the target of the public's ire – her mailbox is full of vicious hate mail. The hate people had for her, the hate she thought was gone, has returned with a vengeance. The shit disturbers have prevailed, and the hatred is more virulent than ever. This time threats of real violence accompany it. The moniker Klunk bestowed on Nan earlier has been resurrected. Nan has once again become the most hated woman in America.

PART XVI

Desperately Seeking Justice

Chapter 81

Mr. Marsteller, Attorney at Law

Nan is in the office of William Fish Marsteller, a Cleveland attorney. She has brought with her the editions of the Evening Graphic which contain the gross fictions about her. She hands them to Mr. Marsteller. He looks at her. "I'm familiar with all this and your story. I'm sure you're not pleased with these articles. That's understandable." He pauses. "So, what do you want to sue them for?"

Nan breathes deeply and tries to respond calmly. "For lying about me and dragging me through the mud. I'm being bullied by them, verbally violated, and threatened with violence." Marsteller considers this, and then says, "Maybe it's defamation and libel, but you will need to be able to prove the claim and the damage you have suffered. The odds aren't good."

"Do I have anything to lose?" Nan asks. Marsteller, an experienced trial attorney, knows the risks well and responds quickly, "More bad publicity I'm afraid. Maybe even a counterclaim. Who knows? Do you have any documents or witnesses?" "I'll be the witness," Nan replies defiantly.

Marsteller offers a quick retort. "Your odds are getting worse. And you got powerful folks that want you to lose. Don't expect justice. Money always trumps the truth in our system. And it'll get ugly, very ugly."

Nan slumps a bit in her chair but then sits up. "Will you give it your all?" Marsteller is taken aback. "Absolutely, always do! Listen, I think they're creeps too. The scum of the earth. I just want to set realistic expectations for you." Nan hands Marsteller an envelope with cash. "Here's your retainer." She gets up to leave. Marsteller counts the money and is impressed. He calls out to Nan as she reaches the door, "Why me?"

Nan looks back at him. "Because I couldn't find what I really wanted." Marsteller is perplexed and slightly insulted as Nan continues, "A woman attorney. Just aren't many around." Nan leaves the office.

Chapter 82
Ways and Means

A few months later, May Dixon Thacker returns to Atlanta's Federal Penitentiary to meet with Gaston Means. This time she is there to discuss his book idea.

The guard opens the door and Means enters the room and sits across the table from Thacker. The guard nods in the direction of Thacker and tells Means, "Here's your visitor." They are now alone in the room, with no one to overhear them. Thacker takes out a pad of paper and pen, is ready to take notes, and tries to smile.

Means looks around. "I didn't properly apologize during our first meeting. I am truly sorry we have to meet here." Thacker responds, "So am I." Means continues, "I'm being held for Prohibition violations. And falsely. But I'll be out in time for the book tour."

Thacker smiles and sarcastically repeats his last words, "Out for the book tour, great." She looks around the penitentiary. "This is a far cry from your days at the White House." Means shrugs. "You know, Miss Thacker, I've got a lot of respect for your organization." Means holds up a copy of the book *The Clansman*. "Fine book your brother wrote. Important story. It needed to be told." He pauses and lights a cigarette. "And so does my story. It needs to be told, too."

He takes a long drag on his cigarette and then dives into his story. "It was a disastrous White House. No one knew what they were doing." Thacker is silent. She is not impressed by this beginning.

Means continues. "Harding was in over his head. His friends were stealing him blind." Thacker starts to pack her things to leave. "Another Harding political scandal. Thanks for reaching out to us." She stands. "But sorry, we're not interested. Try the New York Times."

Means, panicky now, quickly changes strategy and gets aggressive, "Excuse my French but fuck the New York Times." Thacker, surprised by the expletive, turns, "Excuse me?" "Come on, you heard me," Means says, then repeats it louder, "Fuck the New York Times! They're snooty know-it-alls. Their hoity-toity publisher thinks he's cream cheese."

Means has now regained her attention. "Asshole hooty-tooty N.Y. Times editor; thinks he's the cat's meow because he lives in a modest two-bedroom home hours from New York City." Means shakes his head, pauses, and lights a cigarette. He continues, "He should be selling lurid stories of crime, sex and corruption, like William Randolph Hearst. Who cares if he lies? Hearst's got himself a goddam castle. And look at Nan Britton's book, how well it is selling!"

"Yes, I know, Mr. Means. Lies sell," Thacker replies. Means shakes his head. "Oh, Nan Britton isn't lying. It's the goddam truth. My point is that it *doesn't matter*. People want a salacious story – true or false, that's what they'll buy. And it's probably better if they think it's a lie;

they like that more. What I'm proposing is a book that tells the story the public has wanted to hear for so long. The how and why Florence killed him."

Means winks knowingly as he leans closer to Thacker and speaks in hushed tones. "You know, she burned the evidence in the White House right before the funeral. I saw her. She had me light the fireplace. Who lights a fire in August?" Thacker takes out her notebook, "Really?"

Thacker, now with her notebook out, is ready to write. Means starts, "I know - as no other living person - the entire confidential story. The how and why she did it." Means pauses as Thacker is taking notes. She looks up, and Means continues, "'He will die in honor, the stars have so decreed' – that is the proclamation Florence made to Sawyer just as they embarked on the trip he didn't return from." Thacker looks surprised. "Is that true?"

Means shrugs. "I told you already. It doesn't matter." "But why'd she tell Sawyer?" Thacker asks. Means exhales loudly and repeats her question. "Why'd she tell Sawyer? He was in on it. She was just a woman, not smart enough for that kind of crime. Sawyer gave her the poison; showed her how to use it." Thacker is astonished. "Dr. Sawyer? Really??" Means scoffs and nods. "Everyone was corrupt. It was like a rampant disease in that White House."

"And Florence and Sawyer were great friends from way back. He was her doctor and confidant long before she met Harding. He knew her when she was Florence King and was married to her first husband." "She had a previous husband?" Thacker asks. "Yeah, an alcoholic husband. The Republican Party kept all that under wraps, and you never heard about her son from that marriage either. He also became an alcoholic." Thacker shakes her head, incredulous. "Wow, I didn't know any of that."

"Well, Sawyer always hated Harding. Advised Florence not to marry him. Just six months into the marriage, Florence knew Sawyer had been right. Harding's philandering was out of control. She'd been looking for a way out for years, but it was tough, Harding being a public figure and all. The fact that he was President wasn't going to stop her, though. You know, it was Florence that insisted on Sawyer's appointment to the White House. She wanted her co-conspirator close by so they could strike when the time came."

Thacker writes feverishly. Means slows down and is pleased with her interest. Eventually he continues, "But you didn't hear too much about either of them during his Presidency. That was all part of the plan. They were just lying low as best they could, looking for the right moment. And it came when the President had his worst day ever. I was there, and he had just learned of all the financial scandals. Forbes was with him in the Oval Office, and the President was literally choking Forbes to death." Thacker is shocked. "The President tried to kill Forbes and in the Oval Office?"

Means nods his head. "Yeah, he was a madman at that point. It was me and Hoover that broke it up. We saved Forbes's life. And afterward, the President is running around like a nutcase on the White House lawn babbling incoherently and crying. Then he falls to his knees, bemoaning his fate. It was pathetic."

Means takes another drag on his cigarette before going on, "Then who shows up? Florence. She consoles the President and suggests a trip west. Says they need to 'put some distance on their problems.' Distance? I'll say. She and Sawyer were going to put him six feet under and out of his misery. It was perfect. Kill him while out of the White House. When a lot fewer folks would be around."

Thacker recalls, "Sawyer was on that trip." Means nods in agreement. "Absolutely, he came up with the food poisoning story. That was his diagnosis. Remember? Well, it was poisoning, all right, but it wasn't the food. If it had been the food, others would have come down with it. They were all eating the same meals."

Thacker looks up from her notes, "So that's why no autopsy. They would have found Sawyer's poison." Means nods. "Yeah, and they immediately embalmed the body to make sure no one went over their heads and ordered an autopsy. They knew how to cover their tracks." Means shakes his head in disbelief. "A President who dies unexpectedly doesn't get an autopsy? Come on. Got the stink of a cover-up all over it."

"So, it was premeditated?" Thacker asks. "Absolutely, and planned well. You know what Sawyer had as part of the provisions on the trip?" Thacker shakes her head. "He carted a coffin with him from D.C. Now why do that unless you were certain you were going to have a body to put in it? Well, he was certain he'd have a body, and he didn't want any delays. If they went searching for a regal casket or something, that could have delayed the embalming. The Vice President, now President, might have had time to think about it and put out an executive order requiring an autopsy."

"Have casket, will travel" Thacker says, shaking her head. She continues, "So, the good friends conspired to kill the man they both hated, the President of the United States. And they got away with it, didn't they?" Thacker remarks. Means again nods in agreement. "Yeah, and they stuck together afterward. I guess partners in crime do. You remember they were side-by-side behind his coffin at the funeral?" He pauses, giving her a chance to write, then begins again when she stops. "And then they moved in together after."

Thacker is once again shocked. "They were lovers? Sawyer and Florence?" Means smiles. "I like that." Means again motions for her to continue writing. "Were the murderers lovers? Well, he loved *her*. And she used him." Thacker wants to know more. "Why did she want Harding dead then? She'd been living with the asshole for years, and killing a President, even on a trip, is tough to get away with. She could have ended up in jail."

Means nods. "She was pretty sure no one would touch the grieving First Lady. And she was right. The Republican Party certainly didn't want to pursue that line of thinking. It would have been very bad publicity for them. The most powerful man in the world killed by his fragile and feeble wife. That would make them look like weaklings. Awful image for the Party."

Means continues, "As to why she wanted him dead? His womanizing, she hated it. And she wanted him dead before the financial scandals were made public." Seeing Thacker looking skeptical on hearing this last comment, Means adds, "Why would she care about that, you ask?"

Means slows down a bit so she can catch up. "With him gone, the Harding name would be left out of it. Or so she hoped. Let the Cabinet, the Ohio Gang, take all the blame. They're the ones that took advantage of the kind, compassionate and beloved President. That was the story she wanted told, and, in fact, there was some truth to it. But the bozo did hire all these guys. And he was too busy banging prostitutes and too dumb and lazy to know or understand what his cabinet was doing. Way too dumb to be President."

Means pauses, lights another cigarette, and then begins again. "And Florence was shrewd. Some say ambitious too. The women's vote wasn't enough for her. She wanted her own legacy." Thacker is now thoroughly hooked by the story. "Quite the bitch then."

Means nods in agreement. "Then Sawyer dies under identical circumstances just a year later, with Florence by his side. Once you start, I guess you can't stop." Thacker shakes her head. "She killed Sawyer too! Wow! And now *she's* gone." Means replies, "We can make it a double murder-suicide if you like?" Thacker takes notes and nods. The guard knocks and enters, indicating their time is up.

Thacker stands up to leave. "It should be quite a book. Maybe do even better than Nan's. I can see it now: 'Florence and Sawyer, the Most Unlikely of Murderers.'" Means agrees. "Yes, indeed, 'The Evil Murderess and Dr. Killer'. But we got to spruce the President up a bit. She poisoned a great statesman. Saint Warren of Washington." He laughs at his satirical description of the late President.

Thacker smiles too. "Why not, it's your book. Hey, given your circumstances here, I'll come see you daily. You dictate, I draft." "Pretty good offer, I'd say," Means responds. He looks at her as she leaves. "I'll look forward to your visits."

Chapter 83
Nan v. Klunk

It is October 19 1931, and with some trepidation, Nan and her attorney, William Fish Marsteller, walk side-by-side to the Hall of Justice in Toledo, Ohio. Elizabeth Ann, 12 years old in three days' time, trails a short distance behind and is with Nan's sister, Liz. As they enter the Court, angry protestors hurl insults at them. A few of the more virulent protestors toss gum, pebbles and crumbled newspapers in their direction.

Nan tries, as best she can, to shield her daughter from these onslaughts. Try as she might though, the incident is very troubling and shatters her confidence. She hates being hated.

This is the price Nan has been paying since Klunk published the lies about her, and it is the price she continues to pay. But she is finally getting her day in court. Her libel case against Charles Klunk, publisher of the Evening Graphic, begins this morning. He has publicly defamed her, wrongly called her story false, and erroneously labeled her as a cheap, lying, perverted sexual degenerate. And she has suffered horrific abuse on account of Klunk's publications. She is anxious for justice to be done, her name to be cleared, and the truth of her story restored.

Her attorney, Mr. Marsteller, is worried. He knows the justice system is often unfair, especially to women. Things look especially bleak for Nan as the other side is rich, powerful and motivated. And their already bad odds got worse when only two women were selected for the jury. Marsteller also fears that his warnings to Nan about the trial have gone unheeded.

Nan is indeed delusional about the trial, falsely anticipating that the process will be conducted with civility. She naively believes the facts and the law will be discussed calmly and rationally. She is unprepared for the onslaught that will rain down on her, not just from the other side but also from the judge. He will not be the fair, unbiased referee she imagines.

At this point, though, Nan is not the only one anxious for the trial to begin. The courtroom is full. Many arrived hours early to get a seat, and some would-be attendees were turned away. As they eagerly wait for the judge's arrival, Elizabeth Ann entertains them. She skips around the courtroom, declaring to the room in a singsong fashion, "I'm the President's daughter. I'm the President's daughter." The audience laughs at Elizabeth Ann, encouraging her to continue and to do so louder and louder. "I'm the President's daughter. I'm the President's daughter."

The bailiff calls out, "All rise," as Judge John Killits enters the courtroom. His words are not heard over the crowd's laughter and Elizabeth Ann's antics. "I'm the President's daughter," she continues to sing. An angry judge takes the bench and pounds his gavel hard. Nan frantically beckons Elizabeth Ann to sit and be quiet, and the whole courtroom becomes hushed.

Judge Killits then issues his first order: "I need this child removed from the courtroom immediately. Who is her guardian?" Nan raises her hand. "Not you," says the judge. Liz Willits then speaks up, "Your Honor, I am her aunt. I can take her." "Fine," Judge Killits says, "Hurry up."

Liz takes Elizabeth Ann's hand and starts to leave the court. She first stops and speaks quietly to Nan. "We'll see you this evening." The day, with the protestors and now the angry judge, has started worse than imagined, so Liz, to comfort her sister, hugs her. The judge bangs his gavel again. "Get the child out now. I don't have time for a family reunion." Liz leaves with Elizabeth Ann. The judge looks around the courtroom and sees some giggling high school girls. He addresses the courtroom.

"I would like to make some preliminary remarks to set the appropriate tone for the coming days. The case before us, *Britton v. Klunk*, has already garnered a fair amount of notoriety, which is why, I suspect, we have such a large audience in the gallery today. Let me be clear though: the subject matter of this trial and some of the testimony that will be heard is likely to be lewd and degrading. It almost certainly will be to me. There will be discussion of matters and language that is not for the ears of young girls, and I see a number of what appear to be high school girls in our courtroom today." The high school girls giggle. This enrages the judge.

"All girls under the age of 21 are ordered to leave." The judge looks in the direction of the girls in the gallery. "The subject matter of this trial, the plaintiff's book, and the plaintiff's personal life are pornography. This topic is certainly not appropriate for your ears." At this point a few leave as requested, but only a few. Some who are clearly in defiance of the judge's order remain and snicker amongst themselves.

The judge's anger is piqued. Exasperated, he continues, "You know, that's just fine. We aren't here to check I.D.s or to babysit. We are here to uphold the law and do our duty, however repugnant, to God and Country. The fact that pornography has made its way to these hallowed halls of justice is appalling, but it appears that this is the case, so we must all live with it. But by the power given to me, I will set boundaries, at least in this courtroom."

He looks at both parties in the dispute. "Counsel, the parties in this case, the jurors, and the court employees, of course, need to remain, but all others are hereby ordered to leave this courtroom immediately. The only exception I must somewhat reluctantly grant is that reporters can also remain present. I do not want to myself become the subject of a freedom of the press claim." The judge bangs his gavel hard and declares, "This trial is closed to the public." Judge Killits watches impatiently as the courtroom officers clear the gallery of the disappointed crowd.

Nan is concerned by the judge's early display of clear bias against her. How could a supposedly learned man believe her work to be pornography? She looks at Marsteller as the crowd shuffles out and is about to whisper in his ear. He gestures to her not to do so but senses her concern and gives her an imperceptible nod.

Chapter 84
America on Trial

Judge Killits addresses Nan's attorney, "Mr. Marsteller, please proceed with your opening statement." "Yes, thank you, your honor." Marsteller stands and addresses the jury.

Ladies and Gentlemen. First, thank you all ahead of time for your service and the attention I know you will give the parties. I think you will find it interesting, but the task ahead will likely not be easy. Ultimately, you will need to digest a significant amount of evidence and a great deal of testimony (some of it conflicting) to arrive at your decision. My only request is that you be thoughtful and open-minded, and always keep one simple fact about this case in mind.

Marsteller walks over to the defendant, Mr. Klunk.

Miss Britton is not on trial here. You will hear much about her during these proceedings, but you are not here to judge her. So, what you hear about her is irrelevant. It is not Miss Britton who is on trial.

Marsteller pauses and points at Mr. Klunk.

It is Mr. Klunk who is on trial. He is the one who you are judging. And we will help you arrive at your judgment. We will prove beyond a shadow of a doubt that Mr. Klunk has fabricated scandalous lies. He has spun a fantastical tale out of make-believe cloth and, without any evidence whatsoever, maliciously and falsely ruined Miss Britton and her reputation.

He has published these deceits in his newspaper, thereby spreading these lies and slanders right across America, and he has achieved his shameful objective. He has destroyed an honest woman. He has ruined her life with his lies. The lies he has fabricated have destroyed the woman you see before you, Miss Britton. End of story. Those are the facts. No question. The defense will not and cannot dispute any of that.

And what were Mr. Klunk's reasons for destroying Miss Britton? Was this, in his eyes, some supposed moral crusade? Was it a fearless attempt to expose the truth about someone whose life has crossed that of a President of the United States?

No, it has all been for no other reason than to sell newspapers and to make money. Grubby money earned from flagrant lies. Unfortunately, lurid tales sell papers. People love scandal and gossip, as the crowd now cleared from this court testifies. Members of the jury, please put aside any prurient thoughts about the testimony you will hear. Your job is to judge the defendant, his actions, the results of his actions and the harm he did to my client. He lied and his lies caused her serious harm.

Knowingly lying and severely harming someone is detestable, despicable, reprehensible, abhorrent and immoral. Do you know what else it is? It is against the law. It is illegal, and it is called libel.

And that is what Mr. Klunk is on trial for here, breaking the law. He has committed libel. He has published false and malicious statements that have damaged Miss Britton. The incontrovertible evidence will show that he knowingly committed this crime and that my client has undeniably suffered on account of this crime. You have a duty to apply the law, find the defendant guilty and restore dignity to an honest, hardworking woman.

Yes, my client is seeking to apply the law here. But my client wants and deserves something else – she seeks fairness. Miss Britton wants the world to judge her based on her own actions and words and not on the lies spread by a man she has never even met or seen before today.

Miss Britton wants fairness. We all deserve that. Give her the chance to restore her life and be judged by her own words and actions. The starting point for this is in your hands. You must remove the horrific slurs unfairly placed upon her by the defendant. You must find the defendant guilty of the crime he has committed.

Thank you.

Nan is pleased. She sits up straight in her chair, looking confident. This is a very good beginning. Marsteller has laid it out simply and clearly. Klunk did her wrong, and he did so with malice and only because he was greedy. She is certain that by the end of the trial, her name will be cleared. The judge turns to Klunk's counsel, "Mr. Mouser, it is now your turn." Mouser begins, "Thank you, your honor."

Ladies and Gentlemen of the jury, my esteemed colleague here...

He motions toward Marsteller.

Is absolutely correct.

He pauses for dramatic effect and walks over to the jury.

My client is on trial here.

He pauses again.

But far more is on trial than that. My friends, America is on trial. What did Mr. Klunk do? He exercised a cornerstone right of our great nation—his God-given right to free speech.

Mouser picks up some of the copies of the Evening Graphic. He continues, a bit dismissively.

So, what did Mr. Klunk actually do? He wrote some articles. That's it. He wrote some articles-end of story.

I know Miss Britton didn't like the words my client wrote. Well, you can't please all the people. You never will. But we still believe in a free press in this country, don't we? If the press had to please everyone all the time, nothing would ever get written.

Mouser walks over to Nan and points at her.

And this woman. A woman we will prove is a lowlife, lying whore, wants to take this right away from my client with this lawsuit. Think of the irony. She wrote a book. She fabricated a story. Her lies degraded our President, the most important man in the world. She was apparently OK exercising *her* right to free speech.

But now, the shoe is on the other foot, and she wants to take free speech away from another. Is that fair, I ask you? Of course it isn't. What is good for the goose is good for the gander.

He walks over to his client and looks at him sympathetically.

Yes, you must save my client. He has done nothing wrong.

He turns to the jury.

But more importantly, you must save our country. Our founders fought and died for our right to free speech.

He points to Nan.

Don't let this trollop undo the principles they struggled so hard for.

He again looks directly at the jury.

Find for my client and you find for America. It is a formidable task, but I have confidence in you. You can do it. You can save America.

Nan is devastated by Mouser's distortions and distractions, and particularly by his name-calling. She whispers to Marsteller. "Can you request a recess?" Marsteller nods and stands. "Your honor, could we please have a 15-minute break?" The judge looks a bit puzzled. "It's a bit early for that, but I'll grant you this one indulgence. The requested recess is so granted. Court will resume in 15 minutes." The judge bangs his gavel. The courtroom clears.

Chapter 85
Second Thoughts

Marsteller and Nan have adjourned to a private room in the courthouse. Nan is very upset. She sits recounting some of the opening arguments and seeks Marsteller's advice. "He called me a lowlife, lying whore. He's trashing me." Marsteller is frank: "He's far from done."

Nan is frustrated. "This is all so wrong. This isn't fair". Marsteller is again matter of fact. "It's very wrong. It's very unfair. But also very inevitable. From the outset, I warned you this was going to be tough, and here we are." Nan starts to cry. "I don't have a chance! And it's going to be miserable."

Marsteller puts his hand gently on her shoulder. "You could end that misery now. Do you want to withdraw?" Nan, still crying, blurts out, "I don't know."

Marsteller takes her hands, doing his best to be sympathetic. It takes her some time, but eventually she regains at least a modicum of composure. Marsteller then softly speaks to her. "Well?" Nan looks at him briefly. Marsteller asks again, "Should we withdraw?"

Nan looks at him and then again bursts into tears. She gets up and runs from the room. Marsteller looks dumbfounded as he watches her run away.

Moments later, Nan is running from the courthouse. It's oddly quiet outside. The mob and the mob mentality of the morning have given way to a normal setting. Compared to the morning's chaos, the normality makes it seem almost serene.

However, Nan's sense of security is soon compromised as she hears footsteps following quickly behind her. She is apprehensive. She hears a voice calling her. "Miss Britton?" Nan quickens her pace and doesn't look back. Whoever is behind her similarly quickens their pace. Now Nan hears the voice again, "Miss Britton."

The voice, though, is not menacing. On the contrary, it is oddly soft and reassuring. Nan glances behind her and sees that the voice belongs to a young woman, maybe just 17 years old. She is with her mother. Nan is unsure of her intent and though still guarded, is less frightened. The young woman is equally nervous but gets up the nerve to speak to her again. "Miss Britton? Are you Miss Britton, the author of this book?" The teenager holds up Nan's book. "Yes," Nan finally replies.

The young woman, clearly in awe of Nan, nervously holds out her copy of the book towards Nan. "I really loved it. Would you please sign it?" Nan stops in her tracks. She looks at the young woman and senses she is sincere. Nan smiles broadly and takes the book from her. "Of course, I'd be delighted. And what is your name?" "Carolina," the young woman replies.

Nan replies, "Well, Carolina, it's a pleasure to meet you." As Nan signs and returns the book, Carolina says, "I will remember this moment for the rest of my life." Nan can't help herself. She hugs Carolina and reciprocates, "So will I."

"Thank you." The daughter's mother also reaches out and takes Nan's hands. "Thank you for everything."

Chapter 86
Head Scratching in the Courtroom

Nan's absence from the courtroom is, of course, highly conspicuous and regrettable. The judge is angry and impatient. Marsteller is being mercilessly reprimanded, not just for his client's absence but his inability to offer the court any information as to her whereabouts and when, if at all, she will return.

At this point, all Marsteller can do is just sheepishly agree with the judge. "Yes, your honor, I understand this puts us in jeopardy of an immediate dismissal in favor of the defendant." The judge looks angrily at the clock on the wall. "Your client has now turned the 15-minute recess I granted into a 25-minute vacation. Without a good explanation, I will soon hold her in contempt of court."

Marsteller is completely helpless and can only nod, "I understand, your Honor." Marsteller is at a loss and can do nothing. He is, though, the consummate professional and keeps his cool despite the judge's obvious disapproval.

An awkward silence paralyzes the proceedings. It is into this scene that Nan returns. And with new-found purpose, she strides confidently into the Courtroom. "Sorry, I am late, your Honor. Just tending to some feminine matters."

With these words, she immediately and effectively disarms what was, seconds ago, an extremely tense situation. The judge and other men in the room, though unclear as to Nan's precise meaning, are sympathetic and embarrassed. The judge immediately forgets his anger, stammers a bit, and then proceeds as if nothing was amiss. "Very well. Let us continue."

Marsteller looks at Nan and whispers in her ear, "Do you want to proceed?" Nan nods her head. Marsteller addresses the judge. "Yes, your Honor. Let's proceed."

Chapter 87
Daisy's Day

Marsteller calls Miss Daisy Harding to the stand. Despite Nan's strenuous objections, Marsteller has subpoenaed Daisy. He has insisted that she testify. Nan has had no real choice in the matter. Marsteller was going to withdraw from the case otherwise.

Nan has always liked Daisy. Even though they have been effectively estranged for nearly two decades, Nan has always hoped for a real reconciliation. She knows, though, that that hope has now gone forever. Daisy is sworn in, and Marsteller begins his questioning. Nan looks away.

Marsteller: Madam, please state your name and your relationship to President Harding.

Daisy: My real name is Abigail Harding but I go by Daisy. I am President Harding's sister.

Marsteller: I understand that your family and Miss Britton's family have known each other for years and that you all come from Marion, Ohio. Is that correct?

Daisy: Yes.

Marsteller: Is it also accurate that you are a high school English teacher, and that Miss Britton was once a student in your class?

Daisy: Yes.

Marsteller: Do you recall what kind of a student Miss Britton was? If you need help remembering, please refer to Exhibit D of the trial record next to you. It is a copy of her grade reports and graded papers from your classes.

Daisy: That won't be necessary. Nan was an excellent student - one of, if not, my best ever.

Marsteller: I understand you kept in touch with Miss Britton after her graduation, and you were very good friends at one point. Is that accurate?

Daisy: Yes.

Marsteller: Did this good friend ever confide to you about her feelings for, and relationships with, men?

Daisy: She occasionally expressed her views.

Marsteller: In Miss Britton's book, she indicates she was very much in love with your brother, Mr. Warren Harding, from at least her high school days until his death. Is this characterization in her book consistent with her statements to you?

Daisy: Yes.

Marsteller: Did Miss Britton ever express any affection whatsoever with any man other than your brother?

Daisy pauses. She thinks for a moment and then responds.

Daisy: Not that I can recall offhand.

Marsteller: I understand that your friendship with Miss Britton waned, and you two were estranged and did not communicate at all for over ten years. Is that accurate?

Daisy: Well, yes. We were both busy with our own lives. She became more independent as she matured.

Marsteller: Let me ask about some more personal items which friends sometimes discuss. Specifically, sex. Did Miss Britton ever tell you she was conducting an intimate relationship with your brother?

Daisy: Yes, she did say that, but I didn't know if it was true. I never confirmed it with my brother. I didn't know for sure if it was happening.

Marsteller: Did you believe it was true?

Mouser: Objection. The witness's beliefs are irrelevant.

Marsteller: I'll withdraw the question. Miss Harding, after Miss Britton told you of her intimacy with your brother, did you offer her any advice?

Daisy: Well, yes, I thought it a bad idea for both of them. I mean, if it were happening. I suggested she break off any type of relationship, whatever it was, she may have been having with my brother.

Marsteller: How did Miss Britton react to your suggestion that she break off her relationship, whatever that was, with your brother?

Daisy: She said they loved each other very much, and they would continue seeing one another.

Marsteller: Was her unwillingness to break it off the start of your estrangement with her?

Daisy is uncomfortable and pauses before she answers.

Daisy: It may have had something to do with it.

Marsteller: Let's move onto more recent times. After your brother's death and nearly a decade of no contact with Miss Britton, she reached out to you again. Is that correct?

Daisy: Yes.

Marsteller: What did Miss Britton want after all these years?

Daisy: She wanted help in raising her daughter, financial help.

Marsteller: Did she say why she was reaching out to you?

Daisy: She was looking for us to replace the money she claimed, but could not prove, that my late brother had sent her while he was alive.

Marsteller: Why, according to Miss Britton, was Mr. Harding sending her money?

Daisy: She said my brother was the father of her child.

Marsteller: OK. So, she reached out to Mr. Harding's family for money to replace the child support he allegedly previously provided. Did you give her what she asked for?

Daisy: I gave what I could; it was much less than what she asked for.

Marsteller: Did you try to provide more help and arrange for Miss Britton to meet with your other brother, Dr. Harding, so Miss Britton could also ask him for money?

Daisy: I did.

Marsteller: That was very generous of you. Can you recall any similar generosity you have bestowed on estranged former friends you haven't spoken to in years?

Daisy is quite upset and struggles to respond.

Daisy: Not offhand, but Nan was in real trouble, single and with a young child.

Marsteller: A child that by her account was also your niece, your flesh and blood, a family member. So, if her account is accurate, you were helping your own family. Is that correct?

Daisy: By her account, yes, I guess so.

Marsteller: Thank you. No further questions.

The judge turns to opposing counsel. "Mr. Mouser, would you like to cross-examine the witness?" Mr. Mouser stands. "Your Honor, thank you. We have no questions for this witness." The judge raises his gavel. "That concludes proceedings for this morning. Thank you all for your attendance. Please return at 1:30 PM." Judge Killits pounds his gavel, "Court dismissed."

Nan turns to Marsteller. "Why no cross-examination?" Marsteller whispers to her, "To get her off the stand as soon as possible. I would have done the same were I him."

Chapter 88
Klunk

Marsteller announces his next witness. "The prosecution calls the defendant Charles Augustus Klunk." Mouser whispers to his client just before he heads to the witness stand, "No elaboration." Klunk waves him off and heads to the stand, and is sworn in. Marsteller begins his questioning.

Marsteller: Mr. Klunk, your exposés are the subject of this trial. I would like to know the source of the stories you have printed. Where did you get the information?

Klunk: No sources. I just made it up. Dr. Harding gave me some ideas, I guess.

Marsteller: Was he the sole outside source?

Klunk: I guess. But we were both just making things up.

Marsteller: Did Dr. Harding pay you?

Klunk: I don't work for nothing, pal.

Marsteller: Did you make sure the stories were accurate?

Klunk: Why should I?

Marsteller: Did you contact Miss Britton and ask her to verify any claims, to comment, or to offer a rebuttal before you printed your stories?

Klunk: Nope. Never talked with her. But I wish I had. Man, this is the first I've seen her in person - here in court. She's one fine-looking woman. I can see why the President would want a piece of that.

Nan rolls her eyes. Mouser, desperate to rein in his client, stands.

Mouser: Your Honor. As a simple expedience, perhaps the court might want to remind the witness to merely answer the question asked. His elaboration is harmless and does add some interesting color, but the added information might be taking away from the court's valuable time.

Judge: Mr. Klunk, your attorney is offering you excellent advice. I think you'd be well served to follow it.

Klunk pantomimes sewing up his lips and smiles.

Judge: Please continue, Mr. Marsteller.

Marsteller: Just to summarize then, Mr. Klunk. Your work was pure fiction. You made no effort to corroborate your story. You didn't check its veracity. Rather, you simply invented the slander you reigned down upon Miss Britton. Is that correct?

Klunk: That's what I was paid to do. So what?

Marsteller: Did you know your false and malicious statements would seriously harm Miss Britton?

Klunk: I knew they might, but hey, I was just a guy trying to make a buck.

Nan has no respect for Klunk. She jots down the word 'Buffoon' on her notepad.

Marsteller: No further questions.

Judge: Mr. Mouser, would you like to cross-examine the witness?

Mouser: Yes, your Honor.

Mouser has only three questions for Klunk. He has rehearsed these with him over and over. Klunk is to simply answer "Yes" to the first and "No" to the latter two. So, for Klunk, it is only - Yes, No, No – these are the only words Klunk is to utter. It couldn't be simpler, but given his performance so far, Mouser is nervous. He takes a deep breath and approaches Klunk.

Mouser: Mr. Klunk, do you believe in freedom of speech?

Klunk: Very much so.

Mouser is relieved. Not the planned response, but it gets the job done.

Mouser: Did you object to Miss Britton's book when it was published?

Klunk: Not at all. I was impressed. She sold a lot of books. You got to admire that. She did well. My hat's off to her.

Mouser actually likes this response. It is more than he wanted, but complimenting the plaintiff is a nice addition. He now asks his third and final question, hoping for just the simple "No" answer they have rehearsed.

Mouser: Would you describe your publication as serious journalism?

Klunk: Are you kidding? We're a tabloid. We publish junk. Everyone knows that. We write about space aliens, vampires, the supernatural, and gossip. You name it. As I just said, we make up stuff, like the crap we wrote about Miss Britton. We put out anything that will sell, not stuff people should believe. But if someone wants to believe the shit I publish, that's their problem, not mine.

Mouser can't believe the sheer stupidity of his client once again voluntarily reiterating his guilt. Mouser remains unflappable. He smiles and, to bluff the jury into thinking the testimony they have just heard wasn't the disaster to his client that it actually was, offers what he hopes will be viewed as his profuse sincere thanks to the witness.

Mouser: Well, thank you, Mr. Klunk - no further questions for this witness.

Judge: Very well. We will begin with our penultimate witness tomorrow morning and hopefully complete testimony in the next few days. Court is dismissed until tomorrow morning.

The judge bangs his gavel, and the Courtroom clears.

Outside the Courthouse, the reporters buzz around Mouser and Klunk as they rush from the building after the court session. Nan and Marsteller look on. Klunk's damning testimony has Mouser off balance. He tries to shield Klunk from the reporters while defending the indefensible.

A reporter asks Mouser, "Do you regret Mr. Klunk's testimony?" Mouser shakes his head, "Not at all. Why should I? He was refreshing. Spoke his mind." The reporter follows up, "He said he made it all up, lied." Mouser looks angry and moves through the crowd with greater determination. "The only deceitful liar in that courtroom is Miss Britton."

Another reporter follows up. "Your client is on trial for libel. Didn't he pretty much just raise his hand and say, 'I'm guilty?'" Klunk is with Mouser. He shrugs, nods in agreement, and raises his hand. Mouser pushes him aside and responds nervously. "Guilt or innocence is for the jury to decide, thank you."

The reporters rush off. Happy with the reporters' questions and Mouser's defensiveness, Nan smiles at Marsteller.

Chapter 89
May Visits Again

May Dixon Thacker is back at Atlanta's Federal Penitentiary. Today, she hands Means the latest draft of their book. "I am pretty pleased with this; it's now complete and incorporates all your previous edits. I certainly hope it meets with your approval. It was a ton of work, I got to tell you," Thacker says.

Means is profusely apologetic, "I know. Thank you. You're a trooper. Your work is incredible. And I can't tell you how horrible I feel about not being able to pay you yet."

Means continues, "You deserved a generous advance. I am so embarrassed. But look at my circumstances!" Means motions to the prison to which he is confined. "You will be handsomely paid, though, at a first-rate scale. We will split the gross evenly. I'll cover all expenses from my half," Means says. This is indeed a generous offer, and Thacker is grateful. "Thanks, that's appreciated."

Means changes topics. "Look, I assume you've been following the Britton trial." "Of course," says Thacker. Means nods and continues, "It's great publicity for us, and our timing might be perfect. We need to get this thing in the bookstores while the trial is still in the public's eye. And I'll be out of here soon, so I should be available for the book tour." "Well," says Thacker, "Let's hope the stars align. I'll work overtime to speed up the process." "Good," Means says, "I'll look this draft over tonight. I will give you revisions tomorrow. Then we should be good to go."

"OK," says Thacker, "I'll work night and day." "Atta girl!" says Means as Thacker leaves the prison.

Chapter 90

Dr. Harding to the Defense

The court is back in session, and Marsteller has called Dr. Harding to testify. He's been duly sworn in and is now on the stand.

Marsteller: Please describe your relationship with President Harding and your profession.

Dr. Harding: He was my older brother, and I am a medical doctor.

Marsteller: Do you recall meeting Miss Britton in your home on April 17 1924?

Dr. Harding: Yes.

Marsteller: Did Miss Britton tell you that your brother, President Harding, was the father of her child?

Dr. Harding: She offered no proof.

Marsteller: Please just answer the question, Dr. Harding. Did she tell you that your brother, the former President, was the father of her child? Yes or No.

Dr. Harding: Yes.

Dr. Harding turns to the Judge. "Your Honor, may I please elaborate?" "I'll allow it," says the judge.

Dr. Harding: As mentioned, I asked Miss Britton for proof. She had no proof. Zero. And let's face it, women, particularly those that have had a child, struggle with rational thinking.

Marsteller: Objection, your Honor!

Judge: Sustained. The jury is to disregard Dr. Harding's last statement.

Marsteller continues.

Marsteller: Did your sister, Daisy, tell you she was sending child support money to Miss Britton?

Dr. Harding: She told me she was sending money, yes. But look, Daisy is a woman and a good-hearted woman. Too soft if you ask me. And...

He leans forward and speaks in a stage whisper.

Dr. Harding: You see, she's post-menopausal, so often confused.

Marsteller: Were you aware Miss Britton was working on a memoir that would reveal her intimate relationship with your brother?

Dr. Harding: I was aware of her fiction, yes.

Marsteller: Did you in any way try to interfere with the publication of her memoir?

Dr. Harding: Mr. Marsteller, I can assure you that, like any red-blooded American, I did everything I could to protect our family name from false slander.

Marsteller: So, your answer is 'Yes, you tried to interfere with the publication of Miss Britton's memoir?'

Dr. Harding: Perhaps, but I wouldn't personally use the term 'interfere' to describe protecting one's family.

Harding desperately wants to elaborate, but Marsteller holds up his hand to stop him from saying more.

Marsteller: Thank you, Dr. Harding. That is all.

Judge: Mr. Mouser, do you want to cross-exam the witness?

Mouser: Yes, your Honor.

Mouser stands and will use this opportunity to present the defense's case.

> *Mouser:* Would you please remind the court of your occupation and your relationship to the late President?

> *Dr. Harding:* As mentioned, I am a medical doctor and President Harding's brother.

> *Mouser:* How many times was your brother married?

> *Dr. Harding:* Just once, to Florence King.

> *Mouser:* Did he and Florence have any children?

> *Dr. Harding:* My brother, no. But Florence had a son from a previous marriage.

> *Mouser:* So, she was obviously able to have children. Interesting. Was your brother sterile?

> *Marsteller:* Objection. The witness is not sworn in as a medical expert. Furthermore, it is unethical for a doctor to provide medical services to immediate family members. Therefore, he couldn't possibly have the information now being asked of him.

Mouser stands and is about to offer counterarguments. The judge holds up his hand, motioning him to wait as he addresses the objection.

> *Judge:* There's nothing really medical about the question, just common information a sibling might know

about his brother. I'll allow it. Dr. Harding, please answer the query about whether your brother was infertile.

Dr. Harding: As a child, he had the mumps. He was sterile and definitely couldn't impregnate a woman.

Mouser: Thank you, Dr. Harding. On another subject, did you know of Miss Britton's reputation when she was a teenager in Marion, Ohio?

Marsteller: Objection, your Honor. Small-town gossip has no place in a courtroom.

Judge: Where are you going with this, Mr. Mouser?

Mouser: Your Honor, I am trying to disprove Miss Britton's claim of being a virtuous young lady who wasn't deflowered until she was twenty but can do so without involving this witness. May I approach the bench?

Judge: Yes.

Mouser: I submit for the record numerous affidavits from Miss Britton's high school classmates, friends, and teachers, describing her as a very coquettish and oversexed teenager - all long before her alleged rendezvous with the President. These suggest her promiscuity began many years before she claims, and this calls into doubt the credibility of her entire story.

Marsteller: Objection. We've seen the affidavits. They're irrelevant and from questionable sources. And they merely describe an outgoing teenager; there's no indication of intimate relationships with boys.

Judge: Then they are not defamatory to your client. Overruled. Mr. Mouser, please continue.

Mouser: Nothing further, your Honor.

Marsteller: Your Honor. I would like the chance to redirect.

Judge: Go ahead.

Marsteller is about to begin his well-prepared interrogation of Dr. Harding. Of necessity, he must bring up some of the more unsavory personal aspects of President Harding's life. Once again, the late President will be dragged through the mud but this time by Nan's attorney. It is all relevant. But the revelations, though not new, will certainly upset his client, Nan Britton. But Marsteller has no choice. This is his one slim chance to win what is almost certainly an un-winnable case.

Marsteller: Dr. Harding, I assume you're familiar with your brother's philandering and a public statement he once made saying, "It's good I wasn't born a woman. I'd be constantly pregnant."

Nan is upset Marsteller has brought this up. She's not sure he ever said this, but even if he did, she knows it was said in jest. It didn't mean anything. She looks steely-eyed at

Marsteller and quietly shakes her head. Marsteller wisely refuses to even glance at her.

Dr. Harding: He was quite active sexually. That's normal for a man. And the braggadocio? Probably a bit exaggerated. He often spoke like that after drinking.

Marsteller: Did he drink during Prohibition?

Dr. Harding: Well, yes. But it's not like that's a crime.

Marsteller: So, in your mind, breaking the law isn't a crime?

Dr. Harding: You know what I mean. It's all within societal norms for men, the drinking, the bragging, and philandering.

Mr. Marsteller holds up an unflattering photo of Florence Harding, an unattractive woman in any case.

Marsteller: Dr. Harding, do you recognize the woman in this photo?

Dr. Harding: Of course, it's Florence.

Marsteller: Yes, Florence Harding, President Harding's wife. Would you describe her as sexy? Elegant? Chic? Attractive?

Dr. Harding: Florence had many fine qualities. She was more of a business type.

Marsteller: Mrs. Harding was older than your brother and well into her thirties when they married. Correct?

Dr. Harding: Yes.

Marsteller: Were you aware she was in poor health with frequent visits to the sanatorium during her entire marriage to your brother?

Dr. Harding: Yes.

Marsteller: Given her age and health, would pregnancy, even just sexual intimacy, have been advisable or even possible?

Mouser: Objection. Calls for speculation. Dr. Harding was her brother-in-law, not her doctor.

Judge: Sustained. The witness is instructed not to answer.

Marsteller: Can you describe your brother and Florence's bedroom? How many beds were in it and what size?

Dr. Harding: They had two beds, twin beds.

Marsteller: So, they didn't sleep together?

Dr. Harding: They did not share a bed at night.

Marsteller: I see. And you mentioned your brother was given to braggadocio in discussing his sexual prowess.

Did he ever make mention of this activity with regard to Florence?

Dr. Harding: No, of course not.

Marsteller: Dr. Harding, is sexual intercourse a prerequisite to getting pregnant?

Some jury members softly giggle.

Dr. Harding: Yes, of course.

Marsteller: Dr. Harding, would a woman of Florence's age and health that wasn't sexually active likely get pregnant?

The jury laughs.

Mouser: Objection.

Marsteller: I'll withdraw the question.

Marsteller holds up some medical journals.

Marsteller: These medical journal articles discuss cases of men who had the mumps in childhood and who became fathers. Are you aware of this phenomenon?

Dr. Harding: I'm aware of it, yes.

Marsteller: So, to sum up, what we've just learned from you now. Men, like your brother that had mumps, can breed children, but elderly ill women that don't have sex can't. Is that accurate?

The jury laughs, the judge scowls, and a furious Mouser leaps to his feet. Marsteller does not wait for the objection. Instead, he interjects.

Marsteller: I'll withdraw the question - nothing further, your Honor.

Judge: We'll reconvene at 1 PM then, after lunch. Court dismissed.

Nan and Marsteller walk back to the hotel for lunch. There is an awkward silence, "Mr. Marsteller, you did a nice job with Dr. Harding today." "Thanks," Marsteller replies. Nan continues, "But I can assure you that from the day we consummated our love, Warren loved me and only me. He did not stray. We were exclusive."

There is a brief silence, then Marsteller tries to reassure her. "I understand. I am not trying to convince you he was anything but loyal. You're not my audience. The jury is." Nan is thoughtful and responds, "Mr. Marsteller, the world is *my* jury."

They walk in silence. Finally, Marsteller broaches the subject that is weighing on Nan. "I don't have to remind you that you're going on the stand this afternoon. We should go over some things over lunch." "Thanks, Mr. Marsteller," Nan replies, "But I'm having lunch with my sister. I really need her emotional support right now."

Marsteller thinks this a bad idea but capitulates just the same. "OK. I get it. Look, Nan, you'll do fine. You're smart. Just be thoughtful and brief. Answer honestly, and if you "don't know" or "don't recall," just say so. I'll meet you in the lobby at 12:45 so we can walk to court together." Marsteller leaves Nan as she heads to the restaurant.

Chapter 91

A Bit More Blush

Nan, her sister Liz and Elizabeth Ann are in a nearby restaurant at lunch. Nan's dish is untouched. She has no appetite. Her nerves are on edge on account of her pending testimony. She is extremely anxious and apprehensive. She dreads returning to court.

Nan now nervously looks at herself in a hand mirror and asks her sister, "How do I look?" Liz smiles at her and rather unconvincingly says, "You look great." Nan continues to look in the mirror. Liz chimes in, "Well, maybe a bit more blush."

Nan puts down the mirror and reaches out to take Liz's hand. "That bad, huh? I'm a wreck. I don't know if I can do this." Liz looks her in the eye. "My little sister is smart. I have great confidence in you. You'll do fine." "And if I don't?" Nan asks. Liz smiles and then hugs her, "Well then, you'll still be my sister, won't you."

Chapter 92
Nan takes the Stand

An hour later, in court, the afternoon hearing is in session. Nan Britton, the final witness, is now on the stand, and she is responding to the questions, all well-rehearsed, from her own attorney.

Marsteller: Miss Britton, were you a public figure when Mr. Klunk published his story about you?

Nan: Yes.

Marsteller: When and how did you become a public figure?

Nan: The public became aware of me around 1927 with the publication of my book *The President's Daughter.*

Marsteller: Was there much public reaction to your book?

Nan: There was a lot of reaction.

Marsteller: Was the reaction largely positive or negative?

Nan: It was mostly negative.

Marsteller: Did you expect this reaction?

Nan: Not at all. I expected a positive reaction.

Marsteller: Did the negativity continue?

Nan: It died down considerably a few months after the book's release. After six months or so, people seemed to have forgotten. I only occasionally got letters. But very few. It got very quiet, that is, until Mr. Klunk's publication.

Marsteller: And after Mr. Klunk published his articles, did it get better or worse?

Nan: Worse than ever. I received more letters than ever, tenfold more than the previous peak, and the letters were nastier than ever. I was called all sorts of names, names I can't repeat here, and, for the first time, I got threats of violence, even death threats. It was very scary, very horrible.

Marsteller: And your blood pressure reached dangerous levels. Is that what your medical records show?

Nan: Yes, my physical and mental health has deteriorated significantly. I am still suffering.

Marsteller: Your Honor, we note that Miss Britton's medical history and samples of the threating letters she received are already part of the record and these documents corroborate Miss Britton's testimony.

Judge: It is so noted.

Marsteller: No further questions.

Judge: Mr. Mouser, you may begin your cross-examination.

Mouser: Thank you, your Honor.

Mouser stands and approaches Nan.

Mouser: Miss Britton, these nasty letters and threats you received. Who sent them to you?

Marsteller: Objection, your honor. The question is absurd. People don't often sign their names when they make death threats.

Mouser: My mistake, let me rephrase the question. Miss Britton, do you have any reason to believe that any of these nasty letters or threats you received came from my client?

Nan: I have no reason to believe that.

Mouser: To your knowledge, did my client direct people to send you these nasty letters?

Nan: Not to my knowledge.

Mouser: Just to clarify, then. These threats *that you don't believe my client had anything to do with* caused your medical problems. Is that correct?

Nan: Correct, but it was his publication.

Mouser holds up his hands and stops her mid-sentence, frustrating Nan.

Mouser: No buts allowed in court, Miss Britton.

This elicits a few giggles in the courtroom. Nan is now both frustrated by Mouser's characterization of events, and uncomfortable, as the laughter makes her feel like the target of an unwelcome joke.

Mouser: Now, you claim Elizabeth Ann is your daughter. Is that correct?

Nan: Yes.

Mouser: Was she always your daughter?

Nan: Of course. What do you mean?

Mouser: Let me explain. Your honor, may I submit for the record and hand to the witness an article from the New York Daily News dated June 9 1924?

Judge: It's part of the public domain. I will allow it.

Nan is perplexed. She remembers the article but hasn't thought about it or the incident in years. And it was pretty inconsequential. It was just one of those now funny stories of childhood. The fire department had to rescue Elizabeth Ann, then just some four-and-a-half years old, after she locked herself in the bathroom. What could this possibly have to do with this trial?

Mouser: Miss Britton, are you familiar with the article in your hand?

Nan: Yes. It's the story of how the firemen had to rescue Elizabeth Ann after she locked herself in the bathroom.

Mouser: What is the last name of the child, according to the article?

Nan: Willits.

Mouser: Willits. So not Harding, not even Britton. And the article states you were watching over her at the time. Is the article correct in that regard?

Nan: Yes.

Mouser: Is locking a child in the bathroom good parenting, in your opinion?

Marsteller: Objection, your Honor. Counsel needs to stick to facts, not opinions.

Mouser: I'll withdraw the question. Now, this article about the child with the last name of Willits also describes you as her aunt. Were you her aunt then?

Nan: No. I am her mother.

Mouser: I'm confused. Do you know why the article states the child's last name was Willits, and you were her aunt, not her mother?

Nan: I am her mother! I was living with my married sister at the time. For appearances purposes, we said Elizabeth Ann was my sister's adopted daughter, and she took her last name.

Mouser: So, you lied?

Nan: I did what I had to do to protect and raise my daughter!

Mouser holds up a copy of *The President's Daughter.*

Mouser: Did you also do what you had to do, that is, *lie,* when you wrote this book?

Marsteller: Objection, your Honor.

Marsteller's objection is ignored. Nan is now crying, and the heated interchange between her and Mouser is quick and loud.

Nan: No! I did not lie! My book's true. Every word!

Mouser: Every word. Really. We'll see about that, and remember you are under oath and obligated to tell the truth.

Marsteller stands and speaks more forcefully.

Marsteller: Objection, your Honor!

Marsteller is again ignored even though the judge begins to hammer his gavel. Nan blurts out between her tears.

Nan: I am telling the truth.

Mouser: Miss Britton, I am not sure you know the difference between the truth and a lie.

Marsteller is furious. He rises and screams over the argument.

Marsteller: Objection, your Honor, counsel is harassing the witness!

The courtroom goes quiet. Mouser looks at the judge with a false innocence.

Mouser: We are merely asking questions, your Honor.

Judge: Look, it's getting late. This does seem like a good stopping point for today. Let's recess and reconvene tomorrow. Court is dismissed until tomorrow at 9 AM.

Chapter 93
Time to Regroup

Court was dismissed about one hour ago, and Nan is in the hotel lobby with her sister and daughter. Nan speaks to Liz, "I've only a minute. I need to work with Mr. Marsteller. I'm on the stand again tomorrow, and I need to do better."

"Was it that bad?" Liz asks. Nan nods and begins to cry. "It's going terrible. It's humiliating."

Liz hugs her sister. "You're the bravest person I know, little Sis." Nan makes no comment about this, but says, "I am thinking of withdrawing. It's awful on the stand. I'm going to lose anyway."

Liz asks, "What will your life be like if you win?" Nan thinks a bit, then responds, "Probably horrible. People will still hate me." Liz shrugs. "So, same life then, win, lose, or withdrawal?"

Nan nods. Liz then asks, "Ten years from now, which decision would you regret more? Withdrawing or continuing?" Nan pauses, then looks at her daughter. A stranger, a woman, overhearing the conversation, gets up from a nearby table, water glass in hand, and approaches Nan.

This very determined woman speaks directly to Nan. "You're the one that wrote that awful book, aren't you?" Nan tries to calm the woman down. "Ma'am, I'm sorry, I can't talk about that now." The woman snarls and shouts at Nan, "You're a sicko, a disgusting tramp!" She then throws the water from the glass at Nan and scurries away. Nan screams, then grabs and hugs her daughter as onlookers give her disapproving glances.

Nan speaks to her daughter as she holds her. "Elizabeth Ann, someday this might make sense to you." Nan then looks deeply into her sister's eyes. "Take Elizabeth Ann home. Immediately. Leave tonight. I'll see you both in New York when it's over. I can't put her through any more of this."

Nan hugs her daughter and then Liz. Liz takes Elizabeth Ann by the hand and looks back at Nan. "I love you, little Sis. See you in New York." Nan then looks at herself in a nearby mirror and breathes deeply. She then goes to speak with Marsteller, who is sitting at a nearby table in the restaurant.

Chapter 94
Final Testimony

It is the next day, and the bailiff announces that court is in session.

Judge: Would the witness please return to the stand?

Marsteller looks at Nan, and she at him. She nods, indicating she believes she is ready and will continue. She gets up and takes her place on the stand. Mouser holds up a copy of Nan's book.

Mouser: Miss Britton, in this book you claim you had an affair with a married man 30 years your senior?

Nan: The man I loved. Yes.

Mouser: So, let's assume the words of your book are true. If so, did you know you were committing adultery and that doing so was illegal?

Nan: Not initially, but I learned that on the night we consummated our love.

Mouser: And despite that, according to what you have written, you continued this intimate relationship. So, by your second tryst, you were then knowingly committing a crime. Is that correct?

Nan: The President and I knew we were committing that crime. Yes.

Mouser: Miss Britton, yesterday, you told us you lied about Elizabeth Ann's last name. Today you're confessing to a crime. Is this correct?

Nan: I did those things with or on the advice of the President. He willingly made love to me and he was the one that suggested our daughter take the name Willits.

Mouser addresses the judge.

Mouser: Your Honor, would you be so kind as to ask the witness to just answer the question asked? These are Yes/No questions.

Marsteller: Your Honor, may I remind the court that a certain latitude was provided to other witnesses, Dr. Harding, for instance. And not all questions can be answered simply Yes or No. The jury has the right to hear the complete story.

Judge: Gentlemen, I appreciate both of your comments. Would you both please approach the bench?

Mouser and Marsteller walk up to Judge Killits, and he speaks to them in soft tones. "Look, I can't risk a mistrial or easy appeal. That would be in none of our interests. I will gently ask the witness to, if possible, be brief in her responses, but I cannot stifle her. Now, let's continue." Mouser and Marsteller return to their tables, and the judge looks at Nan and continues.

Judge: The witness is directed to do your best and try to limit your responses to your own actions and reasoning. Now, please continue, Mr. Mouser.

Nan is pleased. She recognizes that from this judge, this is only a slight admonishment, and that Mouser has been sent a bit off-balance by her responses.

Mouser: Miss Britton, in your book, you claim you lost your virginity on July 30 1917, at the Imperial Hotel in New York City with then-Senator Harding. And you said he checked in under the name Hardwick or Warwick?

Nan: It was more than a decade ago. I wasn't with him when he registered at the hotel. He told me he used a fake name. As you like to say, he lied. I don't recall for sure what name he used. I think he said Hardwick or Warwick. Maybe it was something else.

Mouser: Your Honor, may I approach the bench?

Judge: Yes.

Mouser: Your Honor, I have an authenticated copy of the Imperial Hotel's guest register on July 30 1917, to enter into the record.

Mouser approaches the bench. The judge looks over the document.

Judge: Bailiff, please enter this into the record.

With the administrative procedure complete, Mouser continues.

Mouser: Please hand the document to the witness.

The bailiff hands the document to Nan.

Mouser: Miss Britton, the court has recognized the document in your hands as the July 30 1917, register of the Imperial Hotel. The date and place you claim you gave up your virginity to then-Senator Harding. Do you understand that?

Nan: Yes.

Mouser: Please look at the guest list and tell me if you see a...

In an attempt to add drama, Mouser looks at his notes and, after a short while, continues.

Mouser: ...guest by the name of Hardwick or Warwick, as you mention in your book.

Nan looks over the list.

> *Nan:* Let's see. In my book, I mention I wasn't with him when he checked in. So my book just passes on the information he gave me. Isn't that heresay?

Mouser is furious.

> *Mouser:* Just please answer the question. Your book listed two names - Hardwick or Warwick. Do you see either name on the list in front of you?

> *Nan:* No but my book is clear. I didn't remember what fake name he told me when I wrote the book and I don't remember any better now some 14 years later.

Mouser is very frustrated.

> *Mouser:* The answer to the question, Miss Britton then is 'No' you don't see either the name Hardwick or Warwick on the document you have in your hands?

She looks over the document.

> *Nan:* No. I don't see either name.

> *Mouser:* So that part of your story doesn't stack up, does it?

> *Nan:* I just don't recall for sure what name he told me he checked in under.

Nan calmly looks over the list. She thinks she recognizes his handwriting and sees the name he did use, 'Harvey,' and begins to offer this information to the court.

Nan: One name here, 'Harvey,' looks like his handwriting.

Mouser (abruptly interrupting): You've already answered my question, Miss Britton! You didn't see either of the names you mentioned in your book.

Nan: Sorry. Just trying to be helpful.

Mouser is about to ask for the last statement to be struck from the record but thinks better of it. He believes he has, in any case, successfully made his point, albeit not as forcefully as he had hoped. He decides to move on.

Mouser: Your Honor, may I approach? I have an affidavit from the New York City Police Department 5th Precinct, the Precinct that encompasses the Imperial Hotel.

Mouser hands the bailiff an affidavit.

Judge: I'll allow it.

Mouser: Let the record show that the affidavit states that the New York City Police Department has no record of any arrest or attempted arrest on the night of July 30 1917, at the Imperial Hotel.

Judge: It is so noted.

Mouser approaches Nan and directs his question to her.

Mouser: So, you made up the police visit. Nice titillating touch, though, handcuffed while naked. I'm sure that lie helped sell a lot of books.

Nan: The cops were paid off. It's in my book. My story is true. We were in love! Real love.

Mouser: And did your lover send you letters?

Nan: Yes.

Mouser: Didn't you save these important mementos?

Nan: I ripped them up as he asked.

Mouser: I see. And did he provide for your daughter?

Nan: He sent me money regularly.

Mouser: Do you have bank records for that?

Nan: No. It was cash. Mr. Gaston Means often gave it to me.

Mouser: Mr. Means says otherwise. You have no doubt seen the affidavit from him.

Nan: Well, one of us is lying. And he's in prison. I'm not.

This comment angers Mouser, but he says nothing.

Mouser: So, you can't prove any of your story, can you?

Nan: How do you prove love?

Nan has been far more effective today than yesterday. Mouser is frustrated. He's not in as strong a position as he had hoped and sees no advantage in continuing with Nan on the stand.

Mouser: Nothing more from this witness, your Honor. The defense rests its case.

Judge: Very well. We will hear closing arguments tomorrow morning, and the jury can begin deliberations immediately thereafter.

Chapter 95

The Close

Nan is both relieved and anxious today, the last day of the trial. She listens attentively as her attorney wraps up his closing arguments. Marsteller is doing well. He is captivating and has the jury's attention.

He holds the stack of affidavits the defense put in the record.

Here's the heart of the defense's case. The affidavits gathered regarding my client's years in high school. And what do these papers prove? They prove Nan Britton was once a teenager.

Marsteller slams down the papers.

Irrelevant and stupid. Now you can believe Miss Britton or not. It really doesn't matter. And by the way, it certainly seems like the person who knew her and the President the best, his sister, Daisy Harding, believed Miss Britton's story. How else do you explain this ex-friend's generosity? Why did she support Miss

Britton's child financially? Financial support she was strapped to provide. But again, whether you believe Miss Britton or not doesn't matter.

Marsteller walks over to and points at Klunk.

It is Mr. Klunk who is on trial here, and he himself testified that he made up, out of thin air, lies that slandered my client.

Klunk, sitting next to his attorney, can't help himself. "Sure I did, but so what? I got the right to free speech."

The judge bangs his gavel. "Quiet, Mr. Klunk."
Marsteller continues.

Mr. Klunk here once again confesses his guilt. His free speech claim is a red herring. Free speech only protects one from Government censorship. Klunk wasn't subject to Government censorship when he, by his own admission, spread malicious lies that seriously harmed my client. He freely admitted his guilt several times here in court, including just seconds ago. In his own words then –he is guilty as charged.

I respectfully ask you to take him at his word. Follow his lead, find him guilty, restore an honest woman's reputation, and strike a blow for the common man's struggle against the powerful and corrupt. Thank you.

The judge nods, "Mr. Mouser, your close."

Mouser stands and addresses the jury.

Ladies and Gentlemen, we have a simple and sad case before us. And let me start by taking issue with what my esteemed colleague on the other side just said regarding the evidence.

Mr. Marsteller and I have a very different interpretation on the affidavits gathered about Miss Britton. They are not stupid. In fact, they tell us a lot. A lot about the plaintiff's character. And what exactly do they tell us?

Mouser pauses for dramatic effect.

How do I say this delicately?

He pauses again.

Well, let's just say the plaintiff was the sort of woman that enjoyed the company of a great variety of men.

He, too, holds up the affidavits.

In fact, it appears she charmed a whole lot of men. Anyone of them could have fathered the child.

Mouser shakes his head.

But the President? I think not. He had no children with his own wife. Certainly, he wanted a legitimate legacy. All men do, especially Presidents. But, as his brother, the doctor, testified, he was unable to father children.

And let's not kid ourselves. The plaintiff is no saint. Not anywhere near the righteous soul her side would like you to believe. Her story is not an exemplary story at all, far from it.

Rather, her story is a rather sad and immoral one. The story of an unmarried woman who gave birth to a child and, by her own admission, lied. And lied a lot. She even lied about her own daughter's name. A child that had to be rescued by the fire department because she was a derelict parent.

Probably on drugs at the time. Shame on her. And what other abominable acts did she admit to? Well, she willingly gave up her most precious gift, her virginity. She shunned laws, societal norms, and values of decency. She is a cheap degenerate pervert who compounded her sin by trying to extort money by spitting on the grave of a great man, our President. A man incapable of even having children. Not only could she offer no substantiation for her claims, what documents we did find refute her story. The hotel did not have the registration she claimed, and there was no record of the police raid that was a key part of her book. Miss Britton is a liar, a cheap, lying, knifing extortionist.

Mouser, now completing his closing arguments, walks over to where Nan is sitting and points angrily at her. Nan looks back at him, outwardly defiantly.

The irony of it all. The guilty one is right here. The accuser, the deranged pervert, Miss Britton. She wrote a fiction and destroyed one of our greatest statesman's legacies, and then she has the gall to complain when my client exposes her lies. Free speech is OK for her but not for my client. In America, we don't live by double standards. Don't let her get away with yet another sleazy deception. Send this useless scum home with nothing, because she is nothing, and allow a great man to finally rest in peace. Do it for my client. Do it for the dead President. Do it for America. Thank you.

Chapter 96
Instruction

The judge offers instructions to the jury.

I want to thank counsel on both sides for their professionalism. I also want to thank the jury for their attentiveness throughout the trial. You have heard a great deal of testimony, have been presented with a large amount of evidence, and listened to arguments and counterarguments. You are now charged with the difficult task of sorting through all this information to come up with a verdict. I have the greatest confidence that you can work together to achieve this most hallowed objective.

I know the parties have offered differing approaches on how to view this case.

The defense prefers a broad view that requires one to look at the many surrounding facts and nuances. They want you to consider not just the defendant but also the plaintiff. They point out that Miss Britton, like

Mr. Klunk, wrote an unsubstantiated sensational story about a public figure. They claim both parties were within their legal rights - just exercising their rights to free speech.

The prosecution suggests a narrow focus. Look at this matter in isolation and focus solely on the defendant, Mr. Klunk. They ask us to ignore what came before and who may have thrown the first punch. They say just look at Mr. Klunk in a vacuum. Was what he did illegal, in other words, was what he wrote libel, and was the plaintiff harmed? Yes or no.

The prosecution's narrow focus is attractive in that it is simple. And I certainly understand why they have made this suggestion. It would be nice if we lived in such a simple and straightforward world. However, we don't. We live in complex times, and I think it wrong to judge this matter, or anything these days, in such a narrow way.

The central figures in this case are people of great public interest: the former President of the United States and this woman who claims to have been his paramour. Clearly, they are both newsworthy figures, and the public would have an interest in knowing about events regarding such individuals. Publishers would want to and have the right to print stories about them.

The question before us is just how far can free speech go before it crosses the line to libel? In our society, the standard, especially when dealing with public figures, is to allow robust room for rhetoric, hyperbole, over-statement, even perhaps misstatements. And I would add that the ceiling for free speech is even higher in this particular case, where the plaintiff herself initiated all this by first making unflattering and unsupported accusations about the late President.

Accordingly, my instructions to the jury are to take the broad view of matters as the defense, Mr. Klunk's counsel, suggests, and carefully consider all the evidence you have heard throughout the trial. Consider both the defendant's and the plaintiff's actions.

Nan catches a glimpse of what Marsteller has written on his notepad - "WF" followed by "WVF." He had told her he would leave such a note if the judge's instructions were unhelpful. He told her "WF" stands for "We're Fucked." He ad-libbed the middle initial, but Nan gets it. She knows it means, "We're Very Fucked."

Chapter 97
Means Book Release

It is late October 1931, and in Toledo, Ohio, word is out that the jury has come to a verdict. The trial will reconvene shortly, and the verdict will be announced.

Meanwhile, in New York City, Gaston Means and May Dixon Thacker are walking to Bretano's Bookstore at 5th Avenue and 27th Street for a book signing. Their book, *The Strange Death of President Harding*, is being released today. Both are a bit anxious. They are uncertain how their book will be received; they fear the worst, but they both nervously smile at each other, putting up a good front.

Means turns to Thacker. "I'm looking forward to this." Thacker concurs, "Me too. And our timing seems good. We're getting so much free publicity from the Britton trial." Means nods in agreement. "Perfect timing for me too. I may be tied up soon afterward." Thacker breathes deeply and says, "I've worked so hard on this, harder than I have ever worked on anything, and I am looking forward to seeing the fruits of my labor." Means remains confident. "You will. And handsomely. Trust me."

Means is lying, and he knows he is lying. He will never pay May Dixon Thacker a cent. He will profess shock, surprise and embarrassment whenever she calls to tell him the funds he has repeatedly promised have again failed to arrive. Each time he will renew his promise, and each time with increased vigor. He will say that he will personally go down to accounts payable or directly to the bank himself to make certain the matter is rectified immediately. Then he will hang up the phone and do nothing. His words will be as empty as his pockets.

Means is a confidence trickster. In fact, J. Edgar Hoover once called him "the most amazing figure in contemporary criminal history" because of his ability to weave a believable, albeit fraudulent, story. In less than a year, he will be back in jail, this time for good and this time for the most outrageous crime of blackmailing the Lindberghs after their baby's kidnapping.

May Dixon Thacker will learn all this in time. On this day, though, she is happy as they turn the corner onto 5th Avenue. Both she and Gaston Means smile broadly in relief as the bookstore is now in view, and they see a long line of people. As they get closer and enter, they also see a substantial queue of folks in the store with copies of their book, waiting for them to be autographed. They both smile broadly. Means sings from the famous song of the time, 'Happy Days Are Here Again'.

They greet the waiting customers and take their places at the table and begin autographing copies of their book: *The Strange Death of President Harding: From the Diaries of Gaston B. Means, as told to May Dixon Thacker.*

More customers grab the book and join the line. While waiting in line, one reads a passage out loud: "'Mrs. Harding was alone with the President. She gave him his medicine. He drank it, laid back for a moment, then suddenly opened his eyes wide and looked straight into her face. Yes, I think he knew." Another woman gasps on hearing the passage, "Oh my!"

At the table, Thacker and Means greet the customers enthusiastically. Two women approach the table to get their books autographed. One of them exclaims to Means, "I knew Mrs. Harding did it from the moment I read about his death!" Means smiles. "You're a very perceptive woman."

Just then, outside the bookstore, a newsboy appears with the afternoon NY Times. He has a number of newspapers in his hands and pitches them by calling out today's very apropos headline, "Nan Britton loses case. Klunk is innocent. Extra, extra. Read all about it. Nan Britton loses case. Jury says she's a liar. Read all about it!" Some customers crowd the boy to buy the paper.

One woman in line is about to meet Means and Thacker and notices the newsboy. "So glad that tart lost her case." Thacker responds to the woman, "We live in interesting times, don't we?" Yet another woman chimes in, "Right decision if you ask me." Not to be outdone, the first woman replies, "It's comforting to know that Mr. Harding can finally rest in peace."

The second woman, intent on getting the last word, continues, "Yes, rest in peace, Mr. President." She then looks toward the heavens and makes the sign of the cross as she holds the book to her bosom. "Those closest to you betrayed you - like Judas betrayed Jesus. This book is your resurrection." Means raises his eyebrows. "That's quite an endorsement, Ma'am." She breathes deeply. "I am sure President Harding is looking down on us right now, smiling, knowing the truth is finally being told." Means smiles broadly.

Chapter 98
Verdict and Beyond

In the Ohio courtroom, Nan is still processing the loss. The court had been open to the public for the reading of the verdict, and the room mostly reacted with jubilation on hearing of Klunk's innocent verdict. This added salt to Nan's wound. Nan was, of course, devastated, even though mentally, she was expecting this result.

After her much improved performance on her second day on the stand, Nan, albeit briefly, fooled herself into believing there might be a different result. She's bitterly disappointed and still hurting after the victory of her tormenters, Mouser and Klunk. Both men, in her mind, are abominations: Mouser a sick and twisted bully and Klunk a blatant and unrepentant liar. She had hoped the bully and the liar would get their comeuppances. She takes a deep breath, though, and turns to Marsteller, waxing philosophically: "The most powerful lessons - the lessons of loss."

Chapter 99

Over isn't Over

The verdict was read some 30 minutes ago, and a crowd of both the press and public gathered outside the courthouse. Mouser, even more bombastic than usual, addresses the unruly crowd. "Today was a great day for justice and a great day for America. But folks, we're not done…". Mouser raises his hands to quiet the crowd so he can make his important announcement, "Today I am proudly declaring my candidacy for Congressman of this great state." The crowd cheers.

Mouser continues, "My platform is to root out the degradation just witnessed in this courtroom. Let's return to the deep moral fiber of our country's foundation, where men went to work and were supported by womenfolk who stayed home and raised children.

"We are now on the brink of living in a Godless society where Satan is our leader. I plan on bringing us back from this brink, introducing laws to restore our morality and return us to a more God-fearing nation. Our problems today are all clearly traceable to the 19th Amendment. It has cast a horrible spell on us, and the centerpiece of my efforts will be for its repeal."

"Women got the vote, and what happened?" He holds up a copy of the book, *The Strange Death of President Harding*. "A woman, the President's wife, found the courage to kill our great leader, Warren Harding."

Members of the crowd shout, "That's right!"

Others shout in agreement. As they quiet down, Mouser picks up a copy of *The President's Daughter*. "And this blasphemous pornography, just proven in court to be one big lie, falsely defamed the President. Yet another example of a woman tearing down American values.

"And then there's that big-bosomed German spy that tried to destroy our country by seducing our President. Yet another shameful snake-in-the-grass tactic by a devious member of the weaker sex."

A crowd member shouts in agreement, "Women are to blame!" A lone counter-protestor, a woman, offers a rebuttal, "Rubbish! Poppycock!"

Nan and Marsteller are leaving the courthouse and try unsuccessfully to slip by unnoticed in the background. A crowd member sees her and calls out, "There she is, the tart!"

A few follow Nan and throw scraps of garbage at her. Mouser beckons to them to come back to him. He wants their attention. "Friends, we've got bigger issues now! Anyhow, she's just a symptom of our broken system. I ask you now to join me in my crusade to fix our system so the likes of her will never again see the light of day."

The crowd cheers. The lone protestor objects again: "Hogwash!"

Chapter 100
Some Homecoming

Nan, still devastated, returns home. She stands silently before the doorstep. In her mind, she still hears Mouser's rant outside the courthouse.

She is frozen as she surveys her porch, now littered with garbage thrown by protestors. A scarlet 'A' has been painted on her front door. A copy of Nathaniel Hawthorne's novel *The Scarlet Letter* is on the doorstep. Written on it is the word "Penance".

Nan is near tears as she picks up the book. For a long time, she can only stare at the cover. Eventually, she opens it to page one. She smiles softly through her tears as she begins reading. Her sister Liz arrives, with Elizabeth Ann in tow. Liz waits on the sidewalk as Elizabeth Ann runs to her mother. Nan hugs her daughter. Elizabeth Ann asks, "Mommy, did you win?"

Nan smooths her daughter's hair with her hand and smiles. "Not yet."

The end

Epilogue

This book is a fictionalized account of historical persons and events. Most characters were living persons, and many pivotal events are consistent with historical records.

President Harding died at the Palace Hotel in San Francisco while on his trip west; he reportedly was a philanderer, and his administration was scandal-ridden. Both Nan Britton and Gaston Means wrote the books noted in this novel. May Thacker did assist Mr. Means in writing his novel. And Nan did sue Mr. Klunk. However, Klunk was not a tabloid publisher. Rather, he was a friend of Harding who sold, in his business establishment, a book counter to Nan's, titled *The Answer to "The President's Daughter"*. *The Answer*'s author, Dr. Joseph De Barthe was deceased by the time of the trial.

Some of the more unusual oddities this book depicts are also consistent with historical accounts. For example, Florence Harding was said to have been very superstitious; she did refuse an autopsy; and she reportedly did burn some presidential documents (though she did so, well after the funeral in Marion, Ohio). A coffin was part of the provisions on the President's trip west, and Harding did write smutty letters to his lovers (though he did so when a US Senator not as President and not under the circumstances described in this book).

The reports of food poisoning and Florence Harding's refusal of an autopsy were part of the public discourse at the time of his passing. These tidbits fueled much of the speculation and rumors surrounding Harding's death. One example of such a rumor is the confrontation discussed in this novel at The Palace Hotel the evening of the President's death, a story that is still part of The Palace Hotel lore.

The ratification of the 19th Amendment, as reported in this novel, is consistent with historical records. The author found no record, though, stating any politician advocated repeal. However, fairly recent articles have noted that some 2016 social media posts suggested repealing the women's vote.

As for the fate of the principals: Nan Britton died in 1991 at 94, unwavering in her love for Harding and her claim that he fathered her daughter. Her daughter, Elizabeth Ann, passed away in 2005. Neither lived to see the 2015 DNA testing proving Harding was Elizabeth Ann's father.

The cause of Harding's death remains a mystery, but most believe he died of a heart attack. The newspaper reports of his health issues were very much as described in this book. He and his doctors stated he had food poisoning. And just before his death, newspaper reports said he was on the road to recovery.

These reports to the press may have painted a deceptively rosy picture of the President's actual condition. In his book, *The Strange Deaths of President Harding*, historian Robert H. Ferrell states that some of Harding's doctors were privately very concerned and questioned his chances for recovery.

Gaston Means died in 1938 while incarcerated in Leavenworth Penitentiary. He was serving time for a con job related to the Lindbergh kidnapping.

Mrs. Philips did successfully blackmail Harding though did so during his run for President. She was a German sympathizer (during both World Wars). She was under federal surveillance most of her life. Though apparently never proven, she was suspected to be a German spy. Harding's steamy letters to her were unsealed by the Library of Congress in 2014.

Acknowledgments

There are many to thank. Certainly, my parents, teachers, friends and others who inspired me over the years. Some are still with us, some gone but all are fondly remembered.

I would like to express special gratitude to a few individuals who were of particular help on this novel.

Sam Pearce of SWATT Books Ltd. was a critical part of this endeavor. Her knowledge and expertise of the book world were invaluable in sorting through the many hurdles of self-publishing. Thanks Sam. Many thanks also to the careful review and editing of Mark Beaumont-Thomas. Mark was appropriately detailed, careful, supportive and encouraging. His input was immeasurably helpful and it was a pleasure working with him.

Also, thanks to Ruth Atkinson of Page-to-Screen. Ruth's advice on the several screenplays I wrote, including the one that was the basis for this book, was invaluable. Miraculously and with her help, two of these screenplays advanced in some prestigious contests.

And, of course, I offer my loving gratitude to my spouse for the encouragement given throughout the years on this and the many oddball endeavors I have attempted.

About the Author

This is E.S. Laurence's debut novel. ES has written screenplays and has performed on stage at the San Francisco Fringe Festival, in student films, music videos, and was a featured extra in some big-time films such as Milk and the Master. In college, ES published cartoons and was a disc jockey. A lot of fun stuff but not lucrative, so ES has made a living doing tax work (ES is a Certified Public Accountant).

Born and raised in San Francisco (the place of Warren Harding's death), the author has an undergraduate degree from UC Berkeley, and went on to earn three graduate degrees. ES is also a member of the US Tax Court Bar (by examination) and once unsuccessfully petitioned the US Supreme Court (go figure).